TARNISHED

TARNISHED

LESIA ANNASTASIA CHYTRA

L Chytra
October, 2015

2015

Printed by CreateSpace, An Amazon.com Company
Available from Amazon.com, CreateSpace.com, and other retail outlets
Available on Kindle and other devices

ISBN 978-0-9948981-0-4

www.facebook.com/TarnishedLAChytra

Author photo: Z.Chytra
Cover & Interior Design: Tanya Mykytiuk for Ptashka
Cover image courtesy of: Adrianna Grod

Dedicated to Anastasia Chytra & Anastasia Gurskyj

To all young women forced from their homes
during World War II

TORONTO

2011

I.

Lively and realistic dreams often filled Anastasia's afternoon naps. An incessant knocking interrupted the middle of her dream. As Anastasia slowly woke up, she realized that the knocking was coming from her front door. There was the sound of a key turning the lock and before she could right herself on the couch, the door swung open.

"Baba! Baaaaaaaba!" a woman's voice called out a chirpy greeting.

Anastasia fought to respond in a positive and cheerful way. It was difficult on so many levels. She was trying to hold onto the dream, to remember the details. She was also still getting used to the lack of privacy that came with being in a seniors' residence. Anastasia had given spare sets of keys to her daughter Alya and granddaughter Sofiya.

As Anastasia clumsily sat up, her granddaughter breezed in. Anastasia did a quick visual assessment of Sofiya. Even with a smile plastered to her face, Sofiya seemed like she was in a hurry.

"You look very nice," Anastasia said to her in Ukrainian before switching into English. "Your hair looks very nice today."

It really did. Anastasia had always admired her granddaughter's long, chestnut-brown hair. When Sofiya was a little girl, Anastasia showed her how red highlights were more noticeable in the sun.

Anastasia sensed that Sofiya felt claustrophobic; the room closing in on her from the second that she had arrived. Even to Anastasia, the place was small and stifling. On that day especially, it was overly bright, overly stuffed, and overly warm. The air was thick with the smells of past cooking.

Anastasia vacillated between feeling depressed that the apartment was not where she had hoped to spend her last few years, to remembering there was always a much more dreary option – one of those terrible long-term care nursing homes. If there was one wish that a woman firmly in her eighties could make, it would be to die peacefully in her new single bed, in her new one-bedroom apartment, rather than wilt away with other old and sick people in some nursing home.

"How are you today?" Sofiya asked her grandmother in English, planting a quick and dry kiss on Anastasia's right cheek. As she straightened, Anastasia noticed that her granddaughter looked sharp and well-dressed as usual. She was wearing jeans with a simple white t-shirt and navy blue blazer. Sofiya always looked so effortlessly put-together. Sofiya had Anastasia's genes – her family had all been tall and slim. Anastasia was still tall compared to the other women her age, but was recently distressed to find that the pants that she had owned for decades were very snug around the waist.

"Oh, I'm fine," Anastasia said, still trying to gain her balance on the couch. "It was raining this morning. I decided to stay in the apartment today. It still raining outside?"

"No, it's not," Sofiya answered. "The rain stopped about half an hour ago, and the sun is starting to peek out. Traffic getting here was brutal, of course. The roads are always chaos when it rains, and Saturday afternoon traffic is bad to begin with." Sofiya fidgeted about, straightening the throw on the back of the couch, and fluffing pillows.

"You should really try to get outside today, Baba," Sofiya continued after a few seconds of silence, still toying with items around the living room. "It's not good for you to sit inside this place all day. You need exercise to keep your muscles active and strong. Remember what the doctor said – at least thirty minutes of activity per day."

Sofiya had only been there for a few minutes, but already Anastasia felt as if it was not going to be a good visit. Sofiya was frequently tense, and today she seemed to be no different. Yet, without her granddaughter, Anastasia didn't know how she would manage even the smallest tasks outside the apartment.

Anastasia watched as Sofiya stopped wandering around the living room long enough to look at a faded and creased photo of two women. It was Anastasia's most precious photograph. Sofiya picked up the photo and peered at it.

"My sister, Kateryna, and my mother, Daria," Anastasia said as if in response to a question.

"Yeah, I know, Baba," Sofiya said, then plunked the photo back down onto the table. "I was just looking for some sort of resemblance to me. Or something. I don't know."

Anastasia reached over to straighten out the photo frame and thought of Warsaw, Poland, where her sister Kateryna had lived out her last few blurry years. Kateryna had been so full of life in her younger days. Her later years made it difficult for Anastasia to reconcile the Kateryna she knew and loved with the shriveled, forgetful old woman that she became. Sofiya had arranged for the two sisters to meet on Skype, just before Kateryna had passed away. Her sister's dry voice had become more distant as dementia took over.

"How old was Ciocia Kateryna again when she died?" Sofiya asked.

"Eighty-eight," Anastasia said as she stretched out her legs, trying to wake them up.

"Oh. That's actually not that old. She always seemed so ancient to me."

"Ha," Anastasia snorted. "You're right – not too old. My mama lived to ninety-eight. That's a miracle."

"Yeah, I know," Sofiya said and then audibly exhaled. "You've told me a bunch of times, Baba."

"Humph."

Her mother and sister may have spent their last years withering away in Poland, but in Anastasia's memories, they would always be young, forever the ages they were when Anastasia left Ukraine. At that time, Daria was forty-one, and Kateryna only twenty-one. But, memories did not keep pace with the march of time, and over the years with each new photograph that Anastasia had received from either her mother or sister, she was jolted back to the hard reality that she had chosen to ignore.

Silence hung in the air. Anastasia was still groggy. She often rehearsed conversational passages in English in her mind before speaking. She needed to be fully prepared in order to get them right.

"How are you?" Anastasia asked, breaking the uneasy quiet. "How is Jeff?"

"Oh, he's fine," Sofiya said. She pulled her cell phone out of the back pocket of her jeans and pecked away at it. "Busy, you know. He's trying to grow the orthodontic practice and establish a second location in Markham.

He doesn't want to work there, but he's busy trying to get the word out."

"I have not seen Jeff in a while," Anastasia said. She spoke slowly, deliberately. She was proud of her English language skills. "He's working every weekend? He should come by here soon. I'll even make him his favourite – *varenyky*."

"Oh, yeah, I'm sure he'll run right over for that," Sofiya said as she rolled her eyes. "Look, Baba, he's busy. We're busy. I'm sure he will try to visit soon, when he gets a chance."

Anastasia knew she was irritating Sofiya, but she felt like picking anyway. Anastasia almost preferred it when Jeff didn't come. For the past few years, visits with Jeff were always the same – he barged in, gave a bored look around, asked Anastasia how she was doing without actually listening to her answer, then flopped down on the chair in the corner. The only time Jeff ever perked up during his visits was when he took the glass of cognac that Anastasia always offered him.

"And your, ah, practice?" Anastasia asked.

"It's going well. There's always lots of demand for dentists."

"Everyone goes to the dentist, *yah*? Young, old. Everyone!"

Anastasia watched Sofiya nod comically, making an obvious show of looking at the time on her iPhone. Jeff was becoming such a sore spot with Sofiya. When Sofiya first introduced Jeff to the family, everyone had seemed so delighted. Anastasia had even affectionately dubbed her granddaughter's new beau 'Canadian Jeff'. Jeff was the first non-Ukrainian who married into Anastasia's family, and even though that seemed like an inevitability in Canada, it was still an adjustment for her. At first, a non-Ukrainian in the close family circle was a novelty. Over the years, however, the very different upbringings of Sofiya and Jeff and the many unspoken values and assumptions that came with them grated and wore thin the fabric of their marriage.

Sofiya shifted her weight from side to side, looking like she wanted nothing more at that moment than to escape home. She and Jeff lived in a tastefully renovated house in an inner suburb of west Toronto, not far away from Anastasia's La Rose Avenue apartment. Their house was a large and airy open-concept bungalow, furnished mainly in white. White was everywhere; the kitchen cupboards, the two couches in the living room, the walls, the side tables, the tile floors.

The house was very beautiful, but Anastasia felt a bit on edge every time she went there. Sofiya and Jeff watched her like hawks each time she had food or a beverage in her hand, falling over each other to hand her a coaster before she could place her drink on the coffee table. Anastasia often clucked that a house was not a home until there were children present. It was such a shame; all that space, a house and yard perfect for little ones.

Sofiya was Anastasia's only grandchild. Anastasia had two children, Alya, now sixty-four, and Bohdan, now fifty-six. Anastasia didn't know if it was due to their age gap, or because they were not the same sex, but her daughter and son were less like family and more like acquaintances. In fact, Bohdan wasn't close to anyone in their family.

"I talk to your vuyko Bohdan today on the telephone. He say *hallo*." Bohdan hadn't exactly asked his mother to pass along well wishes. As if she knew that her grandmother was lying, Sofiya shrugged with indifference. Two decades earlier, Bohdan had moved to South Korea to teach English and now made his life there. Never married, Bohdan enjoyed his bachelor lifestyle and all that went along with it.

"My Bohdan has always been different," Anastasia stated as she heaved herself up from the sofa. "*Yoi!* I remember the fights he and your dido used to have. Like cats and dogs, those two. It was always over Bohdan saying no to go to Ukrainian school, Ukrainian dancing," Anastasia chuckled. "Your dido would yell and stomp around the house threatening to use his belt on Bohdan, but of course he never did."

When she looked over to her granddaughter, Sofiya wasn't even smiling.

"Ok, Baba. Ready to go?" Sofiya asked with a forced chipperness in her voice. "Let's head out to run your errands. I have to get ready to go out. We're going downtown to a restaurant for a friend's birthday."

The two women headed out of the apartment with Sofiya leading the way. Anastasia struggled to keep up with her as they exited the building onto the slippery parking lot. The earlier rain made the asphalt in the parking lot slick. Sofiya yanked out an expensive pair of sunglasses from her purse to shield her eyes. Unexpectedly, she reached over to guide Anastasia by the elbow. Anastasia didn't like being herded around like a small child, but she let her granddaughter do it anyway.

"*Bozhe!* You have another new car?" Anastasia blurted as they approached an unfamiliar vehicle.

"We lease, Baba. I told you. We get new models every two years with leasing, and we can write off the payments as part of our business expenses."

"Leasing?" Anastasia asked, her eyes narrowing. "Isn't that like renting? Why would you rent a car when you can buy one? If you bought the car, you would own it. You pay rent for car?"

"Leasing works better for us. I explained this to you, remember, Baba?"

Yes, Anastasia remembered. However, she couldn't hold her tongue about the leasing arrangement. Anastasia huffed to herself about throwing away money as she struggled with the door of the sleek black car.

As they drove, a ringing sound came from the car speakers. Sofiya pushed a button on the dashboard of the car.

"Hello?" Sofiya asked.

"Can you come by the house?" Jeff's voice boomed over the speakers. Anastasia flinched as Sofiya reached over to turn the volume down. "I have to wait here for the landscape designer and I forgot to drop off my books that are due at the library today. Can you swing by and pick them up?"

"I guess," Sofiya answered. Even from behind her sunglasses, Anastasia saw Sofiya's exaggerated eye-roll. "We'll be there in about ten minutes."

"Do you mind a detour, Baba?" Sofiya asked Anastasia.

"No, no. I want to see that new bedroom set that you were telling me about last week."

Sofiya paused for a second, then replied, "We aren't going to go into the house; I'll just run in and get the books."

Anastasia felt a pang of uneasiness. She was a burden to Sofiya, part of her granddaughter's to-do list before Sofiya was free from her yoke.

Ten minutes later, Sofiya pulled into her driveway.

"Wait here, Baba. I'll just run in quickly!" But, she was too slow for her grandmother, who was already unbuckling her seatbelt.

"Ok," Sofiya relented as they rolled to a stop. "We'll go in real quick for a minute to see the bedroom furniture."

Anastasia took her time shuffling up the wide stone walkway to the front door. It was a glass door, with beautiful and modern wrought iron details. Once inside the house, the front entry was spacious. The entire main living area was visible because there were no walls in that part of the house. Anastasia would never live in a house that allowed dinner guests to view the mess that was in the kitchen, but she didn't think that her busy granddaughter entertained guests for large meals all too often.

The house was very modern and tidy, to the extent that it didn't seem like anyone actually lived in it. The kitchen at the right of the large living area was especially uninviting. It always struck Anastasia as stark with its white tile floors, white shiny cupboards, and white stools at the counter. There weren't even any handles to open the cupboard doors, only grooves to pull them open.

Anastasia spotted Jeff relaxing on one of the large white couches to the left of the living area. A football game blared from the television.

"Hello, Jeff," Anastasia said, careful to leave out her 'Canadian' bit.

"Oh hi, Baba." He turned and gave Anastasia a little wave. "I'm just watching the football match in England. Give me a minute."

"That's okay. You know who used to love football? My husband, Stephan. He was crazy over it, playing all the time until he was an old man. Anyway, Sofiya was just going to show me your new bedroom furniture." Anastasia walked towards him, rounding the couch so that she could properly greet him and stopped cold.

"What are you wearing?" Anastasia asked, squinting her eyes, trying to get a better look at his shirt. "Is that what I think it is?"

"What?" asked Jeff, distracted by his football match. Looking down at his chest, he laughed. "This is a t-shirt I picked up on Queen West a few weeks ago. It's funky. Trying to stay hip, you know, Baba."

Jeff wore a black t-shirt with the words 'I…the 80s' on it. The symbol in the middle of the phrase was of the Soviet hammer and sickle. Anastasia found herself growing upset because she didn't understand why Jeff wore a shirt with this symbol of Russian oppression on it.

Jeff noticed that Anastasia was still standing over him, staring at his shirt. "What's up, Baba?"

"I do not like that shirt you are wearing. Is stupid." Anastasia's accurate use of English tended to leave her when she grew angry. She faced him, waiting for an explanation.

"This shirt? Why, don't you like it? It's kind of funny, ironic even. See, the USSR had the last of its golden days in the nineteen-eighties. I love the eighties. Get it?"

Anastasia had no idea what Jeff was talking about, but she wanted to make sure her point of view was crystal clear.

"So, you do understand what this symbol means. Then you are wearing it as if it is nothing?" Anastasia pointed a finger at his chest. "I thought you were an educated man!"

"It's just a shirt, Baba," Jeff said calmly. "It's kind of funky. It's not like I'm walking around with a Nazi Swastika on me. The Soviet Union was a powerful country until twenty years ago, and, quite frankly, a lot of cool stuff came out of it."

Sofiya appeared at Anastasia's side, library books in one hand as she grabbed Anastasia's elbow by the other, and tried to steer her back to the front door.

"Baba, Jeff doesn't realize how much you hate the hammer and sickle symbol. He doesn't understand everything that the symbol represents, especially totalitarian repression." Sofiya glared at Jeff.

"But you do, Sofiya," Anastasia replied, struggling to get her arm away from Sofiya. "That symbol…is horrors caused by the Soviets. You know all about how they starved us in nineteen-thirty-two and then how they sent everyone who came back from Germany during the war to Siberia. You know all this!"

Anastasia knew that Sofiya was familiar with the history of Ukraine in the 1900s. Years before, Anastasia even helped Sofiya with a project about the man-made famine that happened in Ukraine in 1932 and 1933, which killed ten million citizens.

Anastasia turned away from Jeff, and walked as quickly as she could towards the front door.

"Jesus, Jeff," Sofiya hissed behind her.

Once outside, Anastasia turned to Sofiya, and looked at her directly.

"I do not want to go get groceries today. Take me home," Anastasia said. "I'm tired already. I can go get groceries later, or get someone else to take me. Maybe Alya isn't so busy today."

Anastasia and Sofiya drove back to the senior's residence in silence. The tension was thick between them. They parted ways quickly once back at Anastasia's building. Anastasia rode up the elevator to her apartment by herself. The afternoon sun was glaring through the front living room windows when she walked in the door, momentarily blinding her. She pulled the blinds shut to get away from the sun's harsh light and heat. She cursed the small window air conditioner that sputtered uselessly.

II.

Downstairs in the parking lot, Sofiya sighed and squeezed her eyes shut, resting her head on the steering wheel. She wanted a few moments of peace after her grandmother's abrupt departure. These Saturday visits were often annoying and difficult to handle. For years, Jeff had been borderline rude to Baba, but Sofiya didn't think that Anastasia had noticed, or if she had noticed, that she cared. Sofiya sighed with guilty relief that the unpleasant exchange between Baba and Jeff had at least dismantled the grocery shopping plans for that day. She detested grocery shopping. The hours spent slowly walking down the aisles were painful as she waited for Anastasia to browse. Inevitably, she ended up buying the same dozen items each week.

"I'm so damn tired," Sofiya said out loud to no one. She was disappointed in the exchange between Anastasia and Jeff. Sofiya was Anastasia's only grandchild, and they had been inseparable when Sofiya was a child. Baba took care of her before and after school, and often on weekends. "Thick as thieves," Alya used to say about her mother and daughter.

Sofiya sighed again, and remembered Jeff's ridiculous shirt. She had been with him when he bought it at a trendy boutique on Queen West. It had never sat well with her. She didn't understand why Jeff thought the shirt to be so clever that he had to have it. Sofiya suspected that Jeff had actually grown tired of the shirt, but continued to wear it solely to irritate her.

There was so much of her family history that Jeff just didn't understand. He was keen enough in the beginning of their relationship to learn the basic historical facts of Ukraine, but that interest had totally disappeared. Sofiya remembered how when they first started dating, she and Jeff had wonderful evenings, drinking wine with dinner, then vodka while sitting in the living room. Sofiya's father, Ostap, often told Jeff long, rambling stories of the Cossacks.

Of course, Sofiya knew all about the history of the homeland. She learned it all from an old, long-winded teacher at her Saturday morning Ukrainian classes when she was in high school. At the time, she had viewed the credits that she earned as useful only in counting towards her secondary diploma; otherwise, she would have seen those long hours spent in Ukrainian school as a complete waste of her teenage life.

On the nights that her parents were out somewhere, she slept at Anastasia's where she demanded bedtime stories about her childhood. Even though Anastasia could easily read any of Sofiya's children's books in English, the option of oral storytelling was preferable for the both of them. As a child, Sofiya loved to lie on her stomach in the single bed in Baba and Dido's spare room as Anastasia rubbed her back. Sofiya listened to stories about Anastasia's village in Ukraine; about her siblings, mother, her best friend Hanya, and all the trouble they used to get into together. Sofiya loved the stories about Anastasia and Hanya the best, because they reminded her of the silly antics that Sofiya and her friends got into. Sofiya watched in awe as Anastasia told her stories, appearing to be very far away, as if her spirit was traveling back to that village in Ukraine, while her body remained rooted firmly in Toronto in the eighties.

Sometimes, when Anastasia would tell her stories about Hanya, she laughed so hard that tears came to her eyes. Sofiya found this to be both frightening and fascinating at the same time. How could memories from so very long ago have such an effect on her beloved baba? Sofiya thought of her best friend, Jennifer, and wondered if once she was old, she too would cry when telling her own granddaughter about their antics.

To adult Sofiya, Baba's bedtime stories were a distant memory. Stretching out in her car, looking across the parking lot of the senior's residence, Sofiya tried to remember the name of Anastasia's village, and that friend whose memory brought tears to Baba's eyes. It had been so long since Sofiya had thought about Baba's stories that she couldn't remember any of the specific details. Putting her car into drive, and turning out of the parking lot, Sofiya made a mental note that she really should ask Baba about the details of those stories that she had loved so much. It may have been Baba's life story, but her story was also a part of Sofiya.

Remembering the library books, Sofiya reluctantly directed her new Lexus towards the library.

III.

As Anastasia rested on the overstuffed couch in the living room, she listened to the whirl of the air conditioner fan. She was still riled up with anger towards Jeff and disappointment in Sofiya. She was also, inexplicably, furious at the uselessness of the air conditioner.

"What's the point of you if you don't even work?" she asked out loud in the direction of the air conditioner.

"Now I'm really acting like an old lady. Talking to no one and nothing." Anastasia huffed.

"And to think, I did this to myself."

Anastasia still couldn't believe that the arrangement with the apartment was of her own making. For years, Alya had told her that Anastasia needed to sell her house, that it was too much work for her. Mainly to placate her daughter, Anastasia agreed to sign up on the waiting list for a retirement residence. Almost immediately, after Anastasia received notice that she had been allocated a unit, a huge dumpster appeared in her front driveway. She found herself arguing with both her daughter and granddaughter about what should be kept and what should be thrown in the trash.

Anastasia closed her eyes. Drifting off into a restless doze, Anastasia daydreamed about the memories that had faded with sixty years' worth of life lived in Canada, thinking about a time when she was young and innocent. She had started her life not called Anastasia, but Tasya. It was that young version of herself – of *Tasya*, that she thought about as she drifted off to sleep.

HORAYETZ

1942

I.

Tasya ran on the dirt main road of her village, working hard to keep up with Hanya. The two best friends ran in their light springtime shoes, dust kicking up after them. Their summer skirts flowed. Tasya could feel the thump of her father's heavy gold cross under her shirt with each step she took. From the time that Tasya was first able to walk, she and Hanya had done everything together. Always it was Tasya and Hanya; Hanya and Tasya. They had been best friends forever. The leaves were beginning their slow spring blooms on the oak and linden trees that lined the village streets. Baby's breath and periwinkle flowers were just starting to bud in the shady areas around the small village houses.

"That's enough running," Hanya said. "Let's walk from here, so we don't begin to sweat and smell like horses."

"It's only you that smells like a horse, Hanya." Tasya laughed as she danced around her friend, avoiding Hanya's swats. "Am I going to start to smell like that when I'm your age?"

Hanya was not only older, but taller. At fifteen and seventeen years old, the two friends couldn't have looked more opposite to each other. Older and younger. Darker and lighter. Mature and still learning.

"My age? I'm hardly two years older than you!" Hanya said, dabbing her long sleeve to her thick, dark hairline. "You just don't get as hot as I do."

Tasya laughed again.

"Next you'll tell me that because I have blue eyes that I'm bound to be lazier than you!" Tasya said as she hurried to keep up with Hanya's long strides.

"Let's just stop arguing!" Hanya cried in mock exasperation, keeping up her determined pace. "We need to hurry up and get home and dressed!"

It was a special day for the two of them. It was Good Friday, and they had been chosen as the two girls to carry the embroidered ceremonial banners – the *khorohvy* – in the procession following the Friday Vespers. In every city and village in Ukraine, this was a great honour. This year, they had both been chosen. Tasya was secretly thankful that Hanya was not chosen in the years before her, because the carrying of the *khorohvy* was another thing that they could do for the first time together.

"Is your sister coming to the service this evening?" Hanya asked. Tasya's older sister, Kateryna, had returned home from working in Germany the previous day. One day was all it had taken to upset the established balance in the household. Kateryna brought excitement and life, but also melodrama, to every situation.

"She was in Germany for one year?" Hanya asked.

"No. Nearly two."

"Well, then you must be happy that your sister is finally home," Hanya said, carefully. Hanya and Kateryna had never gotten along. Tasya knew they were both too similar to ever truly get along.

Tasya shrugged.

"I haven't seen that much of her. But, she is anxious to see everyone from the village."

It was Hanya's turn to shrug. It was obvious that Hanya didn't care if she saw Tasya's sister or not.

The afternoon was bright, crisp, and unusually warm, with just a hint of summer on the way. It was a spring day that brought villagers, young and old, onto the doorsteps and roads in celebration of finally casting off the bitterly cold winter. Tasya waved to all of the old men and women sitting on low-backed wooden chairs in front of their houses. She hadn't seen many of them in months, and several called greetings out to her.

Tasya felt an awkward silence settle around them. "It's just that...Kateryna seems so old now! She's only twenty-one, but she acts like because I'm fifteen that I should be treated like the baby of the house still."

Hanya nodded in sympathy. "A lot has changed since she left."

"That's right! I'm not the baby anymore and she doesn't understand that. Mama and I run the house, and we're good at it. Now that she's home, everything feels all wrong."

"Any news of Mychaylo?"

Mychaylo was the middle child, a brother three years older than Tasya, and three years younger than Kateryna; he was their buffer.

"She didn't see him at all. Kateryna says it's different with Mychaylo, because he didn't really volunteer to go to Germany like she did."

Where Kateryna had gone to Germany totally on her own regard, Mychaylo had been more or less forced to go. The German soldiers who occupied Horayetz said that as an able-bodied young male, he would be of good use to Germany.

Tasya loved and adored her brother. When she had found out that he was leaving to work in Germany, she was distraught. Angry at Mychaylo, angry at the soldiers in town, and angry at their mother, she cried hot tears for a week until Mychaylo had departed.

"Tasya, I'll be back. I promise," Mychaylo said, hugging her close.

Tasya clung to him.

"Kateryna is gone. Now you're leaving too. You know you're leaving me all alone with Mama."

Mychaylo laughed.

"Oh, Tasya, you'll be fine. You're Mama's little pet, you know. Besides, the Germans are telling me that if I don't volunteer now, I won't get the same preferential treatment when they have to force me." He lifted up Tasya's chin to look in her eyes. "And anyway, there isn't anything holding me back in Horayetz. I'm ready for the adventure, and to take these boots to places far away."

"But, what if Mama decides to marry the next man who turns his eye to look at her?"

It was her best argument. They had been through enough together, hadn't they? Though it was her best effort, as Tasya peered up at her brother through tear-filled eyelashes, her heart sank. The look in his eye told her not to make parting more painful than necessary. She tried again, becoming increasingly frustrated.

"If that happens, who will I complain to, and who will look out for me?"

Mychaylo sighed and hugged Tasya one last time.

"Listen, Tasya. I think Mama's learned her lesson after Pan Ivan. She's not going to be running into the arms of a man any time soon. You know what?

You'll have her all to yourself! Won't that be perfect?" Mychaylo bent over and picked a small bunch of the periwinkle that grew along the shady side of the house. He presented the flowers to Tasya with a flourish. Against her best efforts not to, she giggled.

As Mychaylo strode away, Tasya picked the deep purple blossoms from the stem. She was still unconvinced that Mychaylo should leave Horayetz, especially since their mother obviously needed a man around the house. The experience of having Pan Ivan as a stepfather had been an unpleasant one for all of the Boyko children. He had been a dairy farmer from the village, and a number of years younger than their mother, Daria. Always blaming others for his problems, Ivan had been a foul and highly unpleasant man.

When their father had died of tuberculosis, their mother grieved terribly.

"Thirty-three years old, and already I'm a widow!" She had cried to all the mourners who came for three days after their father's death. "Now what? How are we going to survive? I can't support the children. I'm a seamstress."

Tasya may have had a strong dislike for Pan Ivan, but Kateryna really hated him right from the beginning. During the time of the brief marriage, Kateryna spent as little time as possible at home, preferring to stay at their aunt's house.

Just as easily as he had swooped into their lives after the death of their father, Pan Ivan took his leave. In a death befitting his life, he died while drunk, and in the most absurd of ways. Ivan had been at the next village, drinking with a group of men, when he mistakenly took Wasyl Suslov's horse home. Suslov's horse had been frightened, bearing the unfamiliar rider into a strange village. Ivan somehow made it home. When he tied up the horse, she grew increasingly unsettled; whinnying and rearing up. Daria went outside to investigate the uproar, warning Tasya to stay indoors.

Daria was halfway across the yard when the horse kicked Ivan. Tasya marveled afterwards how long Ivan remained standing after the kick from the horse. Tasya began to think that he was fine, that the horse had missed him altogether, when Ivan dropped to the ground like a sack of potatoes, never to regain consciousness.

When Kateryna and Mychaylo had left for Germany, Tasya and her mother felt the absence of family dearly. After a year had passed, they decided that Tasya was finished with school and could take over most of the household chores for Daria. That arrangement left Daria to focus on her seamstress piecework. Along with a pittance of an inheritance from Pan Ivan, the two were in decent shape while Kateryna and Mychaylo were gone. Now that she had gotten used to the routine, Tasya wasn't sure that she was happy to have her sister back home.

II.

Any thoughts of terrible step-fathers, the war, or Germany were a long way away for Tasya and Hanya as they walked home together through the village. They strolled up the dirt road without a care in the world, thinking only of the special honour they would have at the church.

While walking, Tasya looked at the familiar houses and sighed happily. All the homes in their area were nearly the same, on identical tracts of land. Each plot of land housed a two to three-room house, whitewashed diligently, each covered by a roof made of straw and mud. Some of the more prestigious families in the village had rough-hewn boards topping their homes. Tasya's family was lucky that their floors were made of concrete, not hard-packed earth. According to Daria, this gave them a higher status than some of their neighbors. Hanya's house did not have a concrete floor. Tasya knew that her friend was embarrassed about this difference, but they had a mutual understanding never to speak about it.

Tasya's house was only one floor with a cramped attic crawl-space, but it had been more than enough room for just Tasya and her mother. The grass around the house was worn thin in several places, including the path that lead from the road to the front of the house. Inside, the house was usually dim, even on the brightest of days, which helped to keep the house warm in the winter, and cool in the summer. Most of the floor space was in the main living and kitchen area, which was one big room. On the right wall was a huge fireplace that held the coal-burning stove. In the middle of the room was a wood dining table large enough to seat eight. Directly next to the front door, a few overstuffed and patched-up chairs were carefully arranged around a low table to form a sort of parlour area for guests. Otherwise, there was one good-sized bedroom and storage area at the back of the house.

Tasya's house was closer to the center of the village than Hanya's family home, and soon they were at the front gate.

"I'll see you back here in one hour!" Hanya called out over her shoulder as she continued down the road. "We will go to the church early together, and sit near the *khorohvy*."

Tasya waved her goodbye as she ran up the path to her house and in the front door. As her eyes adjusted to the darkened room, Tasya saw her mother and sister sitting together at the kitchen table. They seemed to be having a serious conversation and looked surprised to see her, though they should have been expecting her home by then.

Tasya hurried to tell them her good news.

"Mama, Kateryna," she started, breathlessly, "I have to hurry and get ready for Vespers tonight, because Hanya and I have each been chosen to carry a *khorohva* in the procession!"

"Good, child," Daria replied. "You must press your embroidered blouse and hair ribbon."

Daria still appeared preoccupied by the conversation with Kateryna. Normally, Tasya would have expected her mother to fuss over her and bring out the beautiful blouse that she had embroidered. Daria would have made sure that her hair was plaited in just the right way, with the special hair ribbon that she had given Tasya for her twelfth birthday.

Why wasn't Daria busy getting herself and the house ready for Saturday's blessing of the Easter food baskets, and preparing the house for the Easter celebration? Looking around from the middle of the house, Tasya saw that the lunch dishes were still unwashed, the floor not swept, and her mother was obviously not ready to go to church.

"What are you two talking about?" Tasya asked, suspicious. "Are you talking about me?"

"No, no, *donechko*." Daria stood up, and absently planted a kiss on the top of Tasya's head.

"Then why did you both jump out of your skins when I came in the house?"

"For pity's sake, Tasya! Didn't you say that you had some sort of big-deal task to do?" Kateryna snapped. Tasya looked with wide eyes over to their mother, expecting her to reprimand Kateryna for being cruel, but Daria just looked relieved at the distraction and carried dirty dishes to the washing bin.

Tasya scowled at both of them. "You've been back for how long? One day? Already you're irritating me. When are you going back to Germany?"

Kateryna stood up and without meeting Tasya's eyes said, "Actually…I'm not going back."

"What?" Tasya exclaimed. "After all the promises that the soldiers made, and the fight you put up with Mama when you wanted to go...now you are back for good?"

"Things are different now, Tasya. I wouldn't expect you to understand," Kateryna said. Without another word she walked out of the house.

"Now where's she going?" Tasya cried, but their mother ignored her.

Tasya remembered how Kateryna had been drawn by the German soldier rhetoric, and she remembered the pain her leaving had caused their mother, but in the end it had come as no surprise. Kateryna had been wide-eyed with interest whenever the German soldiers were around.

One cold day in February of 1940 as Tasya was walking home from school with Kateryna, they saw a group of German soldiers standing in the middle of the village. They were handing out flyers to a buzzing crowd that had gathered around them.

"Katya!" One of the German soldiers called out to Kateryna. Tasya was shocked, but impressed too. Did Kateryna really know the Germans? It was thrilling knowing that their mother would be angry to know that Kateryna was on such good terms with their occupiers. Tasya remained quiet and tried to make herself invisible.

"Katya, come here! Come see these flyers that just came in!" called another soldier. "They are all about opportunities to work in Germany!"

He handed a flyer to Kateryna, and Tasya stood on her tiptoes to peek at it. It was a picture of three young women, each proudly working at different tasks – one baking, one fixing a machine, and one taking care of small children. At the bottom of the poster, in Polish, Tasya slowly read 'Come to Germany! Your labour will be your help.' The poster was printed in deep and vibrant colours, something that Tasya had never seen before.

Kateryna gazed at the poster for several minutes. The crowd eagerly took every single one the soldiers had.

"Kateryna," Tasya whispered, nervously pulling her away from the growing crowd, and away from German ears. "You know that Mama does not like us to speak to the Germans, and someone might tell her that you are friendly with the soldiers."

"Oh, Tasya! I'm only looking at the flyer. Look, lots of people my age are going to work in Germany and are making good money! I can even make something for myself and bring home lots of money for us."

If Kateryna actually went to Germany, Tasya wondered, might she love it so much that she would never return home? Seeing the determination in her sister's eyes, Tasya knew that Kateryna was weighing the good and bad points. If she decided to go, the battle that Daria was sure to wage was already lost.

Of course, Daria and Kateryna fought mightily about it. Daria couldn't believe that Kateryna would want to go and work in such a distant and foreign place.

"Of course it is unimaginable to you, Mama!" Kateryna had cried. "You have never been further than Peremyshyl. I refuse to live my life that way, and I want to go somewhere that's longer than an hour's train ride!"

Tasya was not surprised that within the week, a triumphant Kateryna marched down to the German recruitment office in the middle of Horayetz with Tasya and Daria in tow. She was promptly registered as a worker with the German administration, and Daria cried for a week straight.

Today, as she put the final touches on her outfit, tucking her blouse carefully into a freshly laundered skirt, and wove her best ribbon through her hair, Tasya stole glances at her mother, still suspicious of what was going on between her and Kateryna.

In less than an hour, Tasya was again outside the front gate, waiting impatiently for Hanya. She ran her fingers over the red and black embroidery on her sleeve. She reached up to pat the ribbon embroidered with red poppies.

Hanya soon met Tasya again, and the girls walked uphill back to the center of the village and to the church. St. Demetrius was a beautiful church, with its three domes topped with three crosses that were visible from all around Horayetz. The church had been built out of timber from the forest around it, and although Tasya had heard visitors from Lviv joke that the design of the church looked to be 'very square', she thought that it was beautiful.

The inside of the church was a hushed, dark space for solemn worship. Tasya and Hanya stepped into the narthex, the vestibule of the church. They were still early for the service. With the sparse attendance, mostly confined to sitting on benches against the outside walls, the nave of the church was nearly empty and silent. Tasya saw the priest and deacon in the sanctuary behind the iconostasis, getting ready for the service to begin. They both held gold censers, suspended on three chains with tiny bells attached. As the priest and deacon whispered prayers around the altar, they swung their censers to and fro, releasing the thick-smoked incense that burned within. The fragrance filled every corner of the church as the smoke curled heavenward.

The girls chose a bench on the left-hand side of the nave, close to the sanctuary, and next to one of the *khorohvy* that they would be carrying as part of the procession of the Holy Shroud. They watched as the church filled with their fellow villagers. Tasya tried her best to look very serious. That Friday, the service was the most solemn of the entire year, and as they sat waiting for the Vespers to begin, they were feeling the weight of their responsibility. The deacon, Father Andrij, usually chose which girls would carry the *khorohvy* in the procession, and the girls wanted very much to please him that evening, as he was much-loved by both of them. As they sat, Tasya spotted Father Andrij, and he gave her a friendly wink, to which Tasya smiled shyly back.

Tasya saw her mother and sister eventually enter the church. Tasya noticed that Daria was glaring at herself and Hanya, and she knew right away that her mother wanted her to stand up from the bench to give her place to one of the older women in the church. Normally, Tasya would be purposely slow to stand, thinking of the long service ahead, but that evening, she felt as if she had transformed from a little girl to a young woman, and she was willing to act in a more adult fashion.

The Vespers began. Soon it was time for each of the girls to carry the *khorohvy* leading the congregation around the church. While it was an honour that many girls bickered over, it was also a tricky job. The *khorohva* was large and heavy. It was a huge piece of white cloth embroidered with images of baby Jesus and Mary. It was tied to an ever bigger and heavier wooden pole. Once Tasya managed to get the *khorohva* out of its holder, it swung around until she found the balance to keep it upright. Tasya's arms grew weak as the shroud oscillated mightily with each step that she took. Sweat broke out under her arms.

Once outside, the congregation processed around the church three times as was the tradition. Tasya walked side by side with Hanya behind the main cross, the priest, Father Andrij, and the Holy Shroud. Once they completed their three turns around the church, they entered through the front doors up to the iconostasis, where the Shroud would be on display until the Resurrection Mass.

After the service, the crowd inside the church drifted outside to form small groups to converse before heading home. Tasya and Hanya's mothers stood talking together.

"I wonder how much longer the Germans are going to let us keep this up?" Hanya's mother, Pani Lida, asked, gesturing to the church.

"The Germans don't seem to care so much about us keeping up with our religion. As long as we keep quiet about it," Daria replied.

In 1939, Horayetz had easily and without much resistance become occupied by German forces. Before the occupation, the people of Horayetz had heard from passing travelers that Hitler's troops were taking over more Polish territory. Doing nothing, they were waiting like sitting ducks when the occupation finally happened. Horayetz was technically in the USSR, but it was so close to the border that it didn't seem to matter to the advancing Germans.

In the early months of the occupation, most of the young people of the village found it exciting to be living and working among the smartly attired and handsome German soldiers. Their uniforms were impossibly clean, sharply pressed, and their tall, perfectly shined boots made the best Sunday shoes of the local village boys look like footwear for cleaning a barn.

The soldiers said that Germany was the land of gold and that there was much money to be made by the boys and girls of the village. They said Hitler's plans required many goods; workers were needed to go to Germany to help in the factories. They passed registration forms to the young people, describing the exciting opportunities for work and leisure in the big, metropolitan cities of Germany.

Now, two years later, things had changed. Here outside the church, Pani Lida peered around as if a German might be listening in to the conversation.

"They *used to* not care, Daria, but with this new administration, we should watch our backs."

Listening in, Tasya considered the new crop of soldiers who were occupying Horayetz. This group was just as handsome and polished as the first, but their tone had dramatically changed. Now, the story was not about convincing the young people to come to work in Germany, it was rather that they *must* go. Tasya had heard their speeches that told villagers every family must send at least one young person to work in the factories. Resistance, the villagers were learning, was futile. To emphasize the point, the Germans threatened that if every family didn't send at least one person, the entire family would have to go. They said there was no choice anymore. No promises of riches, of opportunity, just threats.

Outside of the church, the crowd thinned. Tasya noticed that people were gathering around Kateryna. She looked angry, speaking quickly, waving her arms around.

"What did you say that they call us?" Tasya heard one old woman ask.

"*Zivilarbeiter*. Civilian worker."

"And they made you wear what on your clothes?" The old woman asked again.

"A fabric patch with the letter 'P' on it!" Kateryna yelled. Tasya saw that her sister was frustrated. "Like I said, they labeled me as Polish, if you can believe it!"

The crowd muttered its disgust. Both Ukrainians and Poles lived in Horayetz, but there had always been tension. There was nothing more insulting to the Ukrainians of Horayetz than to be called a Pole.

"When we first arrived on the train, we were told to line up, depending on the type of workers that we were. There was *Zivilarbeiter*, a Polish civilian worker, but I thought I was to be a *Gastarbeiter*, a foreign guest worker, but oh no, that didn't happen."

"What's the difference?" A young man from the edge of the small group called out. Tasya recognized him from the school in the village. There were now at least a dozen people gathered.

"*Yoi*, let me tell you! There's a big difference! There are rules and more rules to follow. *Zivilarbeiter* can't ride a bus, *Zivilarbeiter* are not allowed to mix with Germans, and *Zivilarbeiter* must be paid lower wages. That's just the start of it!"

The crowd collectively made a clucking sound while shaking their heads. Tasya saw that her sister was quickly gaining the sympathy of everyone around her.

"But, they let you leave?" An old woman called out as she pushed for a position at the front of the crowd. She frequently touched the sleeve of Kateryna's coat.

"Well, yes, obviously because I'm here, aren't I? I, uh, told them that Mama was dying and that I had to get home. I had a kind supervisor; otherwise I don't think I would have been allowed to come home."

The crowd murmured its approval once again. More people had gathered to listen. Tasya, at the edge of the group, nervously scanned the road in front of the church yard for patrolling soldiers.

"What did you tell him?" An unknown man's voice called out.

"I promised on my mother's deathbed that I would return to Germany within two weeks."

Tasya heard people draw in a collective breath. She heard many people mutter.

"Oh, two weeks!"

"Are you going back?" Another man shouted out.

"Like hell I am," Kateryna said, shaking her head. "If they want us Ukrainians to come help, then they had better classify us as friendly workers, and pay us appropriately! If they want slave labour, they can get it from the Russians!"

The crowd laughed its approval, and the people joked amongst themselves about Russians.

"Listen, friends! There's more to tell you. Think about what I am about to tell you before you go to register with the German administration. Listen to me...there are other classes of workers, too. Classes that are much more abused then I was."

Tasya then heard the crunch of gravel under boots, and looked up to spot a pair of German soldiers, walking leisurely up the road from the center of the village. They did not appear to be in any hurry, but the sight of their rifles casually slung over their shoulders and their pistols at their waists was enough to frighten Tasya. Her heart stopped and she froze for only a second before she pushed her way through the crowd to Kateryna. "Soldiers, soldiers!" Tasya whispered urgently.

Everyone in the small group looked up and over to where the men were coming.

"Walk away calmly. Do not draw attention to us," Kateryna whispered, but it was already too late. Some of the people who had been listening to her looked like startled rabbits, and quickly walked away. Others looked like they were trying far too hard not to draw the attention of the soldiers.

Daria had also walked away casually after shooting both girls a glare, but Kateryna remained in place with Tasya frozen by her side.

The soldiers approached the group in the church yard. Without looking up at her sister, Tasya reached out and grasped her hand. Kateryna held it firmly in her own.

"*Guten Abend*," one of the soldiers said, looking from Kateryna to Tasya. Tasya saw that he was smiling with his mouth, but not with his eyes.

"What was going on over here?" He spoke in broken and halting Polish.

"We were just all talking. The Vespers just ended." Kateryna answered back in her own rough version of Polish.

"Then why did everyone run away so quickly when we came?" A second soldier, less friendly than the first, interrupted them. Up close, Tasya saw that they were even younger than Kateryna.

"I suppose you make them nervous," Kateryna said. She laughed a low, unfriendly chuckle. Tasya squeezed her hand even tighter, silently pleading to Kateryna that they get away from the soldiers as quickly as possible.

"Why would we make you nervous?" The first soldier asked, forced grin still showing.

"Your rifles are a good start," Kateryna answered.

"As long as nothing is going on that shouldn't be, there's no reason to be nervous, is there?" the first soldier asked, directing his question directly at Tasya.

"Then we have nothing to worry about."

The first soldier looked back at Tasya and laughed. Tasya felt goose bumps growing along her arms.

"You look familiar," the second soldier said, looking Kateryna up and down. "Didn't I see you arrive here on that transport with the soldiers?"

Kateryna paused for several of Tasya's thundering heartbeats before answering. "Yes, you did."

The first soldier raised his eyebrows. "What were you doing coming from the West? That's an unusual sight. Young women like you usually head in the other direction."

"Especially with the new regulations in place," the second soldier interjected, startling both Tasya and Kateryna. The first soldier shushed his partner.

"I'm actually free to come and go to Germany as I wish," Kateryna replied with forced cheerfulness. "I come back every now and again to bring my earnings back to my family."

Tasya knew that was a lie – Kateryna had never returned to bring money home. It was true that she brought back a few German marks that were worthless in Horayetz.

"That must be an old agreement. That sort of thing is very rare these days," the first soldier said, watching Kateryna closely.

"It is. I was a volunteer to go, right in the beginning, and I'm given privileges in return."

The first soldier looked at his partner.

"Well, there you have it. She's been given special privileges."

The second soldier looked like he didn't know what to do. He shrugged.

"Well, you two girls enjoy your evening then," the first soldier said. Tasya saw that the churchyard was now empty. He turned as if he was going to walk away.

"Oh, but don't forget – every family must have at least one volunteer sent to Germany to work, or all of your family must go. Is that clear?" he added. Tasya saw that he was no longer smiling. Kateryna nodded, but didn't say a word.

Once the soldiers began to walk back towards the center of the village, Kateryna pulled Tasya the other way, towards home.

"Why didn't you tell him about Mychaylo?" Tasya hissed at Kateryna, still shaking from the scary conversation with the soldiers. She didn't know why she was so anxious. The first soldier, the calm one with the forced smile, had made her the most nervous. It was as if she didn't know what he was truly thinking, and she didn't like that.

Kateryna didn't answer, but kept holding her hand tightly, dragging her the entire way home.

III.

No matter the time of year, Tasya's favourite sleeping place in the entire house was on the warm hearth in front of the fireplace. It was there, lying on a pile of woolen blankets on Good Friday evening, that Tasya heard what Germany, the so-called 'Land of Gold', was truly about. Tasya overheard Kateryna and her mother talking in whispers. They probably thought she was asleep.

"What are you saying, Kateryna? Everyone is half-starved and being worked to death?" Daria's voice was filled with doubt.

"Mama, you would not believe how people are treated in Germany," Kateryna said.

"Even though you were a volunteer? What about Mychaylo? He's a volunteer as well. Are you saying that you are lumped in the same category of prisoners and Russians?"

"Yes, Mama! *Zivilarbeiter* are no better than dogs to the Germans! Right from when I stepped off the train in Düsseldorf, I saw poor people like nothing I have ever seen here in Horayetz. People everywhere, wearing rags, some even without shoes! And the Jews, *Bozhe*. Don't even ask me about the Jews and their digging, digging all day and night long to build rail tracks."

Kateryna told of the terrible things she had encountered; of her difficult working conditions in a German ammunition factory, the little food or rest allowed. In the early days of the German occupation of their village, the village youth had put so much faith into the words of the handsome German soldiers who said that Germany would be a way to make money for their families.

It was promoted as a way to improve their small village lives.

Tasya remembered the threats, and watching families decide which of their children to send to Germany, yet she had never spoken about this to Hanya. Hanya was the eldest child of the Petrusiv family, and they had not yet sent anyone off to Germany. With no end in sight to the occupation, Tasya kept up hope that her friend would not be chosen to go work in the factories, but that hope became smaller and smaller.

Though Tasya's back was turned towards her mother and sister, she sensed them carefully watching her to see if she was still sleeping. Tasya tried to make her breathing as slow as possible. She reached under her nightshirt to pull her father's gold cross over her shirt. She thumbed it with worry.

"Mama, they don't care where Horayetz is, or that I'm Ukrainian. All they know is that we've been bounced back between the Poles and Soviets for decades. To tell you the truth, I'm lucky they identified me as Polish."

Both Kateryna and Daria stayed silent for several minutes. Were they still there? Tasya kept still just in case.

"So. When are you going to tell her?" Kateryna asked their mother. Tasya's ears perked up, and she strained to listen.

Was that a sniffle? Daria's voice trembled.

"Soon. After the *sviato*. Maybe on Monday, once everything is over. But it will have to be very soon. The German administrator, that godforsaken dog, has already warned me that we must organize ourselves by the end of next week."

Tasya knew who the German administrator was. She had often seen him being driven around the village in a jeep, giving orders, or supervising the soldiers. Tasya also knew that he was in charge of registering the population of the village as well as their comings and goings when traveling.

"He told me tonight, very directly, that if we do not select another family member to take your place by next Friday, that we will *all* be forced to go – you included, *donechko*."

Tasya held her breath. Did Mama mean her?

"I pray it won't be so bad for the poor child, Kateryna. He said that work is needed in the fall harvest, and that she might avoid the factories. If she volunteers now, she will be classified as Polish, rather than Russian."

"They call the Russians *Ostarbeiter*," Kateryna whispered. "We had some of those people in the factory where I worked. Everyone knew who they were because they were forced to wear a blue and white patch on their clothing that had 'OST' on it."

"That was worse than you?"

"Much worse! They were treated like dirt, like sub-human. They had to work in terrible camps, or they were in the factories where they were forbidden to speak to anyone, always supervised by a guard. I heard the German supervisors calling them inferior humans."

"No, that won't do…not for my Tasya," Daria said softly.

"I hope so, Mama. As a *Zivilarbeiter* she will get paid some money at least. The *Ostarbeiter* people don't get paid at all. The only way that they survived was from the rations given to them at their camps."

"Oh God. We have no choice but to send her now," Daria sighed. "If we must sacrifice one member for the good of the rest of the family, what else can we do?"

After another pause, Tasya heard what she had feared to hear most.

"Tasya must take your place."

Tasya couldn't believe her ears, and sat up on the hearth.

"Mama!" she cried. "You're going to send me to Germany to work in Kateryna's place? I'm only fifteen years old!" Rage and terror flooded through her, hot tears burned her cheeks.

Both women looked startled and embarrassed. Daria walked over to Tasya and sat next to her. She reached over to draw Tasya into her, but Tasya shied away.

"Tasya," her mother said weakly. "There's a reason why Kateryna cannot go back to Germany. Your big sister is going to have a baby."

The news struck Tasya like a lightning bolt. Kateryna was with child? By whom?

"Did you lie with a German?!" Tasya spat, turning her sights on Kateryna. She was going to say whatever she wanted.

"Don't accuse me like you would a small child! And no, it's not some German. Ihor is the father. From Liubachiv."

Could it be? Kateryna and Ihor were going to have a child together? Ihor was the son of their fathers' friend. The children of the two families had grown up together. Kateryna and Ihor were the eldest and had gone to Germany on the same transport.

Daria took charge of the conversation again.

"Tasya, I was going to tell you in a few days. There is nothing we can do." Daria reached over to Tasya again, and this time, she let her mother draw her close. "You will have to go to work in Germany in Kateryna's place."

When Tasya didn't answer, her mother continued.

"But I have some good news as well. I have spoken to Hanya's family, and she will also be going to work with you. So you can keep each other company, stay together, protect each other, and be safe."

Tasya looked up from the crook of her mother's arm.

"When?" she whispered.

"By next Friday. You have to register with the *Arbeitsamt* in town. We have to get you a certificate, showing that you are going to Germany to work." Tasya saw her mother look up at her sister. "Kateryna needs one too, showing that she does not have to return."

It seemed that there was no choice. The decision was made. That evening, Tasya thought about the soldiers, their parting warning to Kateryna. She thought about how every single family in the village had been forced to send at least one of their children to Germany. Now, it was her turn to have all choices taken away from her.

IV.

The next week passed by in a blur for Tasya. It was rumoured that there was a shortage of volunteer labour heading to Germany, and that nearly all the young people were being forced to go and work. Entire families were also sent. Ukrainians from all around the region had been sending back word to their villages from Germany of the terrible working conditions, as well as the unbelievably cruel and inhumane policies about the treatment of those who happened to be classified as *Ostarbeiter*. Now, young Ukrainians were running away and hiding. The Germans' reaction was staged manhunts. They went as far as arbitrarily rounding up people in the streets of occupied territories to fill the shortage. The last thing Tasya wanted was to be rounded up like a stray dog in the street. She eventually came to the conclusion that if she didn't want her sister and mother to have to go, then go she must, in their places.

After the initial shock of the news of her impending trip to Germany passed, Tasya began to resent Kateryna. Tasya had always looked up to her older sister, and as a child she had worshiped the ground Kateryna walked on. For her part, Kateryna had been Tasya's protector if children ever teased the younger sister, or if Tasya got into a fight at school. Now, Tasya's world had shifted, and Kateryna was a focus of rage and blame.

Angry and sullen, Tasya watched her mother's preparations for the long journey to Germany. From Kateryna's experience, Tasya knew that although the Germans needed her to work for them, they were not going to make the journey easy. Tasya and Hanya would be traveling by train from Peremyshyl to the far reaches of Germany, into Düsseldorf.

Tasya found herself on the receiving end of dozens of bits of advice from her mother.

"You need to act like an adult, Tasya. Stop crying, please."

"I know, Mama."

"You and Hanya need to look out for one another, Tasya. She will be your family until you come back."

"I know, Mama."

"Take care to make this bread last, Tasya. You need to make it last for two weeks."

"I know, Mama."

"I love you, Tasya."

When Tasya went to register with the *Arbeitsamt*, she was informed that she would be traveling on a train carrying animals, goods, and other workers. She was also given a quick medical examination by a female nurse at registration who proclaimed, despite Tasya's tears, there was absolutely nothing wrong with her to go and work.

The clock steadily ticked towards Friday. Tasya grew more troubled about leaving her family. Most of her life had been spent within the borders of Horayetz or playing in the surrounding forests. Her family sometimes visited Peremyshyl and she always found the experience overwhelming. Düsseldorf sounded unimaginably foreign. Kateryna had not helped when she had warned Tasya that it was a very crowded and busy place.

Tasya didn't sleep well. Every night, she felt the ceiling closing in on her, inch by inch. Could she run? Could she hide? Why couldn't the war just be over? She prayed day and night for a truce to be called so that she could carry on with her life as it was meant to be. Their family and home was all that she had ever known, and she couldn't imagine being away from everything that was familiar to her. Tasya grew terrified; palms and underarms sweating almost constantly. Her heart ached, and her throat felt as if it was closing up even though she was still at home. Her stomach churned, and she felt her upcoming loss acutely, even though she knew that she was aching for a place that she had not yet lost.

Though she had thought of him less in the years after his death, she wondered what would her father say? If he had still been alive, would he have been able to protect her?

Tasya daydreamed that he was alive again, that he saved her from leaving. He was her hero. She imagined his voice, speaking to her softly, saying, *You are my little bird, I will not let any harm come to you. I will keep you safe with me, here at home.*

The Friday morning that Tasya was to leave, she woke up very early from her sleeping place on the fireplace hearth. It was still dark outside. As she adjusted to the sounds around her, she heard Kateryna breathing softly on the sleeping couch, not far from her. Daria was at the other end of the house, in the bedroom. Tasya lay on the hearth and waited for the sun to rise, listening for the first bright chirping of the birds, thinking about how only a week prior, she had been so carefree.

She grew restless. She heard Daria tossing in her bed as well. There would be no more sleep this morning. Tasya heard Daria's bare feet padding across the floor of the kitchen towards the hearth.

"Oh, you're already awake, *Sonechko*," Daria said, using her baby nickname for Tasya. She hadn't called Tasya that for many years. Tasya felt her mother ease onto the hearth next to her.

"The war will be over soon, I'm sure. You'll come back to us," Daria promised as she reached over to rub Tasya's back.

"But, what if the war doesn't end quickly?" Tasya protested. "How long must I stay in Germany? What if something happens to me?" Tasya looked to her mother for reassurance. Her mother was supposed to be her protector from all things bad. Without her support, Tasya was drifting with no tether to her own life.

"Just keep faith in God, say your prayers every day, and you will come back before you know it. I have faith in you, and in God." Daria sounded tired, just as worn down as Tasya felt.

"Will you miss me?" Tasya asked, looking again to seek comfort in her mother eyes.

"I will miss you more than I would the sun if it suddenly disappeared." Daria paused for more than a few seconds. "You are my baby, my special little girl."

Tasya squeezed her eyes together and let her mother embrace her. She knew it was silly, but she desperately prayed to God to be able to see into her future, to know when she would be back with her mother and sister again. If Tasya could ask God for one thing at that very moment, it would have been to know when she would be home again to the warm comforts of her family.

There was little else to be said between Tasya and her mother. Many tears had been shed that week, and both Daria and Kateryna had tried their best to comfort Tasya. Tasya continued to lay on the hearth, while her mother stroked her hair.

On that last morning in Horayetz, they all ate a breakfast of buckwheat porridge, ham, and tea. Tasya prepared herself to leave. Kateryna went out, giving Tasya and her mother a bit of space for a private goodbye.

When Tasya was ready to leave, Daria took her by the hand to the yard out back, sitting her down on the stone bench near the back vegetable garden. Tasya sat silent and tense, feeling that if she said a word, the tears that she had been holding back would break forth and she would not be able to stop them.

"*Sonechko*, this is an important thing that you are doing for our family. If it was not for you going to Germany, all three of us would be sent. You understand why Kateryna cannot have her baby in Germany? She must stay here and wait for Ihor. We will be right here, waiting for you to come home to us." She cupped Tasya's face.

Tasya focused on the feeling of her mother. She wanted to remember the impression of her mother's strong and capable hands.

"Now, *Sonechko*, this is difficult, but I think I should hold your tato's cross with me for safekeeping until you get back." Tasya nodded silently. It was as if she ripped out her entire heart and was handing it over to her mother.

"Stay close with Hanya, and be safe. Always look out for one another. Always remember where you came from, your homeland, and that you are Ukrainian."

Daria kissed both of Tasya's cheeks, then pulled her to her feet before putting the gold cross in her skirt pocket. They walked together over to the well, and Tasya drank the water from it for the last time. Daria took the cloth sack of bread and sprinkled water on all of the small loaves to delay the staleness that would harden the bread over the coming days.

Tasya and her mother then walked together in silence to Hanya's home with Kateryna trailing behind. When they arrived, it looked as if a similar scene of farewell had passed between Hanya and her family members. Hanya's mother, two younger sisters, and her younger brother all stood huddled close to Hanya, while her father stood a ways away, close to his rusted-out farm truck. They all had red-rimmed eyes from crying.

It was time for the final farewells. Kateryna approached Tasya first and gave her a long squeeze. Daria then took Tasya into her arms. Tasya still felt betrayed, but in her sadness, and rising panic, her bad feelings melted away as she clung in her mother's embrace. Next to them, Hanya was saying her final goodbyes to her family, sobbing as they huddled together in one group.

"You will always be my daughter, and my little girl," Daria whispered. "You will one day return to me, I know it." Daria took a step back, squeezed Tasya's shoulders, and turned her towards the truck.

Tasya and Hanya got into the back cab of the truck where piles of itchy woolen blankets had been spread over an old *kylym*. Hanya's father started the engine, and pulled onto the road. Once they were moving, Tasya looked back at the group they were leaving behind, keeping her gaze on her mother and sister. The pair were standing just outside the front gate of Hanya's house. Tasya felt a clutch of jealously when she saw that her mother and sister had their arms around each other. They both had tears streaming down their faces. The Boyko women waved at one another as the truck drove away. As the truck rounded a bend in the road, Tasya's family was lost to sight. Tasya continued to wave at nothing in particular, until Hanya reached up and pulled her hand back down.

DÜSSELDORF

1942

I.

"Name?"

"Village?"

"Skills?"

"Age?"

When Tasya and Hanya arrived at the train station in Peremyshyl, the processing of workers was swift. Shuffling around in an endless procession to German administrators and Polish translators, they answered the same questions over and over again.

It was the question about her age that filled Tasya with growing dread. She felt like every set of eyes in the train station was on her each time she whispered, "Sixteen."

The first time, the administrator looked up from his paperwork, peering over the top of his glasses. "*Heh*? What did you say?" he demanded in Polish. Pinpricks of sweat broke out along the back of Tasya's neck.

"Sixteen," she whispered again.

The administrator looked her over once, and then with eyebrows raised, wrote down her false age. Tasya realized that she had been holding her breath, and tried to exhale without making noise.

Tasya was scared to lie about her age, but she had made a promise to Kateryna late one night. Kateryna was worried that the Germans might not take a fifteen-year-old girl. Their mother had already gone to bed, and the two sisters were lying side-by-side on the fireplace hearth.

"Please, Tasya," said Kateryna. "If they don't take you, what will we do?"

When Tasya didn't respond, Kateryna said flatly, "Do you really want Mama to be sent in your place?"

"Maybe, we could try to tell them that we already have a brother in Germany? Again, I mean," Tasya suggested in desperation.

"We already tried that, Tasya!" Kateryna's voice betrayed her frustration.

At the train station in Peremyshyl, after being asked the same questions for what seemed like a hundred times, they were herded in big groups out to the tracks. Then came the next shock. Along with hundreds of other young Polish and Ukrainian girls, they were loaded onto empty Pullman cars, the kind usually reserved for transporting livestock. It was hard to believe. Though the girls were all different ages, shapes, and sizes, they wore the same wide-eyed expression of awe and fear. Too stunned to know what else to do, the sea of young girls followed orders quickly and quietly.

Tasya and Hanya were directed by a German soldier to a car along with twenty other girls. They had to sit on the dirty floor, which stank of animals. Some girls were alone, openly weeping. Others gathered in pairs or small groups to cry together. Tasya felt badly for one girl, a very young-looking slight blonde, with huge eyes, who sat alone by the wall, repeatedly crying out for her mama. She searched the eyes of anyone who made contact, as if they might help her.

"I feel bad for her; should I ask if she wants to sit with us?" Tasya suggested.

"*Bozhe*, no. I already have you to deal with, and that's about enough for me." Hanya rarely showed sympathy.

"What do you mean?" Tasya protested. She was proud of how little she had cried since arriving at the train station. "I'm keeping myself together. I haven't even cried since we said goodbye to your tato!"

"That may be, but if I wasn't here with you, for certain you would be just like that poor girl, and the other girls here would be trying to avoid you too."

Feelings of shame welled up. Tasya was dismayed at how quickly fear had displaced pity for the distraught blonde girl.

The door was slammed shut by a German soldier. It was still twilight outside, but inside the car was total darkness. Tasya groped around for Hanya, and found her hand. Girls who were crying began to wail.

In the first few days of the trip, the girls in the car were for the most part quiet. Hanya and Tasya each brought with them a thin bedroll of blankets, which they would fold and then sit on for some comfort during the day. At night, they used their bags of clothing as pillows. After two days, the train stopped for the first time at a small village in the Polish countryside, and twenty other girls were herded into the car. They were allowed off for water and to use an outhouse on the far side of the station. The tiny blonde girl all the while kept frozen in one corner. Tasya watched as others grew concerned for her, trying to draw her out of her shell.

A deep, simmering hatred for Germans and Germany began to burn inside Tasya. Who would treat young women, girls really, like animals this way? She prayed to God for the trip to be over, for the war to be over, for anything to end this. What could she possibly have done to deserve what was happening to her? But no answer came to her, and the train rolled on across the unseen countryside.

With the only light coming into the Pullman from two tiny windows at the very top of the car, it was dim during the daytime hours, and pitch black at night. The rise and fall of the sun was the only reminder of their daily lives to Tasya and Hanya, yet they found themselves settling into an unexpected routine. During the day, they tried to keep up a regular breakfast, lunch, and dinner schedule, however meager. Both girls were very careful to ration their bread, and they hid their extra portions from the other girls.

Sleeping on the freight car was not easy, and with the constant moving and jolting, getting any rest became even more difficult. Tasya felt like on most nights she was awake for the entire time, waiting for the light to finally filter through the tiny windows. Every night, she waited anxiously for the daytime light, no matter how weak, to come in. She was never sure that she actually had slept until she remembered fragments of dreams. She tried to hang onto the memories of those dreams, but they quickly disappeared. She couldn't concentrate on anything besides her own exhaustion.

Tasya tried to distract herself by thinking about Mychaylo. Where was her brother, and would she see him in Germany? Hanya had admonished Tasya when she had suggested that they might find Mychaylo, so Tasya kept her fantasizing to herself.

Tasya tried to keep her focus steady on Mychaylo because every time she thought about her mother or sister, she felt sick to her stomach. Her homesickness for her mother and sister had evolved into a sharp and pointed rage. Tasya reasoned that they didn't have to send her. It was what was most convenient for them. They were so selfish!

"What are you thinking about?" Hanya pulled Tasya back from the dark depths of her own thoughts. She was looking at Tasya strangely.

"Nothing." Tasya felt guilty when Hanya caught her deep inside herself, thinking hard about how much she detested her mother and sister at that moment.

"Well, you're looking at the wall like you want to kill it. That's all."

Tasya didn't answer. She hated Daria and Kateryna. She wished the baby in Kateryna would die. No, that wasn't fair. Instead, she wished that Kateryna could be on the train at that very moment back to Germany, and Tasya be safe at home.

The journey wore on, and so did the increasing monotony and discomfort. The worst part was that they were given very little to drink. The forty girls on the Pullman were made to share water from three buckets. There never was enough. Water was all they ever got from the soldiers. Never coffee, never tea, never milk; always water. The bucket wasn't overly large, and it was refilled by the German soldiers only when the train was stopped at stations.

A pair of older girls took charge and tried to ration out the water. No one knew when the train would stop long enough for a refill. Sometimes, there would be a stop, and there was plenty of water still in the buckets. Other times, they would go half a day with dry buckets.

Tasya thought about the times when she was young and begged her mother for a treat, complaining that she was starving. Now, on the train ride to Germany, Tasya discovered what it truly meant to be hungry. However stale and dry her unappetizing bread became, Tasya quickly discovered that hunger was something that she could stand, but thirst was something altogether painful. There was simply no getting used to thirst. Girls lay motionless on the floor of the Pullman. Tasya didn't even have the energy any longer to hate her mother and sister. She prayed for water.

One night, the train arrived at another station in Poland and the girls were allowed to stagger out and drink from a nearby river.

"We would never do this at home!" Hanya said to Tasya as they waded into the river in their bare feet. Tasya couldn't answer because she was so desperate for a drink. It was night, and she hadn't had any water since sunrise. As she drank, her stomach heaved and cramped.

"You had better slow down, Tasya, or you'll be sick!" Hanya said and pulled Tasya away from the water.

Later, while she was back on the train and trying to fall asleep, Tasya heard girls vomiting into the buckets. Tasya cried.

"What's wrong, Tasya?" Hanya asked. Tasya heard the new softness in Hanya's voice. It made her feel even sorrier for herself.

"How much longer?" Tasya asked, her lungs tight from holding back sobs. The others got angry when girls cried too hard and made too much noise.

"A little while longer, Tasya." Hanya answered, but Tasya knew that her friend had no idea how much longer they would be on the train. "Just keep praying. Keep praying that this train will stop soon. Pray that the rest of the road to Germany is fast."

"I can't take it anymore, Hanya!" Tasya allowed herself to wail, and girls from all around shushed her. Quietly, she continued to cry. "My bread is hard like a brick; I'm becoming sicker without enough water, and the toilet. The toilet! I can't take it!"

Tasya knew that she wasn't the only one humiliated with their 'toilet' in the car. At the beginning of the trip, the girls had suspiciously eyed the two buckets that were setup by soldiers in one corner of the car. It took only a few hours for one girl to decide that she needed to use a bucket badly enough to risk the humiliation of being the first. Quickly, the girls on the Pullman came to an unspoken agreement that when someone had to go, she would take a friend over with her, hold up a skirt or blanket, and everyone else would discreetly avoid that area of the car.

Days passed slowly, and during their sixth night on the train, Tasya heard Hanya crying softly into her bedroll. Until then, Hanya had been stoic, the stronger of the two. Tasya was frightened by the sound of Hanya gulping back sobs. She rolled over onto her side and away from her friend. Tasya heard Hanya continue to cry, but she pretended not to hear her. Without Hanya's strength and resolve, Tasya didn't think that she could find the strength within herself to survive.

II.

After their seventh day of travel, the train arrived at a small town in Poland named Skarzysko-Kamienna, and another ten girls got on the already-crowded train car. The new girls looked so clean, so healthy, and they actually looked happy. They explained that they had already been working for the Germans for some time in a factory in their home village. One new girl set her sights immediately on Tasya and Hanya. She headed over to their small claimed area and with a big smile, plopped down on the dirty floor and made herself comfortable in their crowded island of space.

"I don't think I've seen anyone smile in a very long time," Tasya said. "I hardly recognized it."

"Hi, I'm Elzbeta," the girl said in Polish after looking momentarily confused. She was the same size and shape as Tasya. Hanya shifted closer to Tasya.

"I'm Tasya, and this is Hanya," Tasya answered back slowly in halting Polish.

"So you speak Polish?" Elzbeta asked, looking at the pair of them, still smiling brightly. She looked at Hanya.

"I speak a bit," Tasya said, "but Hanya knows more than I do." Tasya nudged Hanya with her elbow for encouragement, but Hanya remained silent.

"Do you two know each other from home, or did you meet on this luxury holiday?" Elzbeta asked, laughing.

"Oh, no, Hanya and I have been friends forever! We decided to go together to Germany together. We do everything together."

"We are actually best friends," Hanya finally spoke.

"Well, that's good that you were able to come together," Elzbeta said, looking around the car and wrinkling her nose. She began to unroll the small pile of blankets that she carried in her arms, partially covering Hanya's. Hanya had to move her bedroll over to accommodate Elzbeta, and she made a face at Tasya while Elzbeta was bedding down. Tasya ignored this. She liked the new girl. In comparison to Hanya, Elzbeta was high spirited and cheerful.

"So, how old are you two?" Elzbeta asked as the train started up again.

"I'm fifteen, and Hanya is seventeen," Tasya said, lapsing into a mix of Ukrainian and Polish.

"And apparently my keeper; I can answer for myself, Tasya," Hanya said in Ukrainian, glaring at her.

When Elzbeta spoke, she continued to direct her conversation at both of them, but Hanya stared at the distant wall of the car, looking bored.

"Did you two work for the Germans in…?"

"Horayetz," Hanya said, taking control. "And, no, we didn't. We were both living at home with our families when we were forced to go. Otherwise, we wouldn't be here right now. Obviously."

"Did you work for the Germans at home?" Tasya asked, hoping that her new friend would ignore Hanya.

"Yes I did. A whole year!"

"Really? Doing what?" Tasya asked, impressed. Hanya rolled her eyes.

"Just outside our village is a munitions factory. For years, Poles from our village have been working there," Elzbeta looked at Hanya, who continued to ignore her.

"The factory used to be owned by the Polish government, and my father had worked there since he was young, but once the Germans took over our village three years ago, they took the factory too. I started working as soon as I was allowed, at sixteen, and liked it at first. The Germans paid us well, and the work was easy."

Tasya asked Elzbeta to go on. "A German foreman who called himself the *Reichswerke* was in charge. He came into our village, and personally invited the women to work there. See, they needed girls since few men were available. We liked him from the start. He was always so friendly! So enthusiastic about helping Germany. You see, we wanted to help him. Help Germany." Tasya scanned Elzbeta's face for signs that she was joking. There were none.

"You wanted to help the Germans?" Hanya asked, her voice full of sarcasm.

"Yes! Why not?"

"Perhaps, because they occupied your village? We didn't love the Germans in our village. But I suppose that's the difference between us and you."

"Ha!" Elzbeta laughed. "That's because the people in your backwater village didn't understand what we did. Germans can provide opportunities!" Tasya grinned while Hanya rolled her eyes. "You don't think so, Hanya? Look around you! You are on your way to a great country! Where would you like to be, sitting in your village, waiting to be married?" Tasya felt some gratification for Elzbeta when she saw Hanya blush.

"The *Reichswerke* was so charming that everyone wanted to come and work for him! Women had always had a difficult time making money on their own in the village, but being invited to do the same work as a man, and getting paid as well as one! Well, it was like a dream come true."

"Fine. Then tell me, what type of work did you do that was so very easy?" Hanya asked after a long pause, her eyes on Elzbeta, but betraying no emotion. Elzbeta either did not notice, or did not care that one of her new friends didn't seem to like her.

"I made some sort of fuse. I got paid better than I would have from working elsewhere in the village, or selling our extra crops, and my work quota was easy. I had to make only two-hundred-and-fifty fuses a day. If I worked quickly and steadily, I could easily make more than my quota!" Elzbeta smiled again at Tasya.

"Sounds too good to be true." Hanya grunted as she squeezed herself between bodies and bags to lie down. The Pullman had become very crowded with close to fifty girls on board.

"Hanya, please," Tasya said, exasperated. "Don't listen to her, Elzbeta. Go on."

"Well, if I had to offer one piece of advice about working for the Germans it would be this. Always try to work hard. As hard as you can! You must keep them pleased with you."

"So," Hanya said, rolling over to face Tasya and Elzbeta. "If you liked working in your factory so much, what are you doing here, being treated like cattle?"

"Hanya!" Tasya again said, chiding her friend.

"That's ok, Tasya. It's a good question, since I'm making everything seem like a time of bread and honey. I'll tell you what happened. Those Jewish bastards took my work from me!" Elzbeta nearly spat. Tasya saw that Hanya was now paying rapt attention, as was she.

"About a year ago, all the Jews in the area were gathered together and sent to live in this crude camp that was constructed outside of the village. I heard from others in the village that they were forced to work for free, for absolutely no pay! What kind of person would agree to work for free?"

Tasya considered Elzbeta's question. "Well, my sister, Kateryna worked in Germany. She ended up earning far less than she thought she would. But she certainly didn't work for free!"

"Of course they paid your sister! Why wouldn't they? Anyway, the more I think about it, those dogs can have my job. I'll go where the real money is made and come back to buy a brick house for my entire family to live in!"

"See that Hanya?" Tasya asked, nudging Hanya with her toe. "We're going to be just fine."

"Yes," chimed in Elzbeta, "I have learned that to be Polish is acceptable with the Germans. They want our help, need it in fact! As long as you aren't a Jew, you will be fine."

"Just because we aren't Jewish, doesn't mean that we are totally safe," Hanya finally said, sitting up. "The way to stay safe is by being loyal to each other, and keeping together. Right, Tasya? Our parents told us to always stay together and to take care of each other." Hanya put a protective arm around Tasya's shoulders. "You know what, Elzbeta? You should really try to find someone to do the same with."

"If safety comes in numbers, then I'll stick with you two!" Elzbeta exclaimed, laughing again. "Three is better than two!"

Tasya smiled. It was reassuring that Elzbeta wanted to be friends with them. Hanya was strong and sure of herself, and that made Tasya feel safe, but she felt drawn to Elzbeta's optimism.

And so a group of three they became. Other groups of girls also bonded and began to look out for each other in small ways. Girls took turns helping their friends use the bucket, shared bread, and shared blankets. Like all other animals grouped together in adversity, the girls were drawn to bond with each other. They faced an unclear future together with the determination and optimism that their youth could afford them.

As the train and its unhappy cargo rattled through the night towards the German border, Tasya thought about God again. Father Andrij at home had told them many times that they were all His children. Tasya considered it. Even bad people like Pan Ivan? But did He love the Germans too? Why did He allow them to treat people like animals, or worse? She fell asleep without an answer.

III.

"Hanya, do you ever feel as if you want to just throw open the door and jump off?" Tasya asked, rubbing her temples. After ten nights on the train, she felt the constant jostling in her bones, the sound of the train wheels on the tracks even when they were stopped, and the smell from the toilet buckets in her dreams. There were times that she wanted to rip open the door and just get out of the crowded cage, no matter what happened after. Knowing that she couldn't actually open the door even if she wanted to made her skin crawl.

"Don't be crazy. The fall at this speed would kill you." Hanya replied calmly.

Then, after two weeks of travel, the train stopped for good. Tasya had expected to find herself dancing with joy, but instead, she felt dread. As the train stopped to the sound of screeching brakes, all the girls in the car did the exact same thing. They sat silently, looking at one another with huge eyes. What was coming?

Some of the girls had been sick for several days. Those girls who were the weakest were unable to sit up on their own. Somehow, Tasya, Hanya, and Elzbeta were all doing fairly well.

The door of the Pullman was thrown open, and the girls were all blinded as sunlight flooded in. Every girl in the car raised her hands to her eyes, shielding herself from the glare of the bright sun.

"Jesus, Christ. It stinks in there," a male voice said in Polish. "Get your things and line up. Quickly!"

Tasya found it difficult to actually stand up and gather her things. The car took some time to empty; the girls were so unused to moving. Impatient with their progress, an apparently high-ranking German soldier in white gloves told them to hurry. A plain-clothed man translated for him between Polish and German. They all lined up in front of the train.

Stunned by the clamor of noise and movement around them, Tasya tried her best to stick close to Hanya as she took it all in. The train station was the busiest place Tasya had ever seen, teeming with activity and people. The train had many, many cars, and all around them, other girls were getting out and lining up. Watching with casual patience were about ten German soldiers. Like those in Horayetz, they all had neat uniforms with tall, shining boots. One soldier had an elegant cape draped over his shoulders. Tasya watched as the others took their orders from him.

In front of them was the biggest building that Tasya had ever seen. The Düsseldorf station was mammoth, made of huge slabs of white stone. It had a grace totally unlike the squat train station in Peremyshyl. As the girls from Tasya's car stood in a silent row, she read the sign that hung across the tracks. *Düsseldorf*, it announced matter-of-factly.

"We are absolutely dirty!" Elzbeta whispered. Tasya looked down at her clothes, then at Elzbeta's. Her friend was right. All the girls were filthy. "We look as if we've been traveling in a Pullman for two weeks!" Elzbeta giggled, but Hanya hissed at her to shut up.

Tasya's legs cramped. She shifted from one foot to another but stopped when she saw a soldier watching her. They waited with their dirty sacks on the ground in front of them. The German soldiers spoke to each other in a clipped, harsh way as they walked to and fro across the long lines of girls. German had an altogether different effect on Tasya's ears than the Ukrainian of her home.

Finally, the soldier with the cape blew into a whistle to get their attention. He gestured for everyone to turn to their right, pick up their meager possessions, and walk in a line into the train station. Tasya walked as fast as she could, but even so, a faceless soldier barked in her ear.

"*Schnell!*"

Tasya jumped.

Inside the station, the sheer size of the building and the height of the ceiling were a marvel. Never in her life had Tasya seen such a huge cavern of a building. Ten of the Peremyshyl stations could have easily fit into this one structure.

They were marched over to a large table in the center of the station, where five officers sat, ready to write down their information. There were two men in civilian clothing, registering the passengers. They were speaking German to the soldiers and Polish to the people lining up.

Tasya saw that everyone in the line was fidgety. Legs ached, backs burned. After two solid weeks of lying about in the Pullman like animals, they were unused to so much movement in such a short span of time.

When they reached the front of the line, Tasya rehearsed her own information in her head as Hanya walked up to the translator first.

"Name?" The same translator from outside asked Hanya in Polish.

"Hanya Petrusiv," she answered. The translator glanced up at her. He looked tired.

"Ukrainian, then. Where from?" he asked.

"Horayetz," Hanya answered uncertainly, sounding more like she was asking a question than stating something that she would have known even in her sleep.

"Where?" asked the translator. Tasya prayed silently for Hanya to speak louder, not to annoy the authorities so quickly. "What is the closest city to your village?"

"Peremyshyl," Tasya said, stepping forward. Hanya woke up from her daze, and shot Tasya a glare.

"Yes, now that is a city that I know," continued the translator. "For your purpose here, you will be known as Polish. Take this," he said handing Hanya a square of fabric with a blue letter 'P' on it. "You are to wear this on your left breast as identification at all times. Next!"

Hanya stepped past the table to wait. While Tasya anxiously waited for the translator to complete Hanya's paperwork, she wanted to scream for him to hurry up. Another soldier walked up to Hanya and nudged her forward with the butt of his rifle. Tasya felt as if she couldn't stand it any longer. Stepping closer to the table, Tasya cleared her throat.

"I'm Tasya Boyko!" she called out.

The translator looked up from his paperwork. He was about her mother's age, and thin as a reed. He wore heavy-looking glasses with huge black rims. The size of his glasses made his small neck appear even tinier. His Adam's apple bobbed.

"Just wait your turn. Didn't your mama teach you any manners in your backwards village?" the translator said. He looked up at Tasya then and visibly softened. "What did you say your name was?"

"Tasya."

"No, no. That's not your real name. What is your baptismal name, the full and proper one your mama gave you?"

"Oh. It's Anastasia," Tasya answered, a lump forming in her throat. The only person who ever called her Anastasia was Daria, and that was only when her mother was angry.

"I suppose that you are also Ukrainian. Same as your friend, you are to wear this fabric patch on your left breast at all times."

When he asked Tasya how old she was, she lied with ease for the first time. The translator handed Tasya a patch identical to Hanya's.

Relieved, Tasya picked up her bag, and ran as quickly as her legs would allow to Hanya, who was walking very slowly, stalling. Where was Elzbeta? Tasya darted looks around the room, but couldn't see her friend.

"Thank God you're here," Hanya whispered when Tasya fell into step with her friend. "I didn't know how much slower I could walk. Listen, Tasya, we have to be careful! We have to stick together."

Tasya and Hanya lined up against a wall at the far end of the processing room with a number of other girls. Each stood with bag in one hand, white 'P' patches in the other. A pair of German soldiers approached. Tasya saw that they were young, and both were handsome.

"Those of you who have registered here, come follow us to the Inspection Room," one soldier called out, smiling. He had neat blonde hair poking out from underneath his cap and his blue eyes sparkled. All the girls in the small group quickly followed the soldier's orders.

Walking into the room, Tasya saw that it was small and without windows. It made her instantly nervous to be in another trapped space. In all, about thirty girls gathered inside the cramped room before the second soldier slammed the heavy metal door behind him. Tasya looked first to Hanya then at the girls around her. Most appeared to be her age, but there were also a few women Kateryna's age as well.

One of the women had a child with her, a daughter. The little girl had dark curly hair that flowed all the way to the small of her back, and huge, watching brown eyes. She clutched a dirty rag doll and hid behind her mother's long skirt as best she could, peeking out with one eye to look at what was happening around her. Tasya felt a mixture of sympathy and envy for the child. She wanted her own mama there as well. Tasya stared at them until she felt hot tears stinging the back of her eyes like the tips of needles and had to look away.

The soldiers spoke quietly to each other. Tasya began to relax until the blonde soldier went over to the door, and turned the lock. The click of the metal on metal made a noise that traveled around the room. Tasya felt the girl to her left jump, and she then realized that it was Elzbeta. Tasya hadn't even noticed Elzbeta had been by her side. Tasya's heart thumped loudly in her ears, and her palms began to sweat.

The smiling blonde soldier announced something in German that Tasya didn't understand to the group of girls. When there was no reaction from the girls, the smile dropped from his face. In a very childish and broken Polish, he said, "You are all beautiful girls."

Long seconds passed with total silence in the room. The girls didn't move a muscle. Tasya heard the sound of her pounding heart so loudly in her ears that she was sure that the soldiers could hear it too. There was no sound at all except for the muffled activity from beyond the locked door. The room that they were trapped in felt a million miles away from anywhere else. Tasya stared hard at the ground, unaware that she had been holding her breath until she took a small gasp of air.

The second soldier, equally as young-looking as the blonde one, called out more orders that no one seemed to fully understand. Elzbeta glanced sideways and whispered to both Tasya and Hanya.

"I think he is telling us to line up."

Following the exaggerated motions of the soldiers, the girls got up and lined their ratty bags along the one side of the wall. Both soldiers sauntered to the middle of the room, dragging metal chairs across the concrete floor. The chairs made a high-pitched whining sound that made Tasya cringe. She closed her eyes. Both soldiers made a great show of sitting down on the chairs, and the blonde one pulled out a pack of cigarettes, offering one to his friend. Taking their time, they lit their cigarettes and reclined in the seats.

The second soldier called out another command, but again, it was not understood. With more softness in his voice, the blonde soldier repeated the command once more, slowly. Elzbeta whispered to Tasya,

"I think he is telling us to take off our clothes. That can't be right – "

The first soldier stood up, lifted the metal chair and slammed it back onto the concrete floor. The sound reverberated around the room for several seconds, and hurt Tasya's ears as she jumped. In Polish he yelled "*Odziez*!" His voice also echoed around the room. All of the girls jumped again.

Hanya turned slightly to Elzbeta.

"What about our clothing? Are they going to take our bags away?"

"No, I think they mean we have to take our clothing off," Elzbeta said quietly.

All of the girls were beginning to understand the commands of the soldiers, but no one moved. They remained frozen in place like trees. Tasya felt like she was in a bad dream, and wanted to pinch herself to wake up.

The second soldier also stood up then, urging "*Odziez, odziez*!" over and over again. Still none of the girls made a move to do anything with their clothing. He took the three strides needed to cross to the closest girl. He tugged at her blouse, hard. Part of it ripped off, and she clumsily grabbed at it, trying to keep it on. The soldier gestured for everyone to follow suit. Terrified, Tasya began to carefully take off her clothing, folding it neatly. She saw that everyone else was doing the same. Unsure of how much the soldiers wanted them to take off, Tasya left on her camisole, slip, and hose. Even though it was warm in the room and she was perspiring lightly, Tasya began to shiver, clutching her elbows.

The soldiers were not satisfied. They gave new orders that no one in the group could understand. The second soldier then said very quietly, "*Nagi*."

"Naked," Elzbeta whispered after a few seconds.

The blonde soldier looked up and down the row of girls and raised his eyebrows, nodding. Slowly, one by one, each of the girls began to also take off their underclothing. Soon, they were all standing in a rigid line, silent, and totally naked. Tasya heard only her own breath in her ears as she tried to control her shivering. She crossed her arms tightly over her small breasts and waited.

Both soldiers sat down again and continued to smoke their cigarettes in silence as they looked at each girl in turn. The blonde soldier then indicated with a lazy rotation of his wrist that the girls were to walk around in a circle, around the chairs. Tasya followed Hanya. Slowly walking one after another, they began to make their rotation around the room.

Smiles grew wide on the faces of the soldiers as they laughed and clapped. Tasya felt as if she had walked around the room a dozen times when she began to shiver more. Some of the girls had begun to cry. After walking around the room so long that her feet went from sore, to burning, to numb, Tasya began to imagine things. This isn't her. She isn't really here. She is watching a play. A disgusting play that will never stop.

The girls walked and walked and walked around the small, windowless, hot room. Sweat ran down the naked backs of all the girls. They walked long after the soldiers stopped laughing and clapping. They were made to keep going. They walked until Tasya totally lost track of time. She snapped out of her reverie and back into her own body. How long had it been? When were they going to be allowed to stop? Panic rose within her.

Tasya needed a distraction. She dared to glance over at the young mother with her daughter. The young woman was walking as well, but clutching her daughter's hand. With no skirt to hide behind, and naked as everyone else, the young daughter walked alongside her mother, sucking her thumb with vigor. As Tasya watched the mother walk, she saw a thin line of deep crimson blood streaming down her leg. The little girl was also staring at the blood that was running around her mother's ankles, and she was terrified.

The blonde soldier then shouted "Stop!" so loud in Polish that some of the girls yelped and the little one began to cry. The soldiers, stood up, laughing as if they had just said the funniest joke in the world. Tasya grew cold. What next? Without another word the soldiers left the room, slamming the heavy metal door behind them with a certainty that made Tasya believe that they were truly gone.

All the girls in the room stayed rooted into place until finally Hanya made a move to get her clothes. Everyone else quickly followed. They were still in the process of getting dressed when the translator entered the room. It was the one from the table who Tasya had given her information to with the huge glasses. He came in looking distressed, but when he saw the girls at various stages of dress he became flustered, pulling at his collar and coughing uncontrollably. He looked down at the floor. With his cheeks red as a flame he cleared his throat.

"The soldiers want me to tell you that your menstruating is disgusting," he said in nervous voice in Polish. "Going forward, you will be given a special medication in your food that will make you stop. Menstruating, that is." As soon as the translator finished delivering his message, he ran out, slamming the door once more. As soon as the door shut, he yanked it open again a sliver and shouted, "You all get out here when you are dressed!"

The girls continued to get dressed in silence. They gradually lined up in single file outside the room, standing still as statues in the active, busy room. Hundreds of other girls streamed past them, and but no one else was going in the windowless room. Hanya and Elzbeta were on either side of her, but Tasya didn't look at them. It was Hanya who finally broke their silence.

"Well, I think that just about shows us what we are in for."

IV.

"Petrusiv!"

"Boyko!"

"Sorowski!"

By some miracle of God, Hanya, Tasya and Elzbeta's names were called in a row for what the translator said was 'labour allocation'. Tasya felt like a tiny child who had no control as she watched the thousands of girls and boys efficiently divided by the soldiers. By the end of the day, every single person from the transport had been assigned to a place of work in Düsseldorf.

The translator had announced to their group that they were close enough to their assigned brick-making factory that they would walk, and were arranged in rows of four across. What had been called a close walk took nearly an hour, and Tasya wanted to cry, the pain in her legs was so severe.

"*Anhalten*!" A soldier finally called out.

As they marched through the gates of a factory and right through the arch of a monstrous red brick building, Tasya forgot all about the pain in her legs. She was dumbfounded. Tasya had never even seen a real factory before, and certainly had never been inside of one. Sounds of banging and machinery bounced off the walls and echoed around the room, louder than anything Tasya had ever heard before. The heat from enormous ovens pressed against every exposed area of skin. Tasya held her hands over her ears and fought back tears.

The girls had another stroke of luck when they were assigned to the same barrack. They were informed by a Polish-speaking guard that the barracks were where they would do their sleeping, and spend their time off. They were drafty wooden structures that were so rickety that Tasya feared that a strong wind might blow them all down. Located right on the grounds of the factory, they appeared to be hastily constructed with little care to the inhabitants. Even though they were not technically imprisoned, Tasya's stomach twisted with worry.

The guard continued their tour by explaining the entire factory compound consisted of a network of the main factory itself; the barracks and a number of additional administrative buildings. The periphery of the compound was staked out by a chain link fence.

"Hanya, is that barbed wire at the top of the fence?" Tasya whispered as she squinted up at the fence. "Why would they bother to put up barbed wire? Who would want to break into a brick factory?"

Hanya looked at Tasya, shaking her head. "It's not to keep people out, stupid. It's to keep us in. They don't want *us* to get out."

Each barrack held forty girls each. In the very center of the barrack stood an ancient-looking black iron stove, the only apparent source of heat. However, to Tasya's delight, the toilets were actually adjoined to their sleeping area.

"Hanya, look! The toilets are right here in this room! We don't have to go outside!" Tasya pulled on Hanya's arm in excitement. She had never actually used an indoor toilet before.

"*Pft*. They are barely inside, Tasya," Hanya said, turning up her nose. "Look at how crude it is."

The washroom was obviously as hastily constructed as the rest of the barrack but Tasya didn't care. Flush toilets that were inside! How could Hanya *not* be thrilled?

"Are you blind, Hanya? Look, there are five toilets, and three sinks!"

Elzbeta had been leaning against the frame of the bathroom door, watching the exchange between Tasya and Hanya with an amused grin.

"So, you still have outdoor privy's at home, *heh*? You should move to my village, *divchata*. We've had indoor plumbing for ten years in my house!"

"Well, good for you, Elzbeta," Hanya had said, pushing her way out past Elzbeta. "Maybe you can talk the guard into getting us a private room too, since you are obviously a princess in disguise."

V.

Their daily brick-making work task was described by the factory foreman to be very simple. Day after day, Tasya threw a mixture of sand and clay into a large pit with water. She then turned on a mechanized tempering wheel that mixed everything together. After the mixture had reached the proper consistency, she and Hanya removed the clay blend and pressed it by hand into a huge mould. They then lifted the heavy mould and struggled to the factory door, where they arranged the moulds in neat rows to dry. After three or four days, they staggered back into the factory with the mould, and baked the brick in the ancient up-draft kiln. A fiery inferno blazed inside the kiln, making that part of the work area unbearably hot. Hanya was put in charge of making sure that the oven stayed at the exact same temperature during the baking process.

"*Beobachten…*" Their foreman had warned, tapping the glass thermometer. "This oven is Satan's playground, and he likes it kept at the exact same temperature. Always." Tasya and Hanya nodded enthusiastically in unison. "Oh. And remember, girls. Be sure to drink water. All day. The last girls who worked here didn't, and they dropped dead on the ground of dehydration. On the spot."

To Tasya's horror, he laughed, and then walked away.

It took only one short day to realize that they were in for dreadful, exhausting work. Each brick weighed twenty kilos, plus another five kilos for the mold. On their first day, Tasya and Hanya both struggled to throw the sand and clay into the pit, and they heaved under the weight of the moulds.

Tasya wiped sweat from her forehead, flicking it away with teary frustration.

"Hanya, this work is so hard!"

"Just shut up and work quietly," Hanya hissed, glancing around, searching for their foreman. "Remember what your friend Elzbeta said? The Germans like workers who work hard, so be quiet!"

Tasya tried to stay quiet, but she was gulping back sobs.

"Do you think we will get a day off soon?" Tasya whined less than a minute later.

"Ha! Does it seem like we are going to have any free time around here?" Hanya struggled to lift her shovel, piled high with sand. Unlike Tasya, Hanya's arms didn't buckle quite as much. Tasya saw that Hanya was sweating too, but she had a look of fierce determination on her face.

"What, then? We have to do this every single day of the week? My back is hurting me already. Look at my arms, they have turned to jelly!"

Hanya scowled but kept shoving.

"Tasya, we are all tired, all aching. Do you really think you are the only one who is struggling right now?" Tasya saw Hanya peek at the silent river of tears running down her cheeks.

"Ok, Tasya, listen. A girl in our barrack told me that there is easier work in the factory to be done." Hanya rested the end of her shovel on the ground and leaned on it. She wiped sweat from her face.

"Be good, and maybe we'll get an easier job soon. You hear that?"

Tasya nodded miserably as she fought to lift her own shovel of clay.

At the end of their first week, Tasya and Hanya returned to their barrack in happy moods. They had found out that after another few days of work, they would get an entire day off. As the girls walked into the barrack, some of the Ukrainian girls were gathered around the stove in the center of the room.

"*Divchata*!" One of the girls called out, gesturing them over.

Tasya recognized the older girl. Luba had introduced herself to the other Ukrainian girls in the barrack during their first days of arriving. The Poles and Ukrainians had been keeping to themselves in separate groups.

"We are organizing a group to speak to the factory commandant," said Luba. "We take issue with being identified as Polish. We are Ukrainian. These factory people need to understand that we volunteered on our own accord to come here to work."

"Oh. What are you going to suggest?" Hanya asked. Tasya looked at

Hanya with surprise. Hanya didn't sound sarcastic or rude; she sounded legitimately curious.

"We want to be identified as Ukrainian, not Polish. We are being forced to follow their decrees."

The group of girls gathered around Luba muttered their agreement. Was Hanya nodding in agreement?

"What do you girls think?"

"Listen, I don't know if talking to the commandant is a good idea," Tasya said as she stepped in front of Hanya. "My sister worked in Germany a few years, and she told me that it is actually better to be identified as Polish. *Zivilarbeiter* is a *good* thing."

"Ha! It's hardly good, Tasya," Luba said. "Yes, I hear it's better than *Ostarbeiter*, but come on. We want to be identified as Ukrainian and get a patch with a *tryzub* on it!"

Tasya burst out laughing.

"Sorry," she said as she saw that no one else laughed.

Getting a *tryzub* patch was a ridiculous idea. Why did they even care? Tasya was exhausted and wanted nothing more than to lie down on her bunk and sleep for a year.

Tasya turned on her heel and headed over to her bed, expecting Hanya to follow. When Tasya flopped down on her bunk, she saw Hanya still stood with the group of girls. Who did they think they were? Tasya closed her eyes as she giggled again. *Tryzub*? What a stupid idea. As she drifted off, she allowed her body to relax into the darkness that overcame her. Tasya was nearly asleep when she heard Luba speak loudly.

"I'm going to go speak to the commandant. Who wants to join me?"

Tasya's eyes snapped open. She sat up, trying to make eye contact with Hanya, trying to get her to come over to their bunk. Instead, she saw Hanya raise her hand as a volunteer.

"Hanya!" Tasya cried out with alarm. "Remember what you just told me? Don't cause trouble!"

Tasya knew that Hanya didn't like being told what to do. Especially by her younger friend. Most especially, Hanya didn't like being told what to do in front of others. Hanya didn't make eye contact with Tasya as she marched out the door and down the barrack stairs with Luba and two other girls. Tasya heard their footsteps echo on the stairs, and then the crunch of gravel as they walked away. When Tasya couldn't hear their steps any more, she flopped back onto her mattress in exasperation. She was too tired to care.

Tasya drifted off to sleep again.

Tasya woke to the ring of the curfew bell. Where was Hanya? When she realized that Hanya still hadn't returned, the knot of worry in the pit of Tasya's stomach grew. She slept in fits and starts the entire night, dreaming something about Hanya that she couldn't quite piece together when she awoke.

The next morning, Tasya was dressed before breakfast. She saw Hanya walk slowly into the barrack. Relief flooded Tasya and she ran across the room to meet Hanya.

"Hanya! Thank God. I was worried sick all night about you," Tasya cried. Hanya didn't say anything in reply to Tasya, and walked right by her as if Tasya was invisible. Hanya went straight to her bunk, gathered her washing rags, and walked in the direction of the toilets.

"What happened?" Tasya asked, as she chased Hanya across the room.

No answer.

Hanya silently washed herself at one of the sinks. Tasya burst into tears.

"Don't cry, Tasya. I'm fine. Don't be such a baby."

"Where were you?" Tasya cried in a high-pitched voice.

"We were locked up overnight. Punishment."

"Locked up?" Tasya asked in horror. "Where? Did they beat you?"

"No, they didn't beat us. I almost wish they did. It would've been better just to get the punishment over with through a quick beating," Hanya laughed bitterly as Tasya stared at her. "No, instead, we were locked up in a cell in an administrator's barrack. And we'll get no food rations for the next three days."

"*Three* days? You'll starve, Hanya!"

"I think that they know that three days is enough to punish us, not kill us."

"Well, I'll give you part of my rations, then. We can share."

"You can't, Tasya. If you get caught trying to help us, then yours will be taken away too. Just let me serve out my punishment and get it over with."

While they were talking, other girls entered the small space of the washroom. The girls stared at Hanya. Some whispered. Hanya quickly walked back towards their bunk.

"See, Tasya? All it took was for them to make an example of us; now everyone is scared to say or do anything. Easy enough, right?"

"Of course it was easy for them, Hanya. I told you it was a bad idea. You aren't going to change the way things are run just because you feel like it." Tasya hadn't meant to, but she was yelling at Hanya.

After a long look at Tasya, Hanya threw her washing rag onto her bunk, and marched out of the barrack.

Word spread like wildfire about Hanya, Luba, and the rest of the protest group. Their overnight detention was enough to scare both the Ukrainian and Polish girls away from any other protests about identification, food, or days off work. Tasya was relieved to see Hanya quietly and bitterly wearing the 'P' patch from that day forward. Hanya also steered clear of Luba and her gang.

A few days after Hanya's brief uprising, Tasya fell into a routine at the factory. The brick-making was hot difficult work however it made for a solid night's rest. Sleep came easy and helped her forget the gnawing hunger in her stomach.

Few of the workers ever left the factory grounds; movements both within and beyond the factory were restricted. A strict curfew was in place for the occasions when anyone left the compound. Even though there were very few places that they could go, Tasya felt the pull of an hour's worth of freedom.

"Hanya, should we maybe ask permission to go out? Go for a walk, maybe?"

"For what? With our patch, everyone would stare, and we don't have any money to actually buy anything, so what's the point?"

Seven days a week they ate, worked, and slept within the arms of the barbed wire fence. In the few hours each day that Tasya wasn't working or sleeping, she was busily occupied in her own misery. She had held out hope to spot Mychaylo among the male factory workers, but after a few weeks, hope had diminished. Now it was totally gone. Where was he? Was he still in Germany? Tasya allowed herself to think about her mother and sister. She missed Daria and Kateryna with every fiber of her being. Tasya had scratched out a number of letters in her childish writing and had given them to the commandant to mail. She didn't know if any of the letters had actually made it back to Horayetz. Neither Tasya nor Hanya heard a word from their families back home, leading them to believe that all life outside of Düsseldorf ceased to exist.

The work was difficult, but both Tasya and Hanya grew accustomed to heavy lifting. But, as she became physically able to lift the shovel and mould, Tasya was less able to deal with constant hunger. There was some food; a quarter loaf of black bread and two bowls of soup per day, but it wasn't enough. The lack of filling and nourishing food was devastating to both Tasya's mind and body. Always very thin, Tasya had been encouraged constantly by her mother to eat more, to fill out a little. At the factory, food rations were pathetic, with each worker feeling the effects of undernourishment within a few days of arrival at the factory. To Tasya, the rations were not even enough to sustain a dog.

"I have no idea how they can call this disgusting brew a soup," Elzbeta whispered at lunchtime to Tasya as they sat on the hard wooden benches of the canteen. Elzbeta pushed around the few chunks of vegetables that sat in a watery brew. Tasya was thrilled to be sitting with Elzbeta, who was normally with the Polish girls. "It has little more than a few potatoes and cabbage swimming around in water. It stinks!"

Each day Tasya finished every drop without complaint. She ate quickly and was sad when she reached the bottom of her bowl. She looked for Hanya seated a few benches over and saw that her friend had also already finished the meager meal.

"I've heard some of the girls call this soupy cabbage water *balanda*. Seems like an appropriate name," Tasya said, gazing with want at Elzbeta's leftovers. She wanted to reach over, grab Elzbeta's tin bowl from her hands, and slurp back what was left of the soup.

"Shit-soup is more like it," Elzbeta said and snorted at her own joke. Tasya was too on edge to laugh. Frustration at the gnawing hunger was building. It made her want to pull at her hair. It made her want to gouge out her own eyeballs to get at the constant throbbing behind them. It was lunchtime. Tasya's next meal of *balanda* would not be until the next morning.

"Why don't they feed us anything for dinner besides the coffee, Elzbeta?" Tasya whined, then panicked when she realized what she had spoken out loud. There weren't any of the guards around but she was so nervous. She couldn't afford to be punished like Hanya had been. Tasya couldn't stand to watch how weak Hanya had become after missing meals for three days. She had tried to make her friend feel better by commiserating with her.

"Hanya, I'm so hungry," Tasya had whispered later that evening as they lay in their bunks, "The water soup is definitely not enough. You really aren't missing much by not eating it and I don't think it's nearly enough to live on. They will have to give us more. At least we have bread."

It was a long time before Hanya responded.

"We're all hungry," Hanya said. "No one here is more or less hungry than the other. Now stop whining, you baby. At least you are getting something."

"Hanya, I know everyone here is also hungry but I'm already so thin. I don't have much fat to live on," complained Tasya.

"I get it – you're hungry. How unusual. Now shut up."

"Why only coffee for dinner?" Elzbeta repeated. "I thought perhaps it was some sort of strange German tradition, but now I think not."

"They are starving us. Do they know that, Elzbeta?"

"Oh, I'm sure that the kitchen is giving us as much food as they can get. It's wartime, Tasya. All of Germany is under strict ration orders," said Elzbeta.

"Don't they know that we work better when we are full?" asked Tasya.

"Of course they do. Don't be mistaken, Tasya. They need us. Not the other way around. Now, cut it out or you're going to start trouble just like Hanya did."

Tasya willed herself to stop complaining.

"Elzbeta, do you ever think about going home?"

"What? No. Never."

"You wanted to come to Germany to work, right Elzbeta?"

Elzbeta paused. "I suppose I did want to come here to work, yes."

"And you're still happy that you did? Hanya and I were more or less forced to be here, but you came on your own."

"I still want to be here, obviously." Elzbeta poked at the last bit of cabbage in her murky *balanda*. "It's fine."

Tasya felt worry work its way up from her stomach. Elzbeta had been so enthusiastic on the train to Germany. She had worked for the Germans before, and was sure of herself. She had made Tasya feel as though everything was going to be just fine.

"When do you think we are going to get paid, Elzbeta?" Tasya whispered. She had been terrified to ask any of the supervisors or her foreman. No one had ever mentioned it.

"Soon, I'm sure. The Germans were very good about paying us on time when I was back home." Elzbeta neither looked nor sounded confident.

VI.

"How about you, Tasya? Anything?"

Tasya froze and tried to avoid Elzbeta's gaze.

When Tasya didn't answer, Elzbeta looked at Hanya. "You, Hanya?"

"Actually, no. Nothing."

"Hmm."

"Elzbeta, might it be from not eating enough?" Hanya asked. Tasya knew that Hanya was trying to redirect attention away from her, and felt immediately grateful. The tiny barrack washroom was crammed with girls getting washed for the day shift. One girl had noticed that she was no longer menstruating and to Tasya's dismay, a conversation had begun.

"No, me neither."

"Not since home."

"I can't remember, but it's been a long time. Since home, maybe? Oh, I can't remember."

"Definitely not since the train ride. It was horrible. Disgusting."

"I did our first week here. But now, nothing."

Tasya realized that the girls had stopped menstruating. Most of the girls actually seemed to be relieved. Tasya scurried out of the washroom as quickly as she could get away. She didn't want to talk about menstruating. She was humiliated that at fifteen years old, she had not yet started. Tears pricked at her eyes as she chastised herself for being such a baby. She tried to cover them up by wiping away the thin veil of perspiration that had already gathered on her forehead. It wasn't even seven o'clock in the morning, yet the barrack was stifling.

The summer of 1942 was hot, making the factory work even more unbearable for Tasya. At the beginning of August, the girls had been at the factory for three months, and while the work continued to be very heavy and difficult, the hunger was getting worse, persisting at all times of day and night. An ever-present nag.

"I don't even feel hungry in the way I used to at home," Tasya explained to Hanya and Elzbeta. In a rare moment, Hanya and Elzbeta were both with Tasya. The three girls were lying on their backs outside of the barrack, looking at the sky change colours from blue to pink and red as the sun set.

"Before, when I used to get hungry, my stomach would rumble and hurt, like it was complaining to get my attention. Now, my stomach doesn't even hurt. But, I know that I'm hungry all the time because I feel so weak. I'm always so tired."

"I know what you mean," Elzbeta said. "My stomach feels like it's dead. I know that I'm slowly starving to death in this rat hole because the bricks feel heavier than ever."

"*Nu*, if you could eat anything right now, what would it be?" Elzbeta asked Tasya, propping herself up on her elbow.

Tasya had thought about it before, and was ready with her answer.

"Chocolate. I've spotted a chocolate shop on one of the streets outside the fence. Maybe I would like a huge piece of chocolate from that shop. Or, maybe a bowl of the German hot chocolate that Kateryna told me about. Yum," Tasya said, wistfully.

"How about you, Hanya. What would you eat?" Elzbeta asked. Tasya knew that Elzbeta was trying to get Hanya to join in on the game, even though Hanya was doing her best to ignore them.

"Me?" Elzbeta continued as Hanya continued her vow of silence, "I would eat a big piece of cake the size of my head! Then, I would wash it down with some of that hot chocolate that you were just telling me about!" Elzbeta laughed, nudging Tasya with her elbow.

Tasya giggled but Hanya sighed audibly. Why was Hanya so sullen? Tasya watched as Hanya opened her eyes, stood up, and walked towards the barrack stairs.

"Oh, come on, Hanya! Where are you going?" Tasya called, laughing even harder. Hanya stopped in her tracks. She didn't turn around.

"This is a stupid game, but if I had a choice, I would eat potatoes. I would absolutely gorge myself. In fact," she said spinning on her heel and facing them directly, "if either of you fools is at my funeral, be sure to put some potatoes in my coffin so that I can be buried with them as well."

Hanya stomped away, leaving Tasya and Elzbeta to exchange grins behind her back.

VII.

There were more signs than ever that war was going on all around them. Tasya was too exhausted to care about the politics of the conflict, but Elzbeta was intrigued by any news that she could get from the Polish guards. The Germans had apparently gone further into Soviet territory, and scored major victories in France. That summer the German army was stronger, and in charge of creating the landscape of borders in Europe. The Germans were successfully advancing towards Stalingrad, pushing the Red Army further back into Russia.

By the end of August, normally upbeat and energetic Elzbeta had joined Tasya in her state of hunger and anxiousness. Elzbeta appeared to lose all hope that they would be paid, that they would get proper rations, that they were anything other than slave labour. Tasya watched as Elzbeta's moods varied dramatically from bubbly and optimistic one day to angry and sullen on the next. Tasya was surprised that on one of Elzbeta's 'happy' days, she suggested that they finally leave the factory grounds. Elzbeta was in such a good mood that she even included Hanya.

"Listen, girls. We'll go after our work shift is complete. We'll only have about an hour or so, but the Rhine is near. I think that I would like to go sit near it, seeing as we've been here for nearly four months."

"No thanks, Elzbeta," Hanya said. At a stalemate, both looked to Tasya.

"Maybe it would help me feel like a regular girl again," Tasya said, shyly. "For a change."

"Tasya, leaving the compound is pretty risky, even with permission."

Hanya said. "What about getting harassed by the Germans? Don't forget, you would still have to wear your ID patch at all times. Do you want to be a target?"

"Oh, Hanya! So what? Then we will wear it, and chase away anyone who tries to bother us," Elzbeta laughed in her usual way, and Tasya was comforted to see her happy. That Elzbeta was not giving in as easily as usual to Hanya's moodiness was a good sign. "We'll go right after our shift, and be back before curfew."

"No," Hanya said. Tasya knew that her decision was final.

"Listen," Elzbeta said. "The German foreman said that us Polish workers are lucky to have the privilege of being allowed to leave the factory, so we should use it. All we have to do is check in with the main gate guard when we leave and again when we return. Easy."

Tasya felt the pull of an hour's worth of freedom from the factory compound. She was penniless, wore the same clothes from the day she had arrived in Germany, and only knew a few words in German, but she wanted to leave. Until that moment, she hadn't realized how badly she wanted to get out from the suffocating factory compound.

"I'm going," Tasya announced, and was happy to see Elzbeta smile.

The very next night after their shift was over, Tasya and Elzbeta ran back to the barrack to wash their hands and arms, and brush their hair.

"You two are acting like you are going out on a double-date," Hanya scoffed, watching them. "You know you have to be back in two hours, right?"

"Yes, Mama," Elzbeta joked, to Tasya's delight. Nothing could make Tasya feel anything but happy at that moment.

Tasya and Elzbeta raced across the barrack to the door.

"Wait!" Hanya called after them. "I'm going to come too!"

"You can come, Hanya, but under one condition," Elzbeta warned as she spun around. "You have to lighten up! We have two whole hours of freedom."

Hanya grunted, and said nothing else.

On their way out, they checked in with a young Polish guard who was friendly with Elzbeta. The two flirted back and forth while they signed their names to the register. Tasya smiled while she watched, butterflies in her stomach. She felt like a regular young girl again.

"Remember, *divchata*, you have to wear your identification patch at all times."

"Of course! We'll do whatever you tell us." Elzbeta batted her eyelashes at the guard.

"I'm being serious, Elzbeta. If you get caught without it, you will be fined twenty-five marks."

"Twenty-five. Five-hundred and five. What does it matter, Antoni? We have *zero* marks to give."

At the use of his first name, the guard blushed and waved them away.

As they took their first steps outside the compound gate, Tasya, Hanya, and Elzbeta were careful to walk closely together. After almost four months within the barbed wire walls of the factory compound, Tasya found herself overwhelmed by all the new sights and sounds. A few steps down the nearest street away from the factory, and Düsseldorf was incredible even with the quiet and darkened streets. The majority of shops looked like they were permanently closed. Those that remained open were sad-looking with very few items stocked. Even so, Tasya easily imagined the great beauty and bustle that must have been a part of daily life in Düsseldorf.

With wide-eyed wonder, the girls darted west along the cobble-stoned sidewalk and narrow streets. When they reached the Rhine, they huddled in one group along the railing that separated the water from the river promenade. Bridges longer than any other that Tasya had ever seen spanned the two shores of the river. The streets around the factory were quiet, but along the river there was a bustle of activity. The river promenade was crammed full of people. Old men walked in small groups having serious conversations. Young women, just like them, walked and giggled together. Children ran, laughed, and played with their mothers. A few couples, holding hands, made their way by.

"For a minute, I forgot that Germany was at war," Tasya said softly when she spotted a pair of soldiers walking leisurely south.

"Everyone's at war," Elzbeta replied, solemnly.

Hanya was also looking at the soldiers.

"They look just like the soldiers from home," Hanya said, then sighed loudly. "Come on, let's get back before we miss our curfew."

As they walked back the same way they came, Elzbeta stopped in her tracks.

"Wait. Before we go back, maybe we could try to find something to eat."

She had a glint of mischievousness in her eyes.

"Yes, Elzbeta, let's!" Hanya said, clapping her hands together. "Why don't we look around for that lovely little café where they sell the doughnuts that you love so much?"

It took Tasya a few heartbeats to understand the depth of Hanya's sarcasm.

"*Bozhe*, Hanya!" Elzbeta said, throwing her hands into the air. "You know that's not what I mean."

As Hanya continued to walk in the direction of the factory, Elzbeta called after her. "See, there? I spot a small bakery. Let's stand outside of it and ask the people coming out if they could spare some bread. Simple."

"Wait. You want us to beg?" Tasya asked. She didn't like the sound of the idea.

"No, we aren't going to beg, exactly. Let's just *ask*. Maybe people have some bread or eggs that they could spare us."

"Elzbeta, I really doubt that a German would sacrifice even a small part of their own bread ration for a raggedy group of girls with *Zivilarbeiter* patches on their chests. They probably aren't even allowed to," Hanya said as she pulled on Tasya's arm. "Come on, Tasya, we really should be getting back."

"Wait! It's worth a try," Elzbeta said, trying to maintain eye contact with Tasya as she was dragged away.

Tasya felt the pressure of being torn between her two friends. Hanya always thought that every single idea that Elzbeta had was stupid. Tasya was tired of being told what to do, and she felt her hunger so acutely that she was beginning to feel desperate. She dug her feet into the cobblestoned street and jerked her arm away.

"I'm going with Elzbeta, Hanya. If you want to come with us, you can, but I'm sick of you treating me like a child!" Tasya shouted. She was secretly thrilled when seconds later, Hanya was again at her side.

All three drifted over to the doors of the bakery, trying their best to appear natural. Tasya's stomach growled, and she clutched at it, feeling conspicuous. Many of the local Germans did not look like they were faring well during the war.

"Maybe Hanya's, right. Let's go, Elzbeta."

But, Elzbeta didn't move. Neither did Hanya. Tasya saw Hanya's gaze glued to the inside of the shop. Both were under a spell.

The girls stood shoulder-to-shoulder, looking in through the front window of the bakery. There were only a few loaves of bread remaining on the shelves, and each looked so much better than their daily black bread from the factory kitchen. As a German woman exited the shop, Hanya stepped in front of her, hand outstretched. Tasya went wide-eyed and looked at Elzbeta, who had the same look on her face. In a split second, Tasya decided that she was ready to run away as fast as she could if the woman started screaming.

The German woman recoiled at the sight of Hanya's dirty hand, but Hanya had surprised her too, and she nearly walked right into the girls as she tried to balance her bags. Tasya saw that the woman wasn't much older than they were – perhaps Kateryna's age. She had dark brown hair with numerous wild bits escaping from the pile on top of her head. From her frayed and tattered clothes, Tasya saw that she was also struggling.

Once the woman got her footing, she looked over towards Tasya and Elzbeta. She looked even more shocked at the sight of two scrawny girls in ragged clothing, the 'P' on their identification patches glaring like a beacon. The woman looked like she was about to keep going as she found her way around Hanya's dirty hand. As the woman made her way past Tasya, she turned to Elzbeta, and without saying a word, dug into her skirt pocket, and thrust a small square of paper at Elzbeta before walking quickly away.

After a few seconds of shocked silence, the girls huddled around Elzbeta's hand. In it was a small square stamp. Tasya could make out the word *Wehrmacht* on it, but didn't understand what it was for.

"Is it a coupon?" Tasya asked.

"I think it's a ration stamp!" Elzbeta yelped, and Hanya shushed her.

"Well, if it is, who is going to go into the bakery?" Hanya asked. "I don't think we should all go in together."

Tasya looked up and down the street. It was deserted, but she felt like a thousand pairs of eyes were watching her from behind the shuttered windows.

"I will," Tasya quickly volunteered.

Elzbeta carefully handed the ration coupon over to Tasya. Taking a deep breath, she held the stamp as if it was a million-mark bill and entered the bakery. Even though the bakery shelves were largely empty, the few remaining loaves called to her. Tasya's mouth watered at the smells of yeast and baked breads. She took one small loaf from the shelf, and placing the stamp on top of it in plain view of the shopkeeper, walked over to the woman behind the counter. The shopkeeper looked Tasya up and down. Tasya again prepared to run, convinced that they had made a huge error in leaving the factory.

After glancing at Tasya's patch, the woman's face softened. She reached across the counter and picked up the stamp. The shopkeeper nodded at Tasya.

Tasya felt herself nodding back in gratitude and relief as she walked backwards towards the shop door.

In her excitement to get out of the shop, Tasya ran right into Elzbeta and Hanya.

"Over there!" Hanya said, as they all regained their footing, pointing further down the street.

While standing in a huddled group around the loaf of bread, they reverently divided the loaf into three equal sections. Tasya tore into her piece of the loaf as soon as she could. It was slightly stale, and not as sweet as the bread that they got in the factory, but it tasted better than anything she had eaten for months. Tasya was so relieved and grateful that she cried silent tears.

"No need to cry, Tasya," Elzbeta said as she hoisted her chunk of the loaf into the air. "It looks like we now have a way to survive," she proclaimed.

VIII.

Tasya and Elzbeta obtained passes to leave the factory at least twice a week. Sometimes a pensive Hanya would tag along. On a good day, they received German ration coupons, or a small bit of a loaf. Once in a while, they managed to get eggs, which they snuck back into the factory and boiled along with their wash. At other times, their begging in the gentle evening sun went ignored. Tasya learned that there were three types of Germans – those who pitied the girls and did whatever small gesture they could to help, those who appeared to feel sorry for the girls but ignored their pleas for help, and those who became angry at the girls and their begging. It was the latter group that caused the most trouble. The girls measured and judged the looks given by strangers. If they judged incorrectly, the police constable would chase them away from their spot in front of the shops.

"What's it to be tonight, *divchata*?" Elzbeta asked as they headed out one warm evening in September.

"Well, aren't you the excited one tonight?" Hanya grumbled in her cranky, sarcastic way.

"It must be that special treat that I got yesterday," Elzbeta said mischievously.

The night before, Elzbeta had gone out on her own, something Tasya had never dared to do. She had returned with some scraps of ham which the three of them had devoured while crammed into a washroom stall, away from the glares of the other girls.

"We'd best make it quick tonight, "Hanya said, pointing at the sky. "Look."

Dark, threatening clouds were approaching.

They arrived at the Rhine bank and sat on the stone blocks that divided the walkway from the twenty-foot riverbank wall. As Elzbeta plunked herself down, Tasya heard her let out a long breath.

"*Owww,*" Elzbeta whimpered.

"Are you alright? What's wrong?" Tasya asked.

"I don't know. All of a sudden, my belly hurts," Elzbeta complained. "It almost feels like I ate some rotten meat or something. Do you think there was some old meat in the soup today?"

Hanya snorted from the other side of Tasya. "I doubt there was any meat in the potato soup they gave us today. Maybe your mysteriously acquired ham is the problem, Elzbeta."

Elzbeta lapsed into a rare state of silence. Hanya followed suit with her usual brooding.

"Well," Tasya said, looking at the dark clouds, "looks like we had better get going if we want to try for a scrap of bread tonight. She watched as Hanya pulled herself up using the walkway railings, but Elzbeta struggled to get her legs onto the sidewalk. Tasya rushed over to help, pulling Elzbeta up carefully by the arms.

"Come on, Elzbeta. Is it really that bad? You were fine five minutes ago," Hanya said.

"Hanya, she doesn't feel well," Tasya said and fixed Hanya with a look that told her to be quiet. Hanya looked away as Elzbeta put her arm around Tasya for support.

"It hasn't been five minutes, actually," Elzbeta said while Tasya struggled under her weight. "I've been feeling it all day. At first, I thought it was because of the ham. Now I'm not sure."

Tasya was surprised when Hanya came over to them and put her arm around Elzbeta's waist. Elzbeta inhaled sharply. "Careful, Hanya."

As they hobbled back in the direction of the factory, they drew curious looks from other people on the sidewalk who had to carefully sidestep around them on approach. A number of passersby looked at Elzbeta with concern.

"Do you need help?" An older woman asked in German before being pulled away by her husband.

"*Lassen Sie uns nach Hause,*" the husband said quietly to his wife. *Let's get home.*

"What's this, now?" Hanya whispered. Tasya looked up to see that they were approaching an intersection. Both sides of the pavement were lined with people who stood in an eerie silence. Tasya saw that all movement had stopped as long rows of people walked down the middle of the usually busy street. Tasya watched men, women, and even some children march down the middle of the street in absolute silence. Even though it was still warm outside, every one of the men and women in the group was wearing a long woolen coat, and everyone, including the women, wore pageboy-style working caps. Their dark coats were dusty from layers of sand and dirt, and the ends of their coats were frayed. Some of the people had leather belts tied around their waists.

"Who are those people?" Tasya whispered.

"It looks like they are being guarded, "Hanya said, scanning up and down the never-ending queue. "See, there are soldiers every ten meters or so, guarding them."

"Those people look worse than us!" Tasya exclaimed.

Elzbeta sighed severely and shifted more of her weight onto Tasya. "They're Jews. See their identification patch? The yellow star? They're Jews."

"How would you even know that?" Hanya asked.

"Because, this is like home."

When Elzbeta didn't say anything further, Tasya met Hanya's gaze over Elzbeta's head

"What are you talking about, Elzbeta?" Hanya asked.

Elzbeta returned from wherever her memories had taken her.

"Remember when I told you about when the Germans came to my village? They made all the Jews live in a ghetto just outside of my village. Every morning and evening they were marched to the factory to work. Like this." Elzbeta kept her eyes closed the entire time that she spoke.

"Why?" Tasya asked.

"I don't know. Maybe because the Jews caused so many problems for the Germans. It was the same in Poland, but no one did anything about it till the Germans came."

Tasya remembered Horayetz and the Jews who lived there. They sometimes had issues with the other villagers, sure. Her eyes flicked to a little boy and girl shuffling by, holding hands. They couldn't have been more than five or six.

"What do you mean, no one did anything about it till the Germans arrived?" Hanya whispered. "It was like this in your village? Under guard like this?"

"Of course. How else do the Jews get from their ghetto to the factory?"

Tasya and Hanya stared openly at the group shuffling by.

"We had issues with the Jews in the village, too. But nothing like this," Tasya said.

"I've never seen a more pathetic-looking group of humans in my entire life," Hanya whispered. "Not even the gypsies, and they are always so poor-looking, *ah,* Tasya?"

The Jews were skinny and pale; their huge eyes looked forward without expression. There were at least a hundred of them, and yet they were supervised by only a few guards. Tasya shivered and leaned into Elzbeta.

"Don't feel sorry for them. What makes you think that they are so unlike us, Hanya?" Elzbeta asked. "We are suffering as well."

"Who do you think *they* are?" Hanya asked, ignoring Elzbeta's comparison. She was staring at a small group of women near the back of the column. They wore the star patch like the rest of the group, but looked to be better off, with cleaner overcoats and boots that were not full of holes. They also walked silently, but had an awareness of their surroundings and the crowd around them that the others lacked.

"Maybe some have an easier job?" Hanya guessed.

"Some Jewish people traded food with the villagers during their march," Elzbeta said quietly. "Maybe they trade." Elzbeta straightened up and both Tasya and Hanya let go of her. "I have an idea. We should try to trade some food for money."

"Don't be stupid," Hanya said. "Look at these people. Where are they going to get anything to trade with us?"

"You'd be surprised, Hanya," Elzbeta said, still clutching her stomach. "The Jews are very crafty people! I'm going to try and barter for something."

With Elzbeta taking the lead and hobbling ahead, they walked to the edge of the sidewalk closer to the road. She led them to the corner of a building where the road made a bend.

"Look. Here the guards can't see them for a few seconds."

Sure enough, as the line shuffled around the corner to go south towards the Rhine, there was a blind spot for the guards.

Elzbeta hissed. "*Brot. Handel. Brot. Handel.*" Bread. Trade.

She repeated this as a number of Jews filed past them. Most completely ignored her. Tasya began to wonder if anyone understood what Elzbeta was saying. She felt embarrassed and sorry for the prisoners. Then, as she was about to drag Elzbeta away, a Jewish woman jumped out of the line. Tasya was shocked to hear her speak in Polish.

"You are Polish, yes?"

"Yes. Do you want to trade with me?"

"Tomorrow. Bring two large loaves of dark bread. Meet me here again, at this same time."

As quickly as the woman had jumped out of the shuffling line, she was back in it, head down. The guards hadn't noticed.

"I told you!" Elzbeta exclaimed, pulling hard on Tasya's arm as she teetered back on the sidewalk. "That woman needs food, and she has something to trade with us! Maybe we'll have some real money, finally!"

Tasya thought Elzbeta might be right – those prisoners were obviously better off than they were if they had money. Perhaps they were paid? Why not trade? As the promise of trade sunk in, she felt elated, until she looked to Hanya to share in the small celebration. Hanya had the opposite expression written clearly on her face.

"How can you trade with someone in such pathetic circumstances, Elzbeta?" Hanya whispered fiercely. "Those people are clearly starving! We should be giving any food that we can find to *them*."

"You are naïve if you don't think that everyone is trading something here," Elzbeta said. Her face was flushed, and Tasya was surprised to find that she looked ready to do battle with Hanya.

"In fact, Hanya, why do you think that some of the Jews look to be better off? You think that they are just sitting back, letting fate take its course, like we are? If that Jew woman wasn't going to trade with me, then she was going to do it with someone else."

"Hanya, I think that Elzbeta has a point," Tasya said, stepping between her two friends. "We aren't saying it's right to trade with someone who is worse off than us, but if you think about it, that woman was most likely searching out someone. We were lucky it was us."

"Yeah, Hanya," Elzbeta said, straightening her shoulders. "You have to admit that subsiding on dark bread and *balanda* was becoming impossible until we started begging."

"We get meat at the factory. Sometimes," Hanya grumbled, eyes down.

"Meat? Those pieces of salted pork that we get if the kitchen commandant is in a good mood? Look at you, Hanya. Even *you* are starting to lose weight!"

"Ok, *divchata*. Enough!" Tasya cried, but neither Hanya nor Elzbeta seemed to hear her.

"Anyway, where do you think you are going to get two extra loaves of bread? We are starving! If we had any, we would eat it. Stupid."

"I've thought about that. There's a woman who works in the factory kitchen, and she is from my village. I might try to offer her a deal. If she can help us, then we will give her half of the money we get."

Tasya knew she had to help Hanya save face.

"Look, it's getting late, maybe we should head back now and talk more about this in the barrack," Tasya said, looking up at the black storm clouds that were gathering above them.

Walking back to the factory in silence, Elzbeta shrugged off any overtures of help that Hanya stoically offered. As soon as they checked back in with Antoni, Hanya bolted in the opposite direction of the barrack.

"I'm sorry, Elzbeta. I don't know what's gotten into Hanya." Tasya apologized on behalf of her friend. Inside, she was teeming in anger. Why did Hanya always have to be so rude to Elzbeta?

"Let her go, Tasya," Elzbeta said, reaching over again to Tasya for support. "If Hanya wasn't your best friend, then I would have smacked her across the mouth months ago. She hates me simply because you like me. She's jealous, don't you see?"

"I know, but, why?"

"She just can't stand to share her best friend. As if by your liking me, you automatically like her less. It's pathetic."

"I'm sorry…again."

The next day dragged for Tasya. She was anxious to see if Elzbeta could get the bread and if they could get passes out of the factory for the evening. She was especially anxious about the Jewish woman. Would she still be there? Privately, she also couldn't help but think about chocolate. The money that they would get might be enough to buy a treat!

Like a miracle, Elzbeta felt well enough to sneak off to the kitchen after their shift was done. Tasya was thrilled when Elzbeta produced fresh, large loaves for her inspection.

"But, how?" Tasya asked. She had to look away from the bread when her mouth began to water.

"I made a deal with that woman in the kitchen!" Elzbeta cried, triumphant. "It's half of what we get, but so be it."

The next evening, both loaves hidden under their shirts, Elzbeta and Tasya headed out, followed by a silent and sulking Hanya. The girls waited for an hour for the gang of Jewish prisoners to walk by. Finally, the sound of the approaching shuffle could be heard long before any of the prisoners could be seen. For a brief instant, Tasya was gripped by a heavy feeling of guilt, but then she looked to Elzbeta's bright and mischievous eyes and managed to convince herself that if they didn't take the opportunity, that someone else would.

Tasya saw the Jewish woman first, and nudged Elzbeta. As soon as the woman entered the blind spot that the corner of the building allowed, she jumped out of the queue.

"Yes," said Elzbeta, who was slightly breathless, "I have the two loaves." She thrust them towards the woman.

Tasya watched in amazement as the woman twisted the heel of her shoe completely off, revealing a hollow cavity. From inside, she shook out a plain gold band. Without another word, the Jewish woman handed the ring over to Elzbeta and picked up the loaves of bread, tucking them into her oversized coat. With one motion, she screwed the heel back onto her shoe and jumped back into the line of prisoners.

The girls quickly walked away from the building. They didn't stop or speak until they were just outside the fence of the factory. Tasya was thrilled with the exchange; however, after eyeing the gold ring in Elzbeta's hand, a pang of guilt twisted her insides again.

"My plan worked!" Elzbeta cried, looking down at the ring with a huge smile.

Though Tasya felt guilty, the thought of chocolate again intruded. She didn't push it away.

"That woman gave us her wedding ring!" The full force of Hanya's accusation was hurled directly to Elzbeta, but Tasya trembled. "Her wedding ring for two loaves of bread!"

"Look, Hanya, I didn't know what her payment was going to be. It happened so quickly that I barely even noticed that it was a wedding band." Elzbeta's explanation showed no remorse and Tasya didn't fault her for that.

Tasya stepped between the two girls. "Keep it down, *divchata*!" Tasya hissed. "Hanya, we don't know that it was her wedding ring for sure. Maybe it belonged to someone else. Maybe she found it somewhere, and that's why she was willing to trade it away for some food."

Hanya shot Tasya a look of disgust, and Tasya felt another tremor of guilt.

"If this is what you two have come to, then I don't want any part of it." Hanya spat. "I'm starving too. Just look at how we're all wasting away. I shake every time I think about food but that doesn't mean that we should take from those who have less than us. And, now…how are you going to trade *that*?"

"Oh, Hanya. You are so naïve," Elzbeta said, laughing. "This is what you call an economy. Times are tough for the Jews, sure, but they are for us as well. If there is a trade that can be made, then why not seize the opportunity ourselves? Everyone in the factory is doing something or other to survive. We do it too, with our begging."

"You can't compare our begging for ration coupons, or the small extras that the Germans bring to share with us at the factory to this, Elzbeta. You are a spoiled sow and you are making Tasya into one too!" Hanya proclaimed before walking ahead to the security checkpoint at the factory.

"Well, Tasya, I for one am not going to let her ruin this!" Elzbeta chirped, again opening her hand to reveal the ring. "I'm going to keep this safe, Tasya. We'll figure out what to do with it together. Yes?"

Tasya nodded and forced a smile. Elzbeta had been so quiet, so sickly that week. Tasya missed her smile, and once again, her friend was bright like the sun.

"Yes, Elzbeta. Remember – I want chocolate!"

IX.

The week after the trade passed quietly. Hanya and Elzbeta actively avoided each other, much to Tasya's relief. Hanya found a group of older girls to spend her time with, and Tasya spent more time with Elzbeta and her Polish friends. Trading the ring proved to be more difficult than expected because none of the other workers from the east had any *Reich* marks, nor did they have anything to trade. Elzbeta enquired with some of the Polish and Ukrainian guards if they wanted to trade, but they also had nothing extra. Tasya and Elzbeta decided that it was too risky to ask any of the German workers or the German guards, so they were stuck. Tasya kept watch each day as Elzbeta hid the ring in the rotting straw of her mattress.

"I don't like hiding the ring each night, then pulling it out each morning," Tasya said as she kept watch while Elzbeta quickly returned the ring to its place one night.

"Me neither," Elzbeta said as she deftly slipped it through the tiny mattress hole. "Each time leaves us vulnerable to someone catching us."

The longer they had the ring, the more a feeling of dread grew in Tasya. She pulled away from Elzbeta to spend more time with Hanya. Elzbeta spent most of her free time with the Polish guards. The guards shared their cigarettes as well as odd bits of bread and even information with Elzbeta. Sometimes Tasya listened as Elzbeta told her second-hand news about the German *Wehrmacht* advancing further into Soviet territory, taking over Stalingrad. She tried to seem interested but she didn't care much for the progress of the German army.

For Tasya, time couldn't go by slower. The four months they had spent in the brick factory felt more like four years, especially since she had so much time to think about home. She wrote to Horayetz but no answers ever came. She missed her mother and sister terribly.

One morning in late September, a Polish girl, Katya, shook Tasya awake.

"Your friend, Elzbeta...something is wrong."

Tasya rubbed her eyes, lifting the heavy curtain of sleep.

"What do you mean? What's wrong?"

"Elzbeta is in bed and she's crying. We are going to be late for work if we stay with her."

Tasya looked to the upper bunk for Hanya but it was empty. Tasya followed the Polish girl over to Elzbeta's bed.

"What's wrong? Are you sick?" Tasya asked.

"My stomach, Tasya," Elzbeta whispered. "I'm in so much pain."

Tasya looked down at Elzbeta's writhing form on the mattress. Panic rose up from deep within her.

"Do you need to go to the toilet?"

"No. It's a different pain. I've never felt this before. Look at my belly, Tasya."

Tasya carefully pulled up Elzbeta's nightgown to look at her stomach. What she saw made her jump and yelp in surprise. Elzbeta's stomach was grotesquely bloated. The skin around her belly was purple and black.

"Elzbeta, when did this happen?" Tasya asked, trying to keep her voice even.

"It got all puffed up during the night. I was hoping it would go away. Oh my God, it hurts," Elzbeta said as she squeezed her eyes shut with pain.

"Just wait. I'll be right back," Tasya said, replacing Elzbeta's nightgown gently around her bloated belly. She tried her best to appear calm as her heart beat against her ribcage like a trapped bird.

Tasya had no idea what to do. She couldn't go to the guards because she didn't know who she could trust. She had heard stories of *Ostarbeiter* workers falling ill, and after being sent away for help, they never returned. There was no barrack matron to help. Tasya decided to find Hanya and ask for her help. She made a beeline to the washroom in hopes of finding Hanya and was flooded with relief to find her there.

"Hanya, come quick! Elzbeta is really sick." Tasya pulled Hanya aside and away from the ears of the others in the washroom. "Her stomach – it's disgusting. It's huge and black."

"What do you mean, huge and black? How bad is it really, Tasya?" Hanya dried her hands on her washing rag. She looked suspicious.

"Hanya, last night Elzbeta was complaining about how skinny we are, and we laughed that we look like little girls. Now, her stomach is huge! It looks awful!"

Hanya rolled her eyes and sighed. "Fine, I'll take a look. Don't her other friends want to help you?"

"Hanya, just help me. No one else seems to want to help her."

"No surprise there," Hanya scoffed. "Elzbeta is about as popular with the girls in this barrack as a disease." Tasya looked at Hanya, confused. "Oh, come on, Tasya! You haven't noticed her spending time with the guards? The others don't like it when one girl is given special attention."

Tasya wanted to ask Hanya what she meant, but then Hanya started to walk in her long strides across the barrack, and Tasya jogged to catch up. When they got to Elzbeta's bed, Tasya pulled up her nightgown again to show Hanya.

"We need to tell the barrack guard," Hanya whispered as she yanked Tasya away from the bunk. "That's disgusting."

"I'm scared that they will take her away," Tasya said as she began to cry. "He will tell the commandant, and then what? I've heard the stories about sick girls."

"That might actually be true, Tasya. Let's think. Why don't we go to the guard with a solution? Tell him that something is seriously wrong with Elzbeta and that we'll pick up her share of work for today so that there isn't any trouble. That might work. Isn't Elzbeta friends with some of the guards?"

Tasya hoped that Hanya was right. She looked outside the barrack door. The boy patrolling up and down the rows of barracks was someone with whom Elzbeta had spent time.

"Hey! Excuse me," Tasya called out in Polish to the guard. He walked over with a self-assured swagger. He was likely not much older than she was.

"What?" the guard asked.

"It's Elzbeta," Tasya said. When the guard's face remained motionless, Tasya whispered, "Your friend." The guard raised his eyebrows.

"Elzbeta. She's very sick," Tasya said.

"What do you mean, sick?" the guard asked. "She can't go to work today?"

"Yes. I mean, no. She's really sick and needs help. It's her stomach. It's huge."

The guard then narrowed his eyes. Tasya saw a flash of fear in them.

"She's in a lot of pain. I don't know what to do!"

"Well, what do you want me to do about it?" the guard asked with a small waver in his voice.

"You need to get Elzbeta help!" Tasya cried.

Hanya shushed her.

"It's just that she looks like her stomach is about to burst," Tasya blurted.

The guard cleared his throat and looked at the ground.

"Well, I'll tell you what you shouldn't do. Don't go around telling anyone that something is wrong. Just tell the foreman that she's sick for today and that's that."

Tasya then remembered the guard's name – Arek. She took a deep breath.

"Listen, Arek. There is something very wrong with her. Who can help her?"

Arek's eyes flashed with anger.

"Don't you dare call me by my first name! Who do you think you are? Don't forget, girl, you are a worker, and I am a guard." He turned to walk away. "I'll tell you what happens to girls with so-called stomach issues. They get sent away, and they don't come back. Do you get it? If Elzbeta is truly sick, then let her rest for today, and she can get back to work when she's better. Believe me, it's the best alternative."

He walked quickly away, darted between the barracks and was gone.

"Now what?" Tasya cried as she spun around to face Hanya.

"Now, nothing. You heard him. We go to work, tell the foreman that Elzbeta is sick, and that's it," Hanya said, grabbing Tasya by the elbow and leading her to the factory.

Throughout the seemingly endless shift, Tasya constantly thought about Elzbeta. She became sick with worry.

"Tasya. Elzbeta is going to be just fine," Hanya said as Tasya worked quietly and quickly next to her. "Elzbeta is annoying, but for God's sake, she'll be fine."

Tasya nodded. She knew in her heart that something was seriously wrong with Elzbeta, but she willed herself to pray for a miraculous recovery.

As soon as the shift was over, both girls raced back to the barrack. They found Elzbeta still in bed. Her skin was grey. Her sweat soaked through her wool blanket into the straw mattress. It was only then that the ring flashed through Tasya's mind.

"Didn't anyone come to see about you?" Tasya asked softly.

"No, no one came here," Elzbeta said in a raspy voice. She breathed in small gasps and gripped her bed sheets. She looked up at her friends with wide eyes.

A number of other girls also back from the work shift came and stood around Elzbeta's bunk, looking at her with open curiosity. Some of them looked worried for Elzbeta, but others looked like they were inspecting an interesting circus act.

"Is she having a baby?" a Ukrainian girl asked. "My sister looked like this when she was having her son."

"I don't think so," Tasya said sharply. She was lying. She'd been wondering the same thing herself. "I would think I would know if she is pregnant!" Tasya spat, defensively.

The other girls drifted away casually, unthreatened by Tasya.

"Now what?" Tasya whispered to Hanya.

"I don't know. Should we ask another guard for help?"

"What about the ring?" Tasya asked. An idea came to her so fast that she couldn't believe she hadn't thought of it sooner. "We could use it as payment for a doctor or nurse to come here to see her!"

"You want a doctor to come here? Plus, why would a doctor accept the ring for payment? What if he thinks we stole it?"

Tasya paused only for a second.

"We could say that it is Elzbeta's. We can make up a story that she is married but willing to trade."

"Hmmmm, maybe. That could be a good idea, especially if she's actually having a baby. We should at least pretend to strangers that she's married now, or at least used to be."

"Let's go now, then. Before curfew."

"I don't think so, Tasya. Only one of us should go."

"You want me to go out by myself? With the stolen ring?" Tasya was wide-eyed with fear.

"Yes. You, alone. It's your ring. Elzbeta is your friend."

"I can't go by myself. I've never been outside the factory fence without at least Elzbeta."

"You'll have to do it, Tasya." Hanya turned back towards Elzbeta and Tasya knew that she had lost the argument. Her heart started again to beat hard in her chest. She pulled Hanya back towards her.

"How will we get the ring? It's in the mattress that Elzbeta is lying on!"

"I guess I'll have to distract the others. Let's do it now, Tasya. You're running out of time," Hanya whispered.

Hanya called out to the girls who gathered around Elzbeta's bunk.

"You're right, Tasya," Hanya said loudly. "Maybe it's contagious,"

The girls around Elzbeta's bunk all took a step backwards and exchanged looks.

"*Divchata*! Take a look at my stomach. Maybe I'm getting it, too!"

As all eyes went to Hanya, Tasya darted around the other girls and went to Elzbeta's side. She easily found the small tear in the mattress just under Elzbeta's shoulders, and quickly dug out the ring from among the damp straw. If Elzbeta noticed Tasya searching around for their one valuable possession, she didn't show it.

With a quick look at Hanya, Tasya walked out of the barrack, and then ran to the guard post at the front gate. She was able to secure a pass easily from Antoni. She walked quickly in the cool evening air, clutching a ratty shawl wrapped tightly around her shoulders. Tasya was terrified of being out of the factory for the first time on her own. She imagined that everyone on the street was looking at her. Even though she knew she could be fined, she hid her identification patch with one corner of the shawl.

With no plan and anxiety clouding her brain, Tasya ran up and down the narrow streets that led from the factory to the Rhine. She looked frantically for any storefront that appeared to be a medical office. Running from door to door, Tasya could hardly read the signs as panic filled her. At one corner, her legs suddenly became stubborn tree trunks, refusing to move even one more step. Her vision blurred with tears, her own strained panting echoed in her ears. Stopping, she exhaled hard. She struggled to breathe normally. Finally, she was ready to run again.

At last, in the distance down one cobblestoned street Tasya spotted a Swiss cross – the sign of a medic. She ran as quickly as she could to the door and pounded as hard as she could with both her fists.

"Help me! Please, help!" she yelled with abandon.

Tasya banged on the heavy wooden door until her knuckles were scraped and bloody. There was no answer. No one opened the door.

Stepping away, she peered through the grime-covered windows. With a great fall of her stomach she realized that the entire building was abandoned. Tasya spotted a long counter and a desk. One chair had fallen on its side, and rested next to the far wall. There was absolutely no one to be found, no one who could help her.

"I hate this place!" Tasya yelled, pounding on the widows, moaning. "You tricked us; you tricked all of us to come here! I hate this country. I hate you people! I just want to go home!" Tasya kicked the wooden door. She fell to the ground, sobbing in frustration.

Tasya wept in the same spot on the sidewalk until dusk turned to dark. Once she felt as if she couldn't cry one more tear, she got up from the cobblestoned sidewalk and began to walk slowly back to the factory. She knew it must have been past curfew. The streets were pitch dark and totally empty.

Antoni at the factory gates looked threatening but his expression softened when he looked at Tasya. She walked by him like a ghost. He did not call after her. Tasya walked back to the barrack.

She entered the barrack still clutching the shawl around her shoulders, and saw that there were several girls still gathered around Elzbeta's bed. When Hanya spotted Tasya, she burst into tears. Tasya had never seen Hanya cry so openly, and she snapped out of her trance. Before she could ask, Hanya cried out, "Elzbeta is dead, Tasya!"

Looking over to Elzbeta's bunk, Tasya finally noticed that the girls who had gathered around were also crying. Some cried softly while wiping away tears; others loudly sobbed their grief for the whole world to see. Tasya wanted to slap the ones who were wailing. They barely even knew Elzbeta. They were just being dramatic. Elzbeta was her friend, not theirs.

Approaching Elzbeta's bunk, Tasya saw that her friend was truly gone. Elzbeta's stomach was still swollen, the covers pulled back as if to show the evidence of what had killed her. At least Elzbeta's face looked peaceful.

"I've already alerted the barrack guard, and he's going to go get the camp commandant," Hanya whispered, joining Tasya. "They are most likely going to come and take the body away soon, so you might want to say your goodbyes."

Death in the factory was handled quickly and without the intrusion of human emotions. The guards swiftly took Elzbeta's still-warm body away while the girls watched, huddled together in the safety of their own bunks. There was nothing else.

After Elzbeta's body was carried away, Tasya laid on top of her bed, still clutching the shawl around her shoulders. She was no longer crying, but shivering and sniffling. The breathing of the other girls in the barracks slowed as one by one they fell asleep. Above her, Hanya tossed and turned. It gave Tasya some comfort to know that Hanya was also unable to sleep. After what seemed like hours, Tasya began to shift around under her blankets. It was only then that Tasya realized that she was still wearing the gold ring on her right index finger. She touched it with her thumb.

Later that night, still unable to sleep, Tasya thought about the deaths that she had witnessed in her life. Her two grandmothers were gone. Her two grandfathers were gone. Her beloved father was gone. She had seen death over and over in her fifteen years. Horayetz was a small village, and when someone in the village died, everyone came out to mourn over a three-day period. Many times, Tasya had spent the first day of mourning with the family. The second day was for the *panachyda* memorial service, and the third was the burial. Afterwards, there was always a gathering with food, vodka, and singing that lasted well into the night. Tasya knew that Elzbeta would have no such mourning.

Seconds later, there was a sharp poke on the side of her body. A hand pushed down over her mouth.

"Don't make a sound," a voice hissed in her ear. "Just tell me where that ring is and I won't tell on you." Tasya's squinted in the near darkness, looking for the owner of the voice. An older woman with grey hair glared back at her. The woman slowly released her grip over Tasya's mouth just enough for Tasya to speak. Tasya thought she'd thumb the ring without the woman seeing. It wasn't on her finger.

"I don't have it," Tasya lied, her throat constricting with panic. She struggled to place the woman, to think of how she might have known about the ring. Then Tasya remembered the Polish woman from the kitchen who gave Elzbeta the bread. With the difficulties trading the ring and Elzbeta's death, Tasya had forgotten about the woman who was owed payment.

"It was in Elzbeta's mattress when she died and I wasn't here. The guards took her mattress outside right after they removed her body, and they burned it. See?" Tasya pointed with a shaking finger over to where Elzbeta's bunk stood naked.

"It was in her mattress?" The woman hissed. "Why would you two senseless girls keep something valuable in her mattress?"

"Because we thought it was the safest place, down in the straw," Tasya whispered. "We didn't know where else to keep it hidden."

"You stupid girls! Didn't anyone ever teach you to keep your valuables close to you, somewhere on your body?"

The woman let go as Tasya shook her head. Tasya remained lying down. She was too frightened to sit up.

Just when Tasya thought that she could relax, the woman lunged towards Tasya and grabbed her hands. She ran her fingers up and down Tasya's hands, inspecting them to the wrists. Finding them unadorned, the woman stood up.

"I had to check that you weren't still holding onto it, of course. You understand." The woman smiled, and Tasya saw that she was missing both of her front teeth. Tasya watched the woman until she slid out of the barrack in total silence. Tasya felt around her thin blanket and mattress. She found the ring under her right leg. She exhaled and slipped it back onto her hand.

"Are you alright, Tasya?" Hanya asked, leaning over from the top part of their bunk. "I wanted to help you. She was scary, ah? I'm guessing she's Elzbeta's friend from the kitchen."

"I don't think she was her friend," Tasya mumbled as she turned over to her side, away from Hanya. She spun the ring around her finger as her heart twisted with grief over Elzbeta. Tasya listened as Hanya shifted back up to the top of their bunk, then she wiped away a tear that started a river worth of tears for her friend.

X.

So, if she wasn't having a baby, then what was wrong with her?" Tasya asked Hanya the next morning. They were partway through their morning work, and Tasya had been sniffling and crying nearly the entire time.

"Who knows?" Hanya was quiet and had stopped crying the night before. "Anyway, the one barrack guard told me that her body was going to be sent back to her family. He actually seemed even more distraught than you, Tasya," Hanya said, then smiled. Tasya didn't return her smile. "Oh, come now. I'm just trying to make you smile again."

Tasya ignored Hanya's joke.

"Do you think that's true, Hanya? She'll be sent home?"

"Actually, I doubt it." Hanya said as she shrugged. "Anyway. I'm taking a water break."

Tasya was left standing at the kiln as Hanya walked away. Tasya noticed Hanya had an extra spring in her step.

Tasya and Hanya settled into their old routine of being a pair. They stuck mainly to themselves, but Tasya missed Elzbeta terribly. She longed for Elzbeta's carefree nature, her laughter and optimism. Hanya was so serious. Hanya hardly ever laughed and never had a sparkle in her eyes like Elzbeta. Once, Tasya even found herself wondering what it would have been like for Hanya to have died, rather than Elzbeta. She felt instantly guilty for even considering it. For the rest of that day, she had been unable to look Hanya directly in the eye.

XI.

Up! Get up!" The barrack lights snapped on. Tasya was heavy with sleep. She was confused. What time was it? Why were there guards in the barrack?

"All of you get up and get outside!"

Tasya sat up in bed and watched the chaos around her. Some girls were already up and running outside in nightshirts; others were gathering some of their things. Others, like her, were stunned. They watched the action in the barrack, frozen in place on their beds. Ukrainian and Polish guards were running around like loose chickens, yelling at the girls to get up.

"What's going on?" Hanya yelled to the girls running by their bunk.

"Bombs! The English are coming to bomb us!"

Tasya jumped out of bed and scanned her bunk. What to take? As she was shifting through her few clothes, Tasya heard the drone of distant airplanes. All the girls in the barrack froze and looked at each other. Hanya grabbed hold of Tasya's arm and dragged her all the way to the barrack door.

"Tasya, just leave everything!"

Outside, it was late in the night, but the streets beyond the factory fence were filled with people running and screaming in every direction. The drone of the planes grew louder. Tasya nearly jumped a foot into the air as the long whistle of a bomb screeched, ripping through a building some miles away.

The crowd paused after the bomb hit for several seconds, and very briefly, there was quiet. Then, full panic erupted. Covering her ears, Tasya looked to Hanya. She looked as terrified as Tasya felt. Everyone was running in the direction of the front gate, and they followed. Tasya watched in disbelief as guards ran out of the main factory gate, the backs of their grey uniform jackets disappearing within seconds. Hanya grabbed Tasya's hand, and she pulled her in the direction that many others were running, towards the Rhine. Stumbling on a rock, but feeling no pain, Tasya realized that they were both barefoot wearing only their nightshirts.

"Where do we go now? How will we be able to escape?" Tasya yelled, clutching Hanya's arm.

"Don't think about that! Let's just try to stick together and make it through this alive. You have to keep a strong hold on me." Hanya yelled back.

It seemed as if every man, woman, and child left in Düsseldorf was running for their lives towards the river. The hard breathing of running people was broken by the few screams that came from women in the massive crowds. Once they reached the bank of the Rhine, the entire British air fleet sounded like they were directly above them. As great flashes of light from the bombs lit up the nighttime, there were hundreds of planes in the sky.

A bomb fell two-hundred meters downriver, destroying one of the stone bridges that Tasya had so often admired on her evenings with Hanya and Elzbeta. Panic set in, with everyone again screaming and running in all directions. Terrified that they might be separated, Tasya grabbed Hanya's hand and clung to her. Hanya dragged her into the first direction that they could go without being trampled. They ran together for what seemed like an hour, still clutching hands, trying to escape the terrifying whistling of the bombs. Tasya wanted to scream but Hanya was totally quiet. The sound of bombs hitting buildings began to fade the longer they ran.

When they came to a fork in the road where the Rhine curved, they chose the direction away from the river and into a residential area. Tasya lost track of which way they were running, and became disoriented, nearly losing Hanya a few times when they accidentally broke their grip on each other. By then, the crowd around them had dwindled. Some older people and children hadn't made it this far, and others were too tired to go on. Though Tasya's legs burned, and her lungs ached, she held onto Hanya for all her life. They passed an old woman sitting by the side of the road, clutching a wide-eyed boy. Tasya stared for a second until Hanya pulled her away.

Just as suddenly as the bombing assault began, it stopped. All at once, everything was silent. Ears ringing, they were enveloped by darkness in the night so deep that they could not even see each other while standing only a foot apart. There was no moon, and no lights anywhere. Tasya tried to get her bearings as her eyes adjusted to the total darkness. The only light was the distant fires burning in the bombed-out buildings.

She realized they were standing on grass, the nighttime dew wet on her feet. She felt a warmth spreading around them, and reached down to feel cuts and bruises that she didn't know she had. The other people gathered around them softly spoke in different languages – Tasya recognized bits of Polish, some German, as well as a multitude of others that she had never heard before. As her eyes adjusted, Tasya saw people sitting on the grass. Most people were silent, quiet in their shock. Tasya and Hanya collapsed down to the ground together, still holding onto one another. It wasn't very cold out but Tasya trembled.

After what seemed like an eternity of sitting, Tasya and Hanya both lay down on the grass, and at one point, Tasya even dozed off. Finally, the sun started to rise in the east, and as the grey dawn began to creep over the horizon, they saw the black smoke that continued to billow from the buildings of Düsseldorf. Even from their distance, they saw the damage that had been done. Everywhere they looked was total destruction. Many in the crowd began to cry, and Tasya heard one man say in Ukrainian, "*Bozhe mylyi*. It's all gone." Tasya began to cry as well.

"I wonder if the factory is still standing," Tasya asked Hanya. She looked over the smoking ruins of Düsseldorf, and wrapped her arms around herself.

"I hope so," said Hanya. "Where will they send us to work if the factory is destroyed?"

Within the hour, a group of German soldiers pulled up in a jeep. With barking authority, they organized everyone by groups. They called out for *Ostarbeiter*, *Zivilarbeiter*, and German nationals. Tasya remained close to Hanya, holding her arm and shivering in the cool morning air. She regretted not taking her shoes when they ran away from the factory.

As the soldiers made notes, another uniformed man roared up on a BMW motorcycle. All the soldiers froze into place, saluting. One soldier with a clipboard addressed the man as General. The General hopped off the motorcycle and asked the soldiers questions. It occurred to Tasya that morning would've been a perfect opportunity to escape and to try to make their way home. She hadn't thought of it, and it didn't appear as if anyone else had considered the option. When the General finished his assessment, he radioed to have supplies brought in. They were given some water, a bit of bread, and a blanket each to keep warm.

They were told to sit and not move far. The day passed slowly. On the roads around them there was much activity. Trucks filled with soldiers were driving in and out of Düsseldorf. Ambulance sirens wailed in the distance. Tasya and Hanya waited while Tasya shivered like a leaf. Everyone around them was abuzz.

In the early afternoon, Tasya spotted a woman approaching on foot, accompanied by the same General from the morning. The woman was dressed plainly, but even from a distance, it was clear that her clothes were clean and of good quality. Her face was bright and cheerful. The woman and General spoke for several minutes while scanning the crowd. Tasya saw the woman point directly to Tasya and Hanya, gesturing for them to come over.

"Hello," said the woman in German. "How old are you girls?"

"I am sixteen in a month," Tasya replied in heavily-accented German. Hanya remained silent. "Hanya is eighteen now. My name is Tasya."

Smiling, the woman turned to the General. "Yes, I will take both," she said. "The older girl is bigger, and looks to be quite healthy. She'll go to the farm, but the younger one will go to the house."

Tasya and Hanya looked at each other. Farm? House? Separation from Hanya was the worst possible thing that could happen to her. Tasya needed Hanya to take care of her. The girls instinctively reached for one another, and clasped hands without taking their eyes off the woman.

"Oh, don't worry, girls," said the woman, "you will be just fine with me!" She laughed; her voice sounded like songbirds. "Look at their faces, General! You would think that we are taking them to a firing squad!"

After the General politely laughed the woman stepped forward and placed her hand gently on Tasya's shoulder. "I'm sorry. You must have been through hell last night." She pulled Tasya away from Hanya. "I will take the younger one home with me now, but the older one will wait for my lead hand to come get her."

Tasya surprised herself by turning and walking away without one word of argument, without even any sign of protest. Tasya didn't argue or fight to remain with Hanya. She simply unclasped the hand of her best friend and limped away.

As Tasya and the woman walked away, Tasya kept looking back at Hanya, but she never managed to meet her eyes. Hanya kept her eyes focused on the ground in front of her own bruised feet, arms hanging limply by her side. Hanya never once looked up.

XII.

The woman walked and Tasya hobbled beside her for ten minutes in silence through eerily quiet streets. There wasn't another soul in sight. Tasya imagined that in different times, the cobblestoned streets and the old buildings with their brightly painted shutters would be charming and full of life. Thoughts of Hanya were tumbling through her mind. The longer she ambled in a daze beside the woman, the more that she began to panic. What had just happened? Why did she leave Hanya so easily? She breathed heavily, and was trying to control it when small black dots fluttered at the sides of her vision.

With a look of alarm, the woman grabbed Tasya's arm and brought her over to a small bench at the edge of a tiny park.

"Are you alright? What's your name, again?" The woman asked in a slow and deliberate German. "You told me, but I can't remember."

Tasya fought to catch her breath and whispered her name.

"Tasya. That is a very unique name." The woman paused. "Actually, it sounds like the name of my childhood friend, Tasi. Would you mind if I called you that?"

Tasya shrugged miserably. She was too tired to care, angry with herself for leaving Hanya behind.

"Wonderful, then!" The woman patted Tasya's hand gently, "My name is Frau Bamm."

Frau Bamm helped Tasya up and they continued walking.

"This is Jüchen, a small suburb of Düsseldorf," said Frau Bamm. "And this is the town square. Have you heard of this place?"

Tasya shook her head, mute.

"Oh, my. You are upset about leaving your friend." Frau Bamm patted Tasya on the back. "All will be right soon enough. Tell me, Tasi, what language do you speak?"

"Ukrainian," Tasya whispered. "Polish, little bit."

"*Aha.* But, can you speak any German?"

"Little bit."

"Well, we speak German at home, and I'm sure you will pick it up quickly. That's the beauty of being so young. Learning anything is possible at your age." Frau Bamm paused again to lift Tasya's chin and looked into her eyes. "I know you've been through a lot, but you'll like it here, I promise. Now, about your friend. Her name, again?"

"Hanya," Tasya said, fighting back tears.

"Hanya. She will be fine, Tasi. Not to worry! We run a small farm where we grow grapes for making wine. Your friend will be treated well there."

Frau Bamm stopped walking. They were standing in front of a line of row houses, bordering the edge of a square which, like the rest of Jüchen, had remained untouched by the bombings. Some of the row houses had planter boxes with beautiful red flowers in them. Tasya inhaled when she saw the flowers. It had been months since she had seen anything of such delicate beauty.

Looking up at the house in front of her, Tasya saw that it was made of a red brick, with dark green shutters framing each window. She then looked up to the upper windows and counted. One, two, three, four, and five! Five windows on the second floor! Tasya had never seen such a beautiful home, and it looked to be ten times bigger than even the loveliest house in Horayetz.

"My husband, Herr Bamm, is a man of considerable influence in Jüchen. We volunteered to help some of the workers after the bombings, and here you are!" Frau Bamm pushed open the heavy wood front door. She reached for a pair of slippers on the ground and handed them to Tasya. "Now, come, child. Tasi. Welcome to our home."

To the left of the entryway was a sitting room, and within it stood a young girl with dark hair with her back to them. The young girl was deep in concentration as she played the violin, carefully following sheet music that was perched atop a delicate wire stand. A very old man listened with closed eyes, head slowly moving up and down to the rhythm of the music.

Frau Bamm stopped and waited for the girl to finish playing, gesturing playfully for Tasya to remain quiet. As they stood there, Tasya looked beyond the girl into a dining room, where another woman was setting the places for a meal, carefully laying out plates and silverware. Tasya smelled food cooking. Her stomach let out a long, high-pitched whine.

The girl playing the violin stopped, turned, and looked up wide-eyed at the sight of Tasya. The old man's eyes snapped open, staring, looking at Tasya as if she were a new creature at the zoo. Filthy, dressed in clothes that were practically rags, and without a proper bath in months, Tasya felt immensely self-conscious. Both the young girl and old man gawked at her for a few seconds before Frau Bamm spoke to them in rapid German that Tasya did not understand. Snapping out of their astonishment, both crossed the room towards them.

In a German slow and precise enough to be understood by Tasya, Frau Bamm explained, "Apologies for the interruption, Herr Vogel. I wanted to introduce someone to you and Adora. This is Tasi. She is going to be working as our new chambermaid now." Tasya didn't know what to do, so she nodded, and stared at the soft slippers on her feet. "She survived the English bombings of the factories near the river. Now Herr Bamm and I have taken her on to work in our house."

The old man nodded with seriousness, then to Tasya's surprise and delight, extended his hand to her in greeting. Tasya watched her dirty hand be enveloped in his for a warm handshake. The young girl was smiling up at Tasya with a wide grin.

"This is my youngest daughter, Adora, and her teacher, Herr Vogel. Now, let's get you acquainted with Isle, our cook."

Tasya waved before she and Frau Bamm continued down the hall to the kitchen at the very back of the first floor. It was the biggest kitchen that Tasya had ever seen, even bigger than the one at the brick factory barracks. Right in the middle of the room stood a large, imposing wooden working block, and directly above were a dozen copper pots and pans suspended from the high ceiling. They shone like so many suns from the light that streamed through the tall windows.

At the working block, a woman was bustling about, preparing the midday meal. With a bounty of food directly in front of her eyes, Tasya couldn't help but stare at it. Frau Bamm left Tasya at the entryway to inspect what the cook was preparing. Tasya tried to follow what they were saying, but found it impossible to concentrate on anything besides the slices of ham, bread, pickles, and potatoes.

"Good God, child, you are looking at the food like a starved animal," exclaimed the cook. "Sit. Sit right here up at the counter, and I will get you something right away."

Tasya sat with relief. The cook immediately sliced a chunk of bread from a loaf and placed it on a plate in front of her. It was a beautiful white bread, still warm. Tasya devoured the hunk as soon as it was given to her, and then devoured a small slice of ham that followed.

"I'm not sure that you heard me with that food in front of you," the cook laughed. "My name is Isle. I'm the cook for the Bamm's." Isle was a plump woman who looked to be in her mid-forties. She had a jolly manner about her that made Tasya feel instantly at ease.

Tasya smiled back shyly, "Tasya. Tasi."

"Ah, well then, Tasi, we have to be careful that you don't eat too much in your first sitting! Give your stomach some time to digest the bread and ham, and then we'll see what else you can handle."

"Isle, give the poor girl some of that soup you made," Frau Bamm scolded gently. "A little bit won't hurt her."

Tasya dove into a small bowl of steaming vegetable soup with doughy dumplings. It was the very best soup that she had tasted in her entire life.

"Good heavens!"

The maid who had been setting the dining table stood at the kitchen door, openly staring at Tasya. She looked to be a bit younger than the cook, Isle, but much more thin. She had a long nose that came to a pointy end. Tasya thought that she looked like a bird, and quickly tried to shake the thought away as a nervous giggle crept up from within her.

"Ah, Frieda. This is the new chambermaid, Tasi." Frau Bamm said with a note of caution in her voice. "She survived the bombing of Düsseldorf last night. Since the factory where she worked was destroyed, she is coming to work here."

"Of course! Pardon me, Tasi. I wasn't expecting anyone new!" Freda gave Tasya a friendly wave and another quick once-over. "Ahhhh. That's right, then. I take care of the main floor."

"And Tasi will help you with dusting and tidying," Frau Bamm said.

"Of course!" Frieda exclaimed again. Tasya giggled as she watched Frieda struggle to recover. "Yes! So! Tell me, how's the soup today?"

"Heaven. Best soup I've ever eaten," Tasya said with grave seriousness. The women laughed even though Tasya had not meant to be funny.

"Alright, I think that's enough for now," Isle announced, taking Tasya's bowl away as she finished off the very last few drops. "I'm concerned about that stomach of yours. You look as if rations were smaller at the factory. We will have to make sure to fill her out, won't we, Frau Bamm? "

"Yes, we will. Don't worry, Tasi, you'll have to actually watch what you eat because Isle is the best cook in all of Düsseldorf!" Frau Bamm said, making her way out of the kitchen into the dining room. "Tasi, I think Isle and Frieda will take things from here, and get you comfortable. I'll be around to see you later on this evening, but for now, you can rest."

"Well," Frieda said, looking Tasya up and down after Frau Bamm had left. "You are a fright, that's for sure. But we can fix that, and thank God a young thing like you survived the bombings. We were all up as well last night, terrified. I hear quite a number of people were killed."

"All those beautiful old buildings, all the factories alongside the Rhine are gone, I hear," Isle added and Tasya nodded.

"So, how old are you, Tasi?" Frieda asked.

"Sixteen. Actually, fifteen."

"Fifteen! Good God, you look closer to twelve!" Frieda exclaimed and Isle shot her a look of warning. Frieda's ice-blue eyes darted around the kitchen as she looked like she was gathering herself together. "Pardon me. With a proper scrubbing, and some food in your belly, maybe you'll start to look your real age soon," Frieda laughed. "Come with me. I have a bedroom that's just down the hall from here. You can get cleaned up, and then have a rest in my bed."

Frieda led Tasya to an indoor bathroom to the side of the kitchen, where she was left alone to bathe in the sit-down tub. Tasya felt as if she had not taken a bath in years. Using the washcloth and bar of soap that Frieda gave her with vigor, the scrubbing turned her skin raw and red, but she was careful around her sensitive feet. Tasya rubbed as hard as she could, yet she could not fully get all the grime off that had built up on her hands. Tasya had to drain the tub of the filth that quickly came off her body and fill the tub again. Looking down at her body as she relaxed in the water, Tasya saw that the few months spent in Germany had made her look even more child-like. What few curves she had before arriving were gone. Her hips were narrow, extending in a straight line down from her waist, and her hipbones jutted out sharply, framing her concave stomach. Tasya's small breasts had shrunk to an even smaller size. She truly did look like a twelve year old.

After the bath, Tasya felt heavy with sleep. Frieda dressed her in a large cotton nightshirt, and put Tasya to bed in her small bedroom. Lying down on Frieda's narrow bed, Tasya was enveloped in softness. The bed was like nothing that Tasya had ever experienced in her entire life. The mattress was not stuffed with straw, but feathers. As she closed her eyes, Tasya unexpectedly remembered Hanya, and jolted awake. Remembering Frau Bamm's reassurances that Hanya would also be safe, Tasya decided that Hanya must be well cared-for. She already trusted the German woman who had shown her much kindness that day. Her guilt eased and she fell into a heavy, dreamless sleep.

XIII.

Tasya woke up and did not know where she was. Was she still in the factory barracks? It was totally dark, and she pawed around the bed trying to get her bearings. She felt a headboard. Then she remembered her rescue and collapsed back into the bed, instantly falling asleep again.

She had vivid and confusing dreams.

In one dream, she was with her mother. They were both working in the brick factory, moving the heavy moulds slowly back and forth. In her dream, Tasya had meant to ask her mother about Kateryna. Daria turned to Tasya, and without expression told her that Kateryna had a baby girl, but that they had both died in childbirth. In the dream, Tasya cried and cried, stuck in place. She badly wanted to be held in her mother's arms, but Daria didn't seem to understand.

Tasya sensed a hand touching her arm, and she tried to turn around to see who it was, afraid it was her foreman. The hand squeezed her arm gently a few times before Tasya realized that she was being pulled out of the bad dream. She tried with all her might to wake up, but she felt like she was covered in a heavy black blanket that wouldn't allow her to open her eyes or move her limbs.

Turning with a neck sore from the long sleep, Tasya struggled to open her eyes. Squinting in the bright light that flooded Frieda's small room, she saw that the hand on her arm belonged to the young daughter. Adora was sitting on a wooden chair right next to the bed, staring with open curiosity at Tasya. She looked so fresh, so unspoiled. A tremor of jealousy ripped through Tasya.

"You were crying as you slept," the young girl said. "What were you dreaming about?"

Tasya wanted so badly to feel her mama's arms around her again, and dreams were the only way that she would be able to. Yet even in sleep, she wasn't able to reach out to find the security and love that she craved. With tears coming fresh into her eyes, Tasya fought to find the proper German words. "I had a dream of my mama and sister. My sister and her baby died."

"Have they actually died? What I mean is, have they already died, or did you just dream that?" the girl asked.

"No, no, they haven't died. At least, I don't think so. No word from my sister or mother since I left home in May."

"That was over four months ago," the girl helpfully offered after a second of calculations.

"Yes, four months," Tasya replied. "Though for me, it feels like much longer. Feels like I've been gone from my home for years." So much had happened in such a short amount of time. Tasya knew in the four months she had been in Germany, she had grown up more than the previous year in Horayetz.

"*Mutter* says your name is Tasi, and that you are going to be the new Ruth."

"The new Ruth?"

"She was our chambermaid. The one before you, I mean."

"Oh. Ruth left?"

"I don't know. *Mutter* said she had to go away, but I don't know why. One day, I woke up, and she was gone."

"Well, I am the new Ruth."

The girl leaned against the back of the chair, looking as though she was ready to trust Tasya with more information.

"I'm eleven years old. Normally, I would have to be in school during the day, but the schools here have closed. Mutter teaches me how to read and write, and Herr Vogel teaches me music. I can play both the violin and piano."

Tasya nodded thoughtfully and struggled to sit up in the soft bed.

"So. Do you have brothers and sisters?" Tasya finally asked.

Adora looked down at her feet.

"I have one sister. Older. Heidi is twelve." Adora paused for a long few seconds. "I also had a brother, but he died. In France. His name was Gerhard."

Tasya remembered her own loss, her Elzbeta, gone now for weeks. She wondered if Elzbeta's mama even knew that her daughter was dead.

"And, of course, there's my father. You'll like him, Tasi. He's very kind and likes to spend time with us children."

There were voices in the outside hallway and Tasya looked up to see Frau Bamm, Isle, and Frieda all rush in together into the small room. They peered down at Tasya with smiles as if she were a newborn baby.

"You are finally awake!" Frau Bamm said. "I was beginning to wonder if you would sleep for the rest of the year. Do you know that you slept for nearly eighteen hours?"

"I was very tired," Tasya said, pulling the thick blanket around her. "My friend Hanya and I ran for hours…that night, trying to escape. Will I have to go back? To the factory?"

"No, the factory was destroyed in the bombings." The women all shook their heads sadly. "Most of that area of Düsseldorf suffered catastrophic damage. No, you will now work for us, here in our house. Better this way, anyway. I'm not sure why a young girl like yourself would be doing brick-making work in the first place!"

Frieda reached over to take Tasya's arm, steadying her as she swung her legs over the side of the bed. "I'm glad you enjoyed my room, but you have your own on the third floor of the house. It's quite nice too."

Tasya wanted to ask Frau Bamm again about Hanya, but something made her hold back. Was it that she didn't want to seem as if she was ungrateful? She only knew that it wasn't the right time to ask about Hanya.

Tasya happily ate a filling breakfast of porridge with milk that made her feel as if she had more energy than she had in her combined months in Germany. She was self-conscious as she used the indoor bathroom more than once that morning as her stomach adjusted to the new foods.

Tasya was taught many household tasks by Frau Bamm, most of which overwhelmed her. She had done very little housekeeping at home; her mother took care of most of it. But she was eager to please, and tried to demonstrate her enthusiasm to Frau Bamm at every opportunity. Hours each day were spent on light housework, yet it was never complete. The more there was to do, the bigger the house felt. The Bamm house was much larger than any of the houses in Horayetz.

Tasya's main duties were to dust different rooms each day, and sweep the floors and front entryway. She was also given the task of helping the Bamm sisters keep their rooms tidy. During each family meal, she was to serve the family at the dining room table.

On her second day at the Bamm household, Frieda approached Tasya with an armful of clothing, setting it down next to her as she ate her lunch.

"Tasya, this is your uniform that you will be wearing each day. Be sure to take good care of it, and wash it every three days."

"Not these?" Tasya asked, looking down at the plain grey dress that she had been wearing since her first morning.

"For serving meals? Absolutely not, you goose! You need to have a more refined uniform since you will be around the family and their guests. Look!"

Tasya put down the soup-spoon, and touched the uniform carefully. It was a clean, well-made frock of plain black cotton. There were two dresses in the pile that Frieda brought to her – one with long sleeves and one with shorter sleeves. Below the two dresses was a starched white apron with ruffles.

"Look. This is how you wear the apron," Frieda said as she tied the long ribbons around Tasya's waist, and then gently pinned the top of the apron just above her breasts. "Oh, and your hat." Frieda added, plunking a small black hat with ruffles on her own head. "Ta, da!" Frieda laughed as Tasya grinned.

Tasya carefully inspected each new garment. Frieda laughed. "My goodness! I don't think I've ever seen anyone smile so much at their work uniform! What's behind that grin?"

"Nothing, Frieda." She fingered the edges of the ruffles that ran along both sides of the apron. Ruffles!

"Well, I'll have to tell Frau Bamm that you are happy with it, then." Frieda said as she patted Tasya's head. "It's the usual uniform that chambermaids wear, but I'm glad you like it."

"It's just…I've never worn something like this before. It's so beautiful." Tasya said as she inspected the small hat. "Even my best Sunday clothes weren't this good."

Frieda's smile changed and she turned away quickly. Before she left the room she cleared her throat, but didn't turn around again. "Well, don't take too much time with your lunch, child," Frieda called as she walked out of the kitchen. "We've got to get you to work!"

XIV.

Of all of her tasks, Tasya soon began to enjoy serving the family their meals the most. She stood next to them as they ate in the dining room, proud in her uniform. Tasya marveled at the grandness of each of their meals. Though the Bamm's were subject to rationing like other citizens, they took great pride in the presentation of the meal, serving the evening supper on fine china, drinking out of crystal goblets. Each evening after serving the family their meal, Tasya enjoyed her own dinner with Isle in the kitchen. If anything else was needed from Tasya, Herr Bamm pulled on a rope that was attached to a small bell in the kitchen. When the bell rang, Tasya jumped up from her own meal, and hurried into the dining room to serve them.

Though she was a servant, Tasya wanted for nothing. She had more than enough to eat, a comfortable place to sleep, and small extras were always given to her. Early on, she quietly decided that she enjoyed her work so much that when she returned home to Horayetz, she would tell her mother that she wanted to work in service at a grand house in Peremyshyl. Her mother would not like the idea of Tasya going so far away, but she decided that she would insist.

As promised, Tasya was given her very own room in the attic of the third floor. It was a small but cozy room, outfitted with a double bed, an old wood dresser, and a small table with a hard-backed chair. Tasya never had her own room before. Some days, she sat still on the bed, listening to the silence that came with having her very own space. Best of all, around four o'clock in the afternoon, the sun would shine directly through the small window above her bed, casting an outline of the rectangular shape of sunlight on the wood floor of the room. As often as she could, Tasya sat directly on the floor, basking like a cat in the filtered sunshine. She remained totally still, breathing in the beautiful silence, enjoying the warmth that crept over her cheeks and arms. In her own room, Tasya was a princess.

In her attic retreat, the mattress was also filled with downy goose feathers, making Tasya feel as if she was floating on a cloud whenever she lay down on the mattress after a tiring days' work. She had two large duvets on the bed – one to lie on top of, and one to use as a luxurious blanket.

The bed was a special place of leisure for Tasya, so much so that even Adora sensed it, and came to visit Tasya in her room. The two girls often sat on Tasya's bed together with the duvet spread across their laps, and they talked for hours together like sisters.

"I want to play violin with the Vienna Symphony Orchestra with all my body and soul," Adora confessed to Tasya. "But, if I'm not good enough to play for the Symphony, then I want to be an equestrian."

"What's an equestrian?" Tasya asked.

"You must know; it's where you ride horses in a competition."

"Really? At home, we only use horses for work, in the fields, or to pull wagons, or for riding places. We never have competitions with them."

"You would love to ride a horse! It's the absolute best thing in the world to do!"

Adora scrambled off to fetch photographs of their horses. The most beautiful photo was of Adora standing next to a fine show horse, looking like a miniature version of Frau Bamm.

"What do you want to be, Tasi? When you grow up more, I mean."

In her heart, Tasya knew that she wanted to continue work in service to a wealthy family in Ukraine, but she was too embarrassed to tell Adora.

"Ummmm. I'm not sure."

"Come on, you must have thought about it at one point or another."

Tasya had spent only seven years in school, leaving when she was thirteen years old, like most of the other girls of the village. She had been helping her mother with her seamstress work and doing odd jobs for others in the village. Like all girls her age in the village, she had been in the in-between place between childhood and her own family. She had been waiting to grow up. She had never thought of anything else.

XV.

The days slipped into weeks, with Tasya enjoying each and every day at the Bamm's. She took great pride in keeping spotless floors and tidy rooms. Her work was light, with ample time for enjoying her meals and for spending time with Frieda, or Isle, or Adora. Tasya spent hours hovering by Isle as she watched how the cook prepared food for the family. With no one to speak Ukrainian or Polish to, Tasya amazed herself by quickly learning the German language, with its hard consonants and drawn-out vowels. Once she did, Tasya tried to please Herr and Frau Bamm by taking a keen interest in the family, asking many questions about their life in Jüchen. Tasya had quickly observed that Herr Bamm was a man of great importance in Jüchen. He was the town *Burgermeister*, the democratically elected leader.

"Ah, Tasi." Herr Bamm said each time he spotted her. "You are enjoying it here?"

"Oh, yes, Herr Bamm. Very much so."

"Very well, then." Herr Bamm nearly always responded with a slight bow.

Not only was Herr Bamm kind, he was also very generous to Tasya, often taking her along on outings with Adora. Once, he even took the girls to hunt rabbits in the public park near the house. Tasya was given an old dress of Heidi's to wear, and they spent the entire afternoon clumsily creeping through the small woods in the park, giving the rabbits more than ample time to run. Herr Bamm gently scolded them for being so noisy, but Tasya and Adora still laughed each time.

Tasya's admiration for Herr Bamm grew. As she answered the many rings of the doorbell during the day, she saw first-hand the number of people eager to ask their *Burgermeister* for his advice on their problems. It seemed as if everyone in Jüchen had many problems during the war but he always listened attentively to his callers, giving what Tasya decided was measured and sound advice.

After a few months with the family, Tasya established a quiet friendship with Heidi, the older daughter. Heidi was not nearly as outgoing and friendly as Adora. She was much more interested in reading and other quiet activities. Even though Heidi was closer in age to Tasya, it was Adora who Tasya became good friends with. Young Adora would often trail behind Tasya as she did her work around the house, talking a mile a minute about anything that popped into her head.

Even with new friendships keeping her occupied and happy, Tasya still constantly thought about Hanya. Her stomach ached with guilt every time that she thought about their last few minutes together. She wondered what Hanya's work was like, and if she also had a supervisor who was kind and caring. After being with the Bamm's for two months, Tasya nervously approached Frau Bamm about going out to the family farm to see Hanya.

"Oh…I don't think it's a good idea, Tasi," Frau Bamm said, shaking her head. "I feel like going to visit your friend would show the inequality between you, since I chose you to come work in the house for us."

"I miss Hanya, though," Tasya said, struggling to hold back tears. "Maybe on my free day I can go out?"

"Tasi," Frau Bamm started, sighing. "I don't even know who would be able to take you out there on your free day. I wouldn't want you to go out there alone, and it's certainly too far to walk."

This surprised Tasya. She had always assumed that Hanya was at one of the farms that were just outside the town square.

"Maybe I can write her a short note," Tasya said, looking at Frau Bamm with pleading eyes.

"Perhaps – "

"If I write one, can you have it delivered to her? Maybe when Herr goes to the farm?" Tasya looked at Frau, hopeful. She took a deep breath and decided to use her best argument. "Frau Bamm, I've lost all contact with my mama and sister, and I don't want to lose my only friend here." Tasya then let loose the tears that had been building up. Frau Bamm looked torn as she patted Tasya on the shoulder.

"Alright, alright. Give me the note, Tasi, and I'll see if I can get it out to your friend."

Later that evening, in her room, Tasya was pensive in front of a spare piece of letter paper that Frau gave her. Was Hanya happy? Was she getting stronger, like Tasya? Did she like the farm even a quarter as much as Tasya loved the house? Tasya stared at the blank page before her – which of these questions should she ask, and how? Even from across Jüchen, Tasya believed that she could feel the weight of Hanya's disappointment in her. She didn't know what to write. Tasya put the piece of letter paper and Frau's borrowed pen in the top corner of her table as gently as she would place a bird with a broken wing. She left them there then slipped into bed.

XVI.

What's this?" Tasya whispered to herself. She held her hand up and squinted. There was blood on her fingers, rust-coloured and dark. She knew it was her own blood. "Oh, no." She groaned.

That morning, as Tasya had used the toilet when getting dressed, she noticed the stain on her underwear. Now, as she quickly wiped the blood from her fingers, she took a large stack of toilet tissue from her rationed pile, stuffed half of it into her underwear, and carried out the other half.

It was still early in the morning. Tasya crept down the stairs towards the kitchen, her cheeks burning with embarrassment as she wondered what to say to Frieda or Isle. Tasya jumped a foot in the air when she nearly collided with Frau Bamm, who was walking up the stairs.

"Oh, good morning, Frau Bamm," Tasya mumbled, trying to get around her.

"Good morning, Tasi. You're up early."

Tasya stumbled around Frau Bamm. She desperately wanted to keep going.

"Where are you going in such a hurry that you didn't even notice me?"

"Just to see Frieda. Or Isle. I need…something. I have to ask Frieda for something."

Frau Bamm's eyes traveled from her face to the stack of toilet tissue that Tasya was still carrying. Tasya cursed herself for holding it rather than hiding it in her uniform.

"Is something wrong, Tasi?"

As much as she tried not to, Tasya burst into tears.

"It's nothing. I just need to go see Isle. Please excuse me, Frau Bamm." Tasya's eyes were glued to the carpet runner on the stairs, focused on the blue and red pattern that she had never really noticed before.

"Tasi, just tell me what is wrong. I'll help you." Frau Bamm's voice was soft. She reached for Tasya's arm.

Tasya's embarrassment tumbled out of her.

"I just got my monthly bleeding. I don't know what to do," Tasya said miserably through her tears.

"Ah ha. Well, what did you usually do, at home? What did your mother teach you?" Frau Bamm asked, letting go of Tasya's arm. Tasya was annoyed that Frau Bamm was smiling. What was so funny?

"She didn't," Tasya whispered, mortified. "I did not start my monthly times when I lived at home. Then, here. With the medicine...you know."

"What do you mean, medicine?"

"The medicine that they gave us in our food. They said we must not have our monthly bleeding. The factory..." Tasya looked back down at the carpet, wishing that she could disappear into the pattern.

"What?" Frau Bamm whispered. "Medication?"

Tasya cringed. "Not getting my monthly time wasn't important to me because I hadn't even started. I almost forgot that I was supposed to have it at all." Tasya shrugged. She was still hoping to get away.

"Tasi, medication? That's ridiculous, not to mention, revolting. I can't believe that they would do that to you young girls. How unbelievable." Frau Bamm looked lost in thought. "I wonder if Herr knows about this."

Tasya was surprised that she could become even more horrified. "Please, Frau Bamm! This is incredibly embarrassing. Don't tell Herr Bamm."

"Of course. I'm sorry Tasi, I'll show you what to do," Frau Bamm said, leading Tasya down the stairs. "We have to gather together rags, and I'll show you how to bind them together. It's extra work for every woman, but it's necessary." Tasya nodded, and sensed her cheeks redden again.

Frau Bamm showed Tasya how to bind together and then wash out the rags when she was finished with them. After her first cycle was complete, Tasya was already tired of her small extra chore. She thought with dread towards another forty years of once a month washing and rinsing. Tasya detected an extra sparkle in Frieda's eye after that day, as well as extra kindness from Isle, though she was too embarrassed to tell them about her change.

With the new change in her, Tasya thought about picking up the pen and writing Hanya a hundred times each day. Something held her back. After weeks of nervously glancing at the paper and pen on her table, Tasya finally scribbled out a quick note and gave it to Frau Bamm.

Dear Hanya,

I miss you. I'm so sorry that I let you go that day after the bombings – I don't know why I didn't try to stay with you. Maybe I was still shocked after running all night away from Düsseldorf.

How is the farm? The house is nice, and the Bamm's are good employers – good people.

Please let me know that you are doing well.

Love, Tasya

XVII.

The Christmas season approached. Tasya learned that unlike her tradition of celebrating Christmas on January 7th, Germans celebrated on December 25th, like the Polish families in Horayetz.

On Christmas morning of 1942, Isle, Frieda, and Tasya were summoned into the front parlour to join the Bamm family in the gift exchange. For her gift, Tasya was given an exquisitely made grey wool overcoat. It had silver embroidered patterns running up the sleeves to the elbow. To Tasya, it was the most stunning thing she had ever owned. Everyone admired it, and Adora commented that it was similar to the overcoats that the Bamm girls wore on cold winter days, which made Tasya smile with shy delight. That night in her room as she stroked her new coat like an exotic animal, Tasya silently vowed to always serve the family with dedication.

In the spring, Tasya was given a new working dress made out of lighter cotton, grey rather than black. Tasya and the other house staff celebrated the Easter meal together with the Bamm's, but did not attend the Resurrection Mass with them. Tasya realized that there was an unspoken understanding between the family and the staff that while they lived together more as equals than most other families with servants, the arrangement was kept private.

As the calendar turned to May, and the weather warmed into the beginnings of a beautiful summer, Tasya increasingly reflected about how much she had gone through that year. She had still not heard from either her mother or sister, and constantly daydreamed about them. At night, her sleep was haunted by them.

Most times, Tasya dreamed that she was walking the narrow cobblestoned streets of Jüchen when she saw her mother and sister approaching. Most of the time, Kateryna was holding a young infant, swaddled in bright white blankets, but in other dreams, Kateryna was empty-handed. No matter how the dream started, the ending was always the same. Tasya yelled out in joy at seeing her mother and sister, and with tears streaming down her face, she ran as quickly as she could towards them. As she approached, the women appeared not to see Tasya, ignoring her cries as they continued to walk down the road. Tasya yelled at them with all her might, though no sound ever found its way out of her mouth. In frustration, she grabbed onto them, hoping to make them somehow see that she was right in front of them. But she never succeeded.

In the few outings that Tasya took with the Bamm family, she continued to half-heartedly look for Mychaylo. Frustration mounting, Tasya convinced herself that in the year since leaving Horayetz that Daria and Kateryna were happily continuing on with their own lives at home. She decided that they had completely forgotten about her, that she had been replaced by the baby. Tasya's bitterness grew like a weed, starting in the pit of her stomach, eventually growing to cover over her heart.

Though her bitterness was sometimes all consuming, Tasya was still curious about Kateryna's baby – her niece or nephew. She guessed that the child was a few months old by the spring of 1943. She wondered if the baby was a boy or a girl, and what its name was. Sometimes, Tasya even allowed herself to fantasize that they had named the baby after her as a way of acknowledging the immense sacrifice that Tasya had made.

One afternoon in May, Tasya was dusting the imposing walnut furniture in Frau Bamm's bedroom, brooding. She was thinking yet again about how her mother and sister appeared to care absolutely nothing about her.

"Tasi, what is it?" Frau Bamm asked, and Tasya jumped.

"Nothing, why?"

"I don't think you've even noticed that I walked into the room. In the past minute, you've sighed heavily at least five times. I thought that maybe you were trying to get my attention."

Tasya shifted uncomfortably. She didn't like to mention her mother in front of Frau Bamm. "I was thinking about my mama and sister. It's nothing."

"From all of your sighing, it doesn't sound like nothing. Go on, tell me." Frau Bamm sat on the nearest armchair. "You've never said very much about your family back home. Tell me about them, even if you don't want to tell me about what's bothering you."

Tasya hesitated. She didn't want to appear ungrateful to Frau Bamm. "Well, I think you know I'm the youngest child of my family. I have an older sister, Kateryna, and an older brother as well, Mychaylo. Kateryna worked in Germany too, also in Düsseldorf, but she somehow managed to get home for a visit. She didn't go back because she was pregnant. I had to come in her place."

Frau Bamm nodded, "Ah, I see now how someone as young as you came to work here. Are you upset that you had to take her place?"

"Yes, I suppose I am," Tasya nervously fiddled with the dust rag that she was holding, scared to look directly at Frau Bamm. "But I love it here! With you." Tasya felt awkward in the silence. When Frau Bamm didn't say anything, Tasya continued nervously. "I'm happy to be here. It's just that I've been gone for more than a year, and I used to send letters back to Horayetz, to home, but I haven't heard anything back from anyone in my family. Or anything from Hanya, either."

"Tasi, you know that mail is intercepted and censored by the Government. As for your friend, I asked Herr Bamm to deliver your note to her, but he didn't say anything about her writing you back."

"Why wouldn't Hanya write me back, though? We were supposed to look out for each other."

"Tasi, you should consider that your friend may not want to actually write you back. I know that parting was sudden for you two, and I'm sure she was upset."

"I know – that's exactly what I'm scared of. I also keep thinking about how my family has forgotten all about me. Especially with the new baby." Tasya was embarrassed. She sounded childish but she didn't care.

"Tasi, let me tell you something," Frau Bamm said, going over to her and taking the rag out of her hands, holding them gently in hers. "If there is one thing that a mother can never, ever forget, it is her child. Even if that child isn't right in front of her eyes."

Tasya nodded, blinking back tears.

"Losing a child has a lasting effect on a mother, believe me. You can see that we are a happy family, and we try to remain modest in our grief, but for me, there is always a certain sadness that hangs like a cloud of smoke around each day, each happy occasion." Frau Bamm paused to make sure that Tasya would meet her eyes.

"Gerhard has been gone from us for over three years now, but the pain is still fresh, and I can see that the pain lives in the hearts of every one of us here. You are maybe too young to understand, but I know that for certain, your mama loves you very much, and thinks every day, every hour about you. Sometimes, I even think about your mother, and know that I have to be kind and fair with you. I would have wanted the exact same thing for Gerhard, or for the girls."

Frau Bamm went over to her bedside table, and picked up a small photo of Gerhard in his soldier's uniform, looking at it for a few seconds before passing it over to Tasya.

"Sometimes, I forget that he's dead. That is the worst thing – forgetting, then the shock of remembering. Most of the time, I feel like I am in an in-between place; I know within my logical brain that Gerhard is dead and will never return, but my heart refuses to believe it." Frau Bamm shook her head, and then looked over Tasya's shoulder at the photo of her son.

"There have been so many of our boys and men lost during this war. The grief of mothers in this country, and many others, has touched so many homes. You know how much I care for you, Tasi, but in my heart, I do hope that you will return to your mother. That way, there will be at least one less house with a grieving mother."

Then, for the first time, Frau Bamm enveloped Tasya in her arms, holding her like no other had since Daria had last held Tasya in her arms. For a few seconds, Tasya felt like she had a mother again, and she hoped that in turn, she could also make Frau Bamm feel a bit better as well.

XVIII.

Spring turned into summer, then into fall, and another pleasant Christmas season passed again. Tasya always tried to please the Bamm family, and in return, they were very good to her, continuing to buy her small gifts now and again. For her birthday in October, Isle baked Tasya a chocolate cake, and the entire family stood around her as she blew out the candles, calling out '*Herzlichen glückwunsch zum geburtstag*'!

Though her life was pleasant, deep down, Tasya had been worried about her existence at the Bamm's. She felt as if she had put in some arbitrary time doing difficult work in Germany, and that her penance was over, but knew that during the war, a dream come true could end as quickly as a dream during the night. With the end of the war nowhere in sight, Tasya sometimes worried about the comfort and safety that she was afforded.

April 6th, 1944, started out as a normal day at the Bamm household. Tasya served the family their customary breakfast, and was cleaning the dishes in the kitchen when the front bell rang. Tasya ran down the hallway and opened the front door. She stopped short when she found two German soldiers standing at the threshold.

"We are here to speak to Herr Bamm. Go get him."

"He is not home, but Frau Bamm is," Tasya stammered.

The soldiers ignored Tasya, and pushed their way past her, into the front hallway. Losing all sense of decorum, Tasya turned and ran back towards the kitchen calling at the top of her lungs for Frau Bamm. Where was Herr Bamm? Had he done something wrong? What had happened?

"Tasi, what's gotten into you?" Frau Bamm asked as she stepped out of the sitting room, a partially completed needlepoint in her hand. When she saw the soldiers making their way into the house behind Tasya, her hands dropped to her side.

"Tasi, go find Isle and sit with her in the kitchen. *Leutnante*, please come with me." Frau Bamm gestured to the sitting room, and closed the doors behind them after they had entered, leaving Tasya still standing in the hallway.

Tasya fled down the hallway into the kitchen, calling for Isle.

"What is it, child? Why are you yelling like that?"

"There are two officers in the sitting room with Frau Bamm."

"Well, child. What do they want?"

"I don't know."

"Relax, Tasi. They scare me too, but just because they are here in the house, doesn't mean that something is necessarily wrong. Just sit still, and we will wait to see what Frau Bamm has to say to us after they leave."

Frieda soon joined Isle and Tasya, and the three of them sat around the working area of the kitchen, waiting anxiously for the officers to leave. After only five minutes, they heard the doors of the sitting room open. Tasya expected to next hear the slam of the front door as the soldiers left, and was surprised to see one officer stride into the kitchen, with Frau Bamm following behind him.

"Now, hold on. Does it have to be right *now*? Can't we have at least a few days to try to get our house in order, everything organized?" Frau Bamm asked the soldier, her voice rising in a sharp pitch.

"No, it must be now."

"But we should at least wait for my husband to get home. I can send someone to get him?"

"Now."

Tasya realized then that the men were of some rank in the army. She stared at their shoulder insignia. "You must go and quickly pack your things. You are being reassigned to different work."

"What do you mean, reassigned?" Isle blurted out. Ignoring Isle, the soldier continued to speak only to Tasya.

"You are an *Auslander*, a foreigner. You are currently assigned to perform household tasks, which are reserved as positions for German nationals only. As a result, you have taken a favourable job away from a German, and this is not permitted under the Decrees." When none of the women moved a muscle the soldier rolled his eyes. "As an *Auslander*, you must work either at a factory, or on a farm. Those are the laws, and they must be obeyed."

At the mention of working at a factory again, Tasya's blood ran cold. She tried to think quickly.

"Then, I can work at Herr Bamm's farm! They have one – my friend works at it. I can go there." Tasya could hear the desperation in her voice.

"You have been assigned to a factory position," said the second soldier, also stepping into the kitchen and glancing at a piece of paper in his hands. "To Ford-Werke, in Cologne."

Tasya couldn't believe what he was saying was true. For a second she wanted to laugh at her own silliness, hoping that she was in the middle of yet another bad dream, but she knew full well that she was awake. Tasya looked to Frau Bamm with pleading eyes, but Frau Bamm did not argue with the officers, nor did she fight.

"You have a few minutes to gather your belongings, and then we must take you to the transport that leaves for Cologne." The second soldier informed Tasya.

Frau Bamm grabbed Tasya and pulled her past the officers, leading her to the quiet of Tasya's third floor bedroom before speaking.

"Tasi, I'm so sorry!" Frau Bamm whispered, choking back tears. "I can't believe that they are taking you away from us, but there is nothing we can do! It was a direct order from the government. All *Auslander*s who are working as house help must be reassigned."

Frau Bamm paced Tasya's narrow room. In a daze, Tasya took her few belongings out of her dresser, packing them up in her pillowcase.

"Should I take this?" Tasya asked, holding up her second dress. When Frau Bamm didn't answer, Tasya decided that she would need every last scrap that she could get her hands on before leaving, and she stuffed them into the pillowcase with the rest of her things.

"Listen, Tasi," Frau Bamm stopped pacing and grabbed Tasya's shoulders. "I will help you. I know where Ford-Werke is. It's actually not too far. I will get Herr to write the factory commandant. Maybe, with some time, we can get you reassigned back to the house." Frau Bamm sounded more hopeful to Tasya than she looked.

Frau Bamm disappeared out of Tasya's room as she packed the rest of her things, returning back with a fistful of *Reichmarks*, and thrust them into Tasya's hands.

"Here. It's not much, but maybe a bit of money can help you until I see you again. If they ask if you have brought anything with you, do *not* tell them about the money."

Discreetly, Tasya hid the marks and the other few things that she counted as her prized possessions in her petticoat before heading back down the stairs, heart thumping in her throat. She was glad that Adora was not home, and did not have to see the sight of Tasya being led away by the officers.

As soon as her feet touched the hallway rug on the first floor, Tasya was grabbed by each elbow by the Officers, and roughly pushed out the front door. As she looked back over her shoulder, Tasya could see Frau Bamm, Frieda, and Isle standing at the doorway of the house, holding onto each other's arms. The officers barked at Tasya to sit in the back seat of a truck. Through the back window, she could see that all three women were gathered, and crying.

Just the same as when she was leaving Horayetz, Tasya looked out the back of the truck window as they drove away, the shape of Frau Bamm in the doorway becoming smaller by the second. Waving the entire time that she could still see her, Tasya continued waving even after the truck turned a corner.

"Stop that. Face forward!"

COLOGNE

1944

I.

"Next. Move up, now. Your nationality."

"*Ukrainisch.*"

"Not Polish? Are you certain?" The administrator was flanked by two interpreters but Tasya's German was good enough that she didn't need their meddling. They looked at her papers.

"*Nein, ich bin Ukrainisch. Nicht Polieren.*" The administrator shrugged and the translators grunted. The administrator gave her an identification card. Across the top was written 'OST'.

"Well, *Ostarbeiter*, you are now reassigned. Ford-Werke in Cologne. Next."

The train ride from Düsseldorf to Cologne was mercifully short. Arriving amongst hordes of girls and young men in Cologne, Tasya was disgusted by the newcomers. Weepy and vulnerable girls clutched their cloth bags to their chests. Tasya was an old, world-weary woman compared to the weak recruits.

Tasya and a group of a hundred other girls assigned to Ford-Werke marched the short distance from the station to Henry Ford Strasse. It took ten minutes to arrive at the imposing iron gates.

The factory was much larger than the brick-making compound in Düsseldorf, with additional crude plywood buildings for barracks spreading out well past the imposing main building. Tasya counted twenty before she lost track of the number of barracks.

Tasya's group was directed to an open yard just inside the front gates where they were told by the *Werkschutz* security guards to wait quietly. After an hour of standing and waiting, some of the girls became brave and spoke quietly among themselves. Tasya fidgeted in her maid's uniform as many of the girls stared at her with curiosity. She knew that compared to the others, she must have looked like royalty. The others were ragged, dirty, and thin. They clutched filthy bags to themselves. She cradled her clean white pillowcase, digesting the visual contrast. Tasya warily ignored getting involved in the conversations around her. She wanted nothing more than to be alone as the other girls looked for company and solace.

"I was caught on the street by the Germans, and they sent me here. I didn't even say goodbye to my mama," one girl sniffled in Polish.

"I was at a camp, Wuppertal. Have you heard of it?"

"I came from home. They said I had to."

Finally, the *Werkschutz* guards came back, and handed out cards with worker numbers on them. Looking down at hers, Tasya saw that she had been assigned worker number 897. Closing her eyes to fight back the tears, Tasya couldn't believe that when she had woken up that very same day, everything in her life had been in order. She had been happy.

A small group of men in civilian clothing walked out of the factory. One carried himself in a manner of refined confidence, and it reminded Tasya of Herr Bamm. She felt like she was going to be sick. Ripped away from the only home that she knew in Germany, every person or item that reminded Tasya of the Bamm house was like a dagger in her chest. Another man stood on top of a crate, waving to get the girls' attention.

"Excuse me, girls," he announced, still waving his hands in the air even though the group was silent. "Thank you. I am Schmidt, and I am the head foreman here. By here, you must know by now that I mean the Ford-Werke factory. You are to assist us in making some of the best trucks for the Reich, which is a very noble job indeed," When his announcement was met with more silence, Schmidt cleared his throat and continued, "You will all be working on the line that produces the Maultier truck!"

A girl poked Tasya in the arm, and whispered in Ukrainian, "What is he saying?" Tasya waved her away.

"You are all *Ostarbeiter* workers, and by far our largest group here at Ford. For your information, there are other classifications of workers here as well, including the *Westarbeiter* groups, and we have a small contingent of Italian workers. *Ostarbeiters* are to live in the Russian camp, and the other classifications will have their own camp as well." Pausing to look around carefully at the group of girls, the foreman then said slowly and carefully, "There is to be absolutely no mixing of the groups of workers. Each of you has your own rules which you must follow."

With that, the foreman got down from the crate, and the group of men walked away. Tasya heard other girls whisper.

"What does it mean to be *Ostarbeiter*?"

"I think it's better than *Westarbeiter*, no?"

"What rules do we have to follow?"

"It doesn't look so bad here, to me. Look at the flowers outside the gate! Look at that girl...Look how nice her uniform is."

A *Werkschutz* guard barked from a script the many rules that the *Ostarbeiter* workers were to follow. Tasya saw from the looks of confusion on the faces of many of the girls that they didn't understand what he was saying.

"You are not to use public transport. You must not attend cultural events. You may not own or ride a bicycle. You have a curfew in your barracks of eight p.m. Your mail will be censored. You are *Ostarbeiter*, and may therefore not leave the factory, or the camp. You may not, under any circumstances, mingle with Germans. Relationships with a German will be punishable by death."

Tasya shook her head at the ridiculous rules.

"They really are giving us too much credit," Tasya said out loud. A few of the girls around her took a step away. "Really, do you think that we will have a bicycle? Mail?"

Everyone jumped as a loud whistle blew from the factory roof. Then a large gang of girls in rows of four were led from the factory to the barracks by a *Werkschutz* guard. A girl standing next to Tasya jabbed her in the ribs, raising her eyebrows at the women who were walking to the camp.

"Look. Women in pants! Can you believe it?" The girl looked at Tasya with excitement. "Do you think that we will also have to wear pants?"

Tasya had never seen girls in pants either, but she was too exhausted to care. She edged her way to the periphery of the group, and closed her eyes, exhaling hard. She just wanted to lie down and put her head against her clean pillowcase.

The *Werkschutz* guards came over and had everyone line up two-by-two. They were then led over to a set of office barracks closest to the factory. They were sent inside, one pair at a time, to a table with factory administrators in civilian clothing. The girl next to Tasya remained silent as they waited.

Finally it was their turn to enter the barrack and approach the table. Both men looked at Tasya with surprise.

"Where did you get that uniform?" one administrator asked her in German as she handed over her paperwork.

"From my employer, obviously," Tasya answered in an even tone.

"Fine, but who was your employer before Ford-Werke?" the administrator asked, with a note of caution in his voice.

"The Bamm family. Herr Bamm is the *Burgermeister* of Jüchen. Do you know it?"

"Name?" The administrator sighed.

"Tasi."

"Again. Your name. Not your nickname, but your real name."

For the second time since leaving the Bamm house, Tasya felt tears pricking the backs of her eyes. She answered the rest of the questions as quickly as she could, and prayed that she wouldn't cry. She asked if she could keep her maid's uniform.

"Keep it if you want," the administrator said as he handed over a bundle. "For your factory uniform, one set is for wearing, and one is for washing."

Back outside, Tasya examined the uniforms – two sets of dark blue jackets with 'OST' sewn directly above the breast, wooden shoes, and dark blue pants. Her very first pairs of trousers. She examined the unusually rough fabric.

Once all of the girls were processed, they were again lined up in pairs and taken away from the factory to the *Ostarbeiter* camp. There was only one gate. It struck a note of fear in Tasya when she realized that the gate was actually located within the security barrack. They were on lock-down, and the rules were going to be very different than at the brick factory.

Once inside the Russian camp, the entire group of *Ostarbeiter* girls was split into two smaller groups by number, and each group was led by more *Werkschutz* guards into empty sleeping barracks. Even though it was sunny outside, Tasya's eyes took a minute to adjust to the dimness of the barrack. The space was extremely Spartan. As far down the walls as Tasya could see, there were three-tiered sleeping bunks, and in the very middle of the cavernous room was a small iron stove, with one long wooden table sitting next to it. Otherwise, it was completely empty.

Tasya hung back as the other girls scrambled to claim bunks for themselves. Once the initial rush had died down, she took a middle-tier bed. She touched the mattress gingerly, and it barely gave way to her hand. It was filled with sawdust that would soon crumble until there was barely any padding left. Stretching out on the mattress with closed eyes and clutching her pillow case of precious goods from the Bamm's, Tasya remembered the few valuable items that were hidden in her petticoat. She waited for a good time to hide them elsewhere. She kept her eyes on the three guards who hung around, watching.

The two taller guards gave the smallest one a little shove towards the long wooden table in the center of the room. He stood on it, calling for attention.

"We have some specific instructions we must give you," he began in a high-pitched tone in Polish. "First, about pay. You will be earning a wage, but there are deductions that Ford must take before you receive your final pay. There will be several deductions for taxes, insurance, lodging, and food. Then you will be given what's left."

One girl across the barrack put up her hand to ask a question. "Is there a camp commissary for us to buy things, then? Where is it?"

The guard making the announcement looked down to the other guards for an answer, and they whispered something back to him.

"You will get all of that information later. For now, you are under curfew. You will be awoken by the morning bell at six a.m. Your shift tomorrow begins at seven a.m."

After the guards left, with no evening meal, there was nothing to do but lie down on the bunk and wait. The first night was long, drawn out, and punctuated by muffled crying from girls all around the room. Sleep was elusive for Tasya, kept just out of reach by a combination of heartache and the lumpy hardness of the sawdust mattress. Worst of all was adjusting to the nighttime noises that went along with sleeping among hundreds of other girls. As she laid in the miserable darkness, Tasya was lost in her own sadness. She thought about her room at the Bamm's, and how she was unsure if she would ever see anyone from the household again. What punctured her heart the most was the loss of safety, and knowing that she had been cared for.

The next morning, the bell went off at 6 a.m. Without any time to rouse or to wash, the girls were told to line up for the morning roll-call. With the impatience of the guards growing steadily, many girls were lost in the confusion about lining up in order, and it took forever for the guards to ensure that the workers were all present and accounted for. Within the large group, Tasya called out the number 897 each time she was required. Her heart lurched each time there was a roll call, knowing that a number was now her new identity. Her identity was no longer Tasya, and not even Anastasia, not even Tasi.

II.

On the first march from the barracks to the main factory, Tasya was able to get a better look at her surroundings. Armed guards with dogs patrolled the area inside the chain link fence. The men looked like they were barely older than Tasya as they walked with arrogance and carefully held rifles across their chests.

Three of the four corners of the Russian camp had tall guard posts. *Werkschutz* guards with rifles on display watched every movement in and out of the camp. The guards on the ground laughed and chatted with each other during the march. The girls were silent.

At the canteen hut, the girls were each given a bowl and spoon. It was announced that holding on to the bowl was very important because without it, getting the ration of daily soup would be nearly impossible. The eating area was sparse - no tables, just rows of benches. Workers lined up at a small window to receive their food ration.

Tasya sat down at one of the benches and looked at her ration. Three thin slices of bread, a tiny pat of butter, and nothing else. No coffee, no tea. It had been nearly an entire day since her last full meal. Tasya's hands shook. The girls around Tasya quickly ate up their bread, including all of the crumbs. When the meal was over, the girls sat uselessly, fiddling with their empty bowls. Some of them relaxed, turning to one another to chat quietly. A girl who was sitting on a bench across from Tasya leaned over.

"Hello, I'm Inna. I'm from Chmelnizka. This is my first time being in a work factory, but I've been in a holding camp for months." Waiting for a reply from either Tasya or the girl next to her, Inna sat smiling.

"I'm Alyona," the girl next to Tasya whispered. She was a slight, thin wisp of a girl with poker-straight brown hair and huge brown eyes. "My family was living in Rostov, in the eastern part of Ukraine, when I was taken away. I just got transferred to this camp yesterday."

"How old are you?" Inna asked both Tasya and Alyona. Tasya looked at Alyona and saw the girl was working hard to blink back tears.

"I'll be eighteen this year," Tasya replied as she patted Alyona's knee. "My name is Tasya, and I'm from Horayetz."

"So, Tasya. Why were you transferred to this camp? Were you in one of the other camps?"

Tasya thought of her time with the Bamm family, and a lump rose up in her throat. She was saved from replying by the interruption of another long whistle. The girls all rose. Obediently they followed instructions to get into formation outside of the canteen. They followed the guard towards the factory like newly hatched ducklings.

The factory buildings of Ford-Werke were huge and imposing structures. Outside of the main building, in the courtyard where Tasya had stood for hours the day before, a number of male German workers waited. Different groups of workers arrived in the yard. Tasya's group of fifty girls entered through a door that had 'Department 13' painted on it. They were led inside by a short German man, who had a completely bald head and a stomach that protruded as if he had a ball under his shirt. His uniform was similar to theirs in colour but was a better quality material and he didn't have the OST patch.

Inside the factory, and away from the hundreds of workers gathering in the yard, it was surprisingly quiet. Aside from the few civilians who were organizing workers, the factory was empty. Conveyor belts ran everywhere, linking different areas of the factory.

The short man who led the group of girls inside waited for everyone to enter before he jumped up onto a small platform.

"Quiet, please," the man said in a loud voice that echoed and bounced off the walls. He was unnecessarily loud given the silence in the cavernous building. He cleared his throat and fidgeted on the platform.

"I am Lars, the Foreman of Department Thirteen. I have been working on the line in Department Thirteen for nearly twenty years." Lars gestured around to the machinery in the department with pride. "We are an assembly line that puts front glass into the two-ton Maultier trucks."

Tasya watched as Lars used his hands to emphasize everything he said. He mimed with his hands what Tasya assumed was putting a sheet of glass onto a truck, nodding vigorously the entire time.

"I'm sure that none of you are familiar with the Maultier. We call it the 'mule', because it works as hard as one! Ha, ha!" Lars cleared his throat, but began to cough as something caught. "It's what we call a half-track truck, modified from an Opel model. Though you don't know it now, you will soon be more familiar with a truck than you ever thought possible! You will all be working at different stations on the assembly line, and then the part must go through inspection before it moves on to Department Fourteen."

Lowering his voice, and with a wagging finger, he warned, "We must work carefully and be sure to keep up to our quota. Mistakes and laziness will put everyone behind on the quota, and then there will be repercussions. Repercussions!"

With Tasya's command of German, she more or less understood most of the instructions. Others translated for those who looked around quizzically when Lars' miming ceased. Lars continued nodding, allowing the time for explanations in Ukrainian and Polish, waving his hands around in the air with enthusiasm.

"Recently, our department has been processing only thirteen to fifteen of our parts each day, because we've had only four men working in Department Thirteen for the last year or so. Fifteen parts a day is an unacceptable level of production, and we must get up to at least one-hundred-and-fifty parts, per day. I will be your fearless leader in our goal, because your production reflects directly back on me."

Lars then stopped and stooped over slightly. Tasya found herself, along with all the other girls, leaning in attentively to hear what Lars would say next.

"Quiet, please," Lars repeated again, unnecessarily. "Understand this: if you do not work well, I am to report you to the camp security or the factory foreman. They tell me there are consequences for those who do not follow orders, and those who do not perform well." Lars gave his warning with his eyebrows far in the air, looking down at the group of girls from over the tip of his nose.

After his opening speech, further assignments were made, allocating the girls into different groups along the assembly line. Tasya and the girl named

Alyona happened to be standing near one another, and as a result were put on the same station. They were taught how to insert the pane of glass onto the metal frame of what was to become a truck, then send their part down the conveyor belt to the welders. After that, there would be a final quality check. Tasya realized that with the machinery the work was not difficult, but moving the glass from the inventory pile made for a very heavy task.

Along with the fifty girls who worked in Department 13, there were the four older German civilians. The men kept to themselves, and took to speaking only to the *Ostarbeiter* girls when absolutely necessary.

By the end of the first morning, training was complete. The assembly line was working on what Lars called 'slow-production-mode'. The noise level of the factory slowly rose throughout the mid-morning hours as hundreds of workers ran their machinery and conveyor belts. In addition to the noise level increasing, the temperature also went up. By the end of the day, Tasya was sweating through her uniform.

At noon, all workers were marched back to the canteen barracks. The German workers sat in the grassy shade of the factory walls, eating and playing cards. Watching them laugh together made Tasya think of Adora, and her heart hurt from missing her friends. The smell of *balanda* hit Tasya hard as she walked into the canteen, and she retched from the stink of it. Stomach twisting, Tasya knew that she had to eat something in order to stay healthy, or as healthy as possible. After staring at the bits of cabbage and potato floating in the weak broth, she drank it as quickly as she could, making sure to get every last drop from her bowl. As she reached the bottom of the bowl, she gagged.

At the end of the shift, Lars once again stood on his crate, waiting for the attention of his workers. The German men did not pay attention to him, and headed straight out of the factory once the whistle blew. Lars made sure all the female workers were gathered around before making further announcements, again with great flourish.

"Quiet, please. Your shift is now over. Before you go back to your camp, you may get yourselves cleaned up in the washroom here. It is up the stairs, near the toilets. You have ten minutes at the end of every shift to do so."

When Lars nodded for them to go, the girls hurried up the narrow wooden staircase. Next to the washroom with three stalls was a large bathroom with eight sinks, and a sectioned-off room with ten showers. There were no towels, only some rags in a box in a corner near the showers along with bits of old soap. Tasya washed as quickly as possible, taking turns under a shower head with Alyona. At exactly ten minutes after the end of the shift, the guards blew their whistles. The entire group of girls was marched in rows of four through the security barrack back to the Russian camp.

Tasya lay down on her bunk, trying not to think about her hunger. Resisting at first, she allowed herself to daydream about what everyone in the Bamm household was doing right at that very moment. She imagined that dinner service was underway with the family gathered around the table. Her eyes flew open as she remembered her mother and sister. She closed them again, feeling guilty when she realized that she had not thought of them in days. Tasya also let herself think about Hanya. With the great shuffle of thousands of workers, perhaps Hanya was also at Ford-Werke? Now Tasya had both Mychaylo and Hanya to look for.

Feeling the corner of her mattress sink down with someone's weight, Tasya was surprised to find Alyona had climbed up from the first bunk and was now perched on Tasya's bed. Tasya didn't feel like making new friends, but after the girl's quiet tears that morning, she felt sorry for Alyona.

"Can I sit on your bunk with you?" Alyona asked with a soft smile.

"Sure," Tasya said. Tasya sat up with her legs crossed, and Alyona facing her. Alyona looked in good health, and Tasya guessed that she hadn't been gone from home for too long.

"Did you come here straight from home, Alyona?"

"Sort of. I was in a holding camp for two weeks. They said it was for quarantine to make sure that we were not going to pass along any diseases."

"What kind of diseases?"

Alyona shrugged. "I have no idea. We sat around, mostly, and took turns in teams helping with the cooking and cleaning. The food there was bad, but this is much, much worse." Alyona looked stricken.

Tasya couldn't help but laugh and felt sorry for Alyona. She remembered how difficult her own transition had been.

"Listen, Alyona. I've been here a while. The first few months away from your family will be hard. It's something you will need time to get used to, though you never really will. Do you have any brothers or sisters?"

"Yes. Two brothers and a sister. All younger than me. That's why I had to come, to spare the rest of them." Alyona paused and Tasya let her blink back more tears. "They told my mother if I didn't come then I would be shot. Just like that. I remember it so clearly. *Schieben sie*."

"Well, I more or less volunteered. The soldiers in Horayetz never threatened to kill us. At first," Tasya said, "we actually liked having them there. Handsome, charming. What's not to like?"

"It wasn't the same for us. With the Germans, there was no point in trying to hide because they knew I was there. I was scared that something would happen to my brothers or sister, so I went peacefully with the rest. We looked like a herd of cattle when we were gathered at the train station."

Alyona looked down at her lap, and didn't continue. Tasya blinked back tears as her own memories resurfaced of gathering at the train station and saying goodbye to the only people and places that she had ever known. Tasya looked down. Both girls sat quietly for a long while on the bunk until the curfew bell rang. Alyona quietly got down and returned to her own bunk.

III.

The work routine in the factory began, and week by week, more and more young male and female workers arrived. Soon there were so many that they were divided into alternating shifts – one twelve hour shift during the day, and one twelve hour shift at night. The night supervisor, Hans, was an easygoing older man with ruddy cheeks and a kind manner, who often commented how he had been called out of retirement. Content to spend most of the shift chatting with the girls in bits and pieces of German, he kept an unhurried pace of work. As long as the shift made its quota, Hans was happy.

"Which shift to do you like to work the most – day or night?" Alyona asked Tasya, a few weeks after the schedule of alternating shifts began. She had come out of her shell, and the girls spent most of their free time together. The more time that Tasya got to spend with Alyona, the more impressed she became. Alyona's true intelligence was masked by her quiet nature, but as she got to know her, Tasya saw just how mature and thoughtful Alyona was.

"I actually like to work the night shift. After it is done, I can sleep all day in the barrack. Don't you find it was easier to forget the hunger if you sleep all day? Being up and working during the night seems so unnatural in the first place, but I don't feel as desperate for food during the night."

"You mean starving *and* working during the day is a much more dreadful combination?" Alyona asked, laughing.

"Exactly!" Tasya answered. "Plus, you can sneak naps during the night shift."

It became known that Hans did not mind if his workers disappeared for a half hour during their shift.

"We're lucky that Hans is so easy-going. I don't think that Lars would let us sneak off like that."

When she had been at Ford-Werke for two months, Tasya was surprised to be handed a note by Lars, directing her to the Camp Commandant's office after her shift. Tasya was terrified of him. Everyone was. He had been spotted only a few times by the *Ostarbeiter* workers, but held a commanding presence. He was always accompanied by two deputies who looked like they would be the type to shoot first and ask questions later. Behind his back, the Commandant was called 'The Boss' by all the workers and seemed to be feared by everyone in the Russian camp, including the guards.

Tasya was both puzzled and alarmed to be called in to see The Boss. She felt the eyes of all the girls in her work shift watching her as she went, escorted by one of his personal deputies, back in the direction of the *Ostarbeiter* security barrack.

"Come in!" The Boss commanded when the deputy knocked on his door. The deputy opened the door, and gestured for Tasya to go inside, but he didn't follow. The door slammed shut behind her as she stepped over the threshold.

The Boss sat behind a large wooden desk. Two windows overlooked the camp yard. Besides two green filing cabinets next to the desk, there was very little in the room. Tasya felt nervous at the starkness of it.

The Boss glanced up from paperwork for only a second. "You are Anastasia, number 897, yes?"

Surprised to be called by her given name, Tasya froze.

"Yes, I am," she said in German.

"Well, number 897, I have been asked to create a special work arrangement for you, for *Burgermeister* Bamm." He looked at her. "Do you know him?"

"Yes." Tasya could barely speak at the mention of the Bamm name. The Boss looked like he expected more of an explanation from her.

"I worked for them as a servant in their home before coming to Ford-Werke."

"Then I have a very unorthodox arrangement for you. You are to go there on your off-hours here. I have made concessions for you to travel to their home to work during the daytime hours on the weeks that you work the night shift." The Boss looked directly at Tasya. "This does not in any way take the place of the usual work that you must do here. Do you understand?"

"Yes, I understand," Tasya replied in a serious manner, trying desperately to keep the emotion out of her voice. She very much wanted to get back to the Bamm house again. Images of food and her bed flashed through Tasya's mind, and she suppressed a smile.

"You have this special arrangement as a favour, but do not think that you may begin to disrupt the system in my camp. First rule," The Boss said, pointing his index finger at her like a gun, "you may not bring goods into the camp to trade on the underground market that you Russians have running here."

Tasya nodded. She had no idea of the illicit market.

"Second," he said, holding a second finger up, "you may also not tell *anyone* of your special privilege. If you do anything that disrupts the peace in my camp, I will be forced to punish you. Have you heard what happens to those who upset me?" Tasya shook her head. "I refer that person to the police, the Gestapo. I can assure you that you do not want me to have to do that."

The entire time The Boss was talking, Tasya was nodding enthusiastically in agreement, her eyes open wide. The absolute last thing on her mind was selling items on some underground market. She wouldn't know how to do it even if she desired.

"Good." The Boss must have concluded that Tasya didn't intend to cause trouble for him. "On the weeks you will work the night shift, you may come by the security office to get your day pass to leave the camp, as well as your train pass. It will not take you long to get to Jüchen from here. One way, it should take approximately forty-five minutes. That will leave you plenty of time to travel, work, and then to come back for your next night shift." It occurred to Tasya that sleep was not factored into the equation, but she pushed the thought from her mind.

With that, The Boss looked down at his paperwork and dismissed her with a wave of his hand. Walking back to the barrack alone, Tasya marveled at her good fortune. She was deep in thought about how she would soon be reunited with Frau Bamm, Isle, and Frieda. As Tasya approached the barrack, she saw Inna was sitting outside with a group of other girls. They had been friendly in their first days at Ford-Werke, but then Inna gravitated towards an older group of girls.

"So?" Inna called out. "What did The Boss want with you? Are you in trouble?"

"No." Tasya froze. She hadn't decided what to tell the other girls. "Um… it's a long story."

The other girls assessed Tasya with expressions of either boredom or mild curiosity. Two of the girls were smoking. One of the girls saw Tasya watching her smoke, and walked slowly over. Tasya knew that the girl was named Stefa and she had already been in a few fights with others in the barrack.

"You look to be fine, so you couldn't be in too much trouble." Stefa blew some of the smoke directly in Tasya's face. Tasya coughed, and took a step back. She was surrounded. Stefa looked Tasya directly in the eye. "Plus, you haven't been sent away somewhere else. What really happened?"

The threats uttered by The Boss still rang in Tasya's ears. She was terrified of upsetting the order of the camp. Tasya saw suspicion in the eyes of every girl in the group, including Inna.

"Well, I'm not sure why, but I have to do an extra work assignment." Tasya knew that she wasn't a good liar. She felt her cheeks redden as she spoke. "The Boss told me that because I had been caught sleeping on the job during my last night shift, I now have a bit of extra work to do."

"You were caught? When?" Inna asked. Tasya wished that she had thought of something that sounded clever.

"Well, I'm not exactly sure of the details, but I have to go to clean houses for German nationals during the daytime hours. After my night shift ends."

It was a half-truth and the story seemed plausible to Tasya. Stefa was not going to let her off the hook. House cleaning was an unusual punishment for falling asleep during a shift. More common punishments doled out by the guards included beatings with the rubber truncheon or solitary confinement for a few days. Never work outside the factory.

"What are you talking about?" Stefa asked. "Your punishment is to go do light work as a maid in a *house*? What kind of punishment is that?" Stefa stepped closer to Tasya again. "In fact, why don't you tell me how I can be punished like that?"

The girls surrounding Tasya giggled.

Tasya tried her best to look innocent and confused.

"You see, I still have to do my usual work in the factory. The housework is on top of all of that. The weeks I work the night shift, I have to go and do work during the day. I think the lack of sleep will be the punishment."

"Which house will you be so busy cleaning during the days? The Boss's?"

Tasya felt her cheeks redden again.

"I don't know whose house but I know it's not for The Boss. He said for some sort of German General."

"You heard about what happened to the Russian girl who was getting special favours from the guards, yes?" When Tasya shook her head, Stefa punched her fist into her other palm. "She had to be taken away after. Just a warning to you, Tasya."

Stefa broke her stare and stepped back towards the other girls. Tasya quietly exhaled. The other girls went back to chatting among themselves as Stefa struck a match to light another cigarette that she pulled from inside her wooden clog. Tasya felt Stefa's eyes on her until she got back to the safety of the barrack.

She desperately wanted to go to the Bamm house again but now faced a different threat besides malnourishment. She had heard of the young Ukrainian men in the other barracks begging German workers for some of their food. She didn't want to be targeted by the other girls as a possible source for additional bread or potatoes.

Alyona came into the barrack a few minutes later, and headed straight over to Tasya's bunk.

"That unpleasant girl, Stefa, just threatened me when I walked by her. She said something about keeping an eye on you because you are up to something. What's she talking about?"

"Oh, Alyona. I don't want to cause you trouble. The Boss has given me a new work arrangement. I have to clean a German's house after my night shifts."

"You have extra work, then? What's Stefa's issue?"

"I think she believes that there is more to it than extra work, like I'm getting special privileges or something," Tasya said.

"I don't know about you but I would try to steer clear of that girl. She's always going on about having her eyes and ears open."

Alyona pulled herself up to Tasya's bunk and lay down next to her.

"This is a world unlike anything that we are used to, that's for sure," Alyona said. "We live like prisoners, with no food, no family, no love. It's awful."

"Food is our big problem, I'm not so sure about love."

"You're wrong, Tasya. We need food to survive physically, but what about our other needs?"

"Sometimes I only care about getting food. Maybe surviving the shift without collapsing. I actually forget about my mother and sister for a few days. I forget about the Bamm family and how happy I was there."

"I miss my sister the most," Alyona said, wiping away her tears. "We were always together, day and night. I find sleeping alone the most difficult, because we always slept in the big bed together."

"It will get better, Alyona, I promise," Tasya said. "I've been here for two years now, and I've changed so much, but I don't feel less like a daughter or a sister. I still miss my mama's love and guidance."

"Sometimes, at night, I try to stay close to my family, in my mind at least, by playing a game that I made up. I try to imagine my village, in every detail that I can remember, and then I think of every detail of each person of my family."

Tasya laughed.

"I've done that, too," Tasya said. "I would have thought that I would start to forget details as time went on, but as long as I keep thinking about Horayetz, about Mama and Kateryna, the more I actually remember."

"I sometimes can even remember smells!"

"Me, too. My favourite daydream is walking through the village on a beautiful summer's day and imagining the smells; wildflowers, grass, small bush fires, and the best smell of all, bread baking."

Tasya looked at Alyona, who had her eyes closed, so she continued. "I then imagine myself walking up to our cottage. The sounds and the smells that I sense as I walk up the path to the door. Inside, Mama is making the evening meal of soup, and not like *balanda*, either. She's making a warm and rich potato and chicken stew."

"What happens next?" Alyona asked, still lying down with her eyes closed. When Tasya didn't answer, she propped herself up on her elbow. "Keep telling me what you see and hear. It's good for both of us."

"Next, I go over to the fireplace – my special spot in the house. I lie down, then Mama comes over and rubs my back, asking me how my day was, or what I had been up to that afternoon with Hanya."

"See I'm right – you miss love just as much as food. In your daydream game, you don't go over and eat the stew; you have that special moment with your mama."

Tasya knew that she wasn't the only one feeling deep loneliness because she could always hear crying scattered around the barrack throughout most of the night. Some girls cried lightly, and then fell asleep quickly, while other girls tried to keep their long sobs muffled by pillows made of rags.

Knowing that Alyona was right, Tasya lay down next to her again, but that time, she let the tears fall openly down her cheeks.

IV.

Tasya began to count the days until her return to the Bamm household. She quickly realized that counting only made time go more slowly, so she counted down the quarter-days. She had to keep her excitement a secret around everyone except for Alyona, who knew that Tasya was allowed to leave the factory but not where she would be going.

The morning of her release, with a train ticket in hand, Tasya skipped as she rushed to the train station. Just the thought of the familiar sight of the beautiful square surrounding the Bamm house, or of the smells of Isle's cooking caused a flutter in her heart. She couldn't wait to finally be with Frau Bamm, Adora, and the others.

Arriving at the station in Jüchen, Tasya jumped off the train and ran as fast as she could to the Bamm's. She had to keep slowing down when her legs would not keep up, and once, stopped altogether to rest. She cried tears of frustration at being unable to move her body as quickly as she wanted it to move.

When she finally staggered into the familiar square, Tasya made for the Bamm house and pounded on the front door. When Frieda's face appeared, Tasya burst into tears, and collapsed into the older woman's arms.

"Oh, my dear girl. Come in, quickly, and we will take care of you. You look like the tiny waif that you were two years ago!" Tasya let Frieda half-carry her through the front entryway to the back, and into the kitchen.

There was a joyful reunion between Tasya, Frieda, and Isle, filled with hugs and tears. Tasya was given a small bowl of porridge, with promises of more to follow. Isle made sure that she ate slowly, just like her first time at the Bamm's. Tasya took in the sight of the familiar copper pots suspended from the ceiling, the sight of Isle and Frieda bustling about the kitchen. She smiled. She breathed in the warm scent of the bread that was baking in the oven, and closed her eyes. Enjoyment of the moment was paramount and Tasya savored every second of it.

Frau Bamm rushed into the kitchen, smiling. "Tasi, you've finally arrived back to us! Thank God that you are here, and safe. I wasn't truly sure if we would be able to get permission to have you leave the factory. Herr Bamm finally managed it, and now, here you are."

Hugging Frau Bamm, Tasya laughed and tears again filled her eyes.

"I was told about a week ago that I could come here after my night shift."

Lowering her voice so that only Tasya could hear, Frau Bamm leaned in to Tasya. "When you have a moment, please come see me, in private." Frau Bamm straightened herself back up and turned to the others.

"Alright, let Tasi eat and then rest for now. Please send her to see me when she is ready."

Tasya finished eating her small portion, but took her time rising from the table. She watched Isle peel and cut potatoes into tiny cubes. She took note of how the morning sunlight streamed in through the two tall windows behind the sink. She wanted to pinch herself at her good fortune, but was afraid that she would then wake up from a beautiful dream.

"Tasi! Where have you drifted off to?" Isle watched her with open curiosity. Tasya smiled and blushed. "As I was saying, we've been put under an even stricter rationing program by the government, but don't worry, Tasi, there will always be something for you."

Later, Tasya knocked on Frau Bamm's bedroom door.

"Come in, Tasi. Close the door. Quickly."

Tasya stepped into the warm comfort of Frau Bamm's room. She was again surrounded by the plush femininity that she had missed so much. Tasya glanced at the beautiful green velvet armchair that Frau enjoyed reading in. A small fire burned in the fireplace. Tasya looked at the photos in the silver frames that Frau Bamm arranged after each time Tasya dusted. In the room, Tasya was safe.

"Tasi, I apologize that I haven't spent more time with you this morning, but I have to be careful of who is watching." Tasya looked at Frau Bamm quizzically. "After you left, we were forced to hire a local girl. She is nice enough, a war widow at only twenty years old, but I don't fully trust her. Also, I know this is difficult, but I don't want her to know how fond we are of you." Frau Bamm stepped forward, and engulfed Tasya in a warm hug.

Frau Bamm sat on the bed, gesturing for Tasya to sit next to her.

"Tell me, what's it like at Ford-Werke? Are there many like you? From Russia?"

Didn't Frau Bamm know that she was Ukrainian? Tasya tried to keep her face neutral.

"We are all classified as *Ostarbeiter* workers, no matter if we are from Russia, or Ukraine," Tasya said. "And, no, it's not good there. The work isn't too bad, very boring, but the worst is the food. The food is awful."

"What do they give you?"

"We only get soup and bread, and one cup of coffee per day. The soup is *awful*."

Frau Bamm shook her head, looking Tasya up and down carefully.

"It looks as if you've lost some of the weight that you put on here. We'll have to get you into good shape again."

Tasya laughed, looking down at her skinny frame. "Thank goodness, because I don't know what I would do, otherwise. The rations aren't enough to exist on for any real length of time. Everyone is starving. Others have begun to resort to find ways to get extra food but I'm terrified of getting caught."

"What do you mean?" Frau Bamm asked, raising one eyebrow.

"Like, sneaking into the kitchen barrack to get extra potatoes, bribing the kitchen staff, or…becoming friendly with the guards," Tasya looked down, blushing. "But that's not something I want to have to do."

"No, of course not," Frau Bamm said quickly. They both paused before Frau Bamm hugged Tasya again. "Did you use the marks that I gave you before you left?"

"I did…but I'm sorry, Frau Bamm, I don't think I used them wisely."

"Tasi, I gave you enough marks at that time to buy the entire household food for three days. What did you do with them?"

Tasya paused, and felt ashamed. "I bribed a kitchen girl, and she gave me four potatoes for the marks." She couldn't meet Frau Bamm's eyes, and fiddled nervously with the cuff on her jacket.

"Four potatoes!" Frau Bamm exclaimed. "Tasi, those marks weren't much, but you could have bought more than four potatoes."

"I'm sorry, Frau Bamm, I didn't know," Tasya whispered, looking down again.

"Oh, all right. It's no matter now, at least it helped a bit," Frau Bamm said, patting Tasya's hand. "Before you go, let me warn you, watch out for Berta, your replacement. I do not know what it is about her, but I don't trust her completely. She's heavily involved with our Nazi party, and tensions there are running high right now."

Tasya nodded, curious to meet the girl who had joined the Bamm's in her absence. As if she could read Tasya's mind, Frau Bamm shook her head.

"Everyone is on edge lately, actually. I don't know if you've heard, but we lost our hold on Paris a few days ago."

Tasya shook her head. She could not care less what was going on outside of the Ford-Werke factory.

"It's just that things are not looking so good right now, and I don't want to draw attention to our family."

Tasya knew Frau Bamm had been through enough in the war to last a lifetime. Frau Bamm looked down at the ground, quiet and distant for a few seconds before she looked at Tasya with a smile again.

"Anyway, Berta has your old room and does all of your old duties, so we have to try to find you something new to do while you are with us. Why don't I assign you light work? Tell the staff that you are doing other work as well."

Tasya nodded. "I'll have to sleep for a few hours during the day since I still have to work my night shifts."

"Yes. I assume that you'll have to continue your regular factory work, but we will do everything we can to make you comfortable during your hours here." Frau Bamm reached over to hold Tasya's hand. "I can't believe that we had to send you away so suddenly, and we miss you very much around here. I was told that you are allowed to come once during your night shift schedule."

"Only once?" Tasya asked, feeling her enthusiasm deflate. "The Boss said every time after my night shift."

"The Boss? No, I'm sorry, but I was given very clear outlines. You are only allowed once on your night-shift weeks."

Tasya looked at Frau Bamm with open devastation. "What do you mean, once?"

"That's what we've been told. Once each night shift schedule. That's it.

That's every two weeks, I believe."

Tasya nodded as tears pooled in her eyes.

"Oh, dear. But, think of it this way," she said, lifting up Tasya's chin to look into her eyes, "we get to see you every other week, and we will try to take care of you as best that we can."

At lunch, Tasya joined the rest of the staff in the kitchen for lunch, including Berta. The usually lively group sat in complete silence during the meal. Tasya was uncomfortable and aware of Berta's eyes on her, but as soon as Isle put a bowl of potato and pork stew in front of her, she devoured it. When Berta was finished her meal, she left, scraping her chair across the floor. Frieda and Isle comically exhaled when she was gone.

"So, tell us," Frieda asked as she carried the dishes over to the sink, "Are the factories as bad as I have heard?"

Tasya answered their questions. They paid close attention as Tasya told them about the barracks and the terrible *balanda*.

"I haven't been working in the factory for very long, and was in good health when I arrived, so I haven't had do what that others have to do to get extra food."

"Do they have to steal?" Isle asked.

"Sort of. If they are lucky, it's as simple as getting one of the Germans to take pity and give them an extra slice of bread or a potato. The guards aren't all monsters, either. I've heard that some of them allow the boys to sneak out under a spot in the fence at night."

For every story of desperation that Tasya told, there was also one of kindness by the German people to the hungry foreigners.

"The German workers have to eat in a separate area, but they do what they can. The Ukrainian boys climb over the roof of the German eating area, and maybe someone sneaks some soup out the window to them. Sometimes, they get the rolls from the German canteen. It depends."

As Frieda and Isle smiled at her, Tasya thought of the stories that she purposely didn't tell. Those who bravely snuck over to the German eating area were often rewarded with food, but they were also often punished. There was a factory security guard who had a notorious reputation of being an absolute savage towards any of the *Ostarbeiter* workers. If he caught a Russian or Ukrainian boy with food, he struck them across the backs of their heads. Tasya had heard that older German workers would often try to stop him, but the guard held the power.

"So, who is this Berta?" Tasya whispered.

Frieda came over from the sink, shaking her head, and leaned in to Tasya. "There is something in that girl's eyes that just does not sit well with me, and Tasi, you would be wise to give her a wide berth."

"Everyone in the house, even Frau Bamm, seems to be intimidated by that girl!" Isle added. "Imagine that – being intimidated by your chambermaid! The world has gone completely mad."

Two hours before her factory shift was to begin, the small satchel she carried filled with bread, potatoes, and a bit of cake, Tasya returned to the train station, feeling bittersweet. Her reprieve from the factory was a Godsend, and the food she carried would be enough to get her and Alyona through the next two weeks. She knew that without it, there was no telling what would become of her.

V.

The first winter in the camp arrived, and it was marked by incredible cold and hunger for everyone. Tasya's existence revolved around making her quota, attempting to stay warm, and getting any food she could lay her hands on. Finding warmth began to overtake hunger needs when the small stove in the barrack proved itself completely inadequate. Fuel shortages meant that often, there was no coal at all.

Snow fell heavily that entire winter and bitterness grew in the *Ostarbeiter* camp. Workers from the French and Italian camps were permitted to receive care packages from their families. One day on her way into the factory, Tasya saw the Red Cross distributing packages to the other workers. A few weak protests by the *Ostarbeiter* workers sprang up, but were quickly squashed by the guards. Ten Russian and Ukrainian boys were taken away in full view by the Gestapo. After that, there were no more protests, but the grumbling continued.

As the cold winter dragged on mercilessly, Tasya watched as greater risks were taken by the workers for warmth and food. A girl from Tasya's barrack, Slavka, was kept in solitary confinement for two days when she was caught boiling a potato with her laundry. Boys were subjected to much harsher punishment. One boy from Inna's village, Mykola, was caught sneaking out of the camp twice. After the second time, the *Werkschutz* guards turned him over to the Gestapo. Inna cried for a week.

With the warnings of The Boss still resounding clearly in her memory, Tasya was careful that only Alyona knew that she was carrying food. If anyone else found out, Tasya knew there would be chaos and her privileges would be revoked.

Desperate and foolish, a few girls from the *Ostarbeiter* camp tried to escape in February of 1945. Rumors had swirled around the camp that farmers in the countryside were aiding and hiding escaped workers in exchange for help with their work. Some girls were fortunate, and with luck on their side they got away, but most were caught by the guards in one of the three stations around the factory perimeter. Word traveled back to the *Ostarbeiter* camp that three boys who were attempting escape to the countryside were shot on sight by the city police.

Escape was something that Tasya never considered and felt detached from when she heard stories of punishment. Then, in late February, Stefa and a second girl, Vera, attempted to escape. The *Werkschutz* guard who found them was thought to be in a foul mood, because he took them directly to the penal barrack. Their cries got the attention of some of the Russian girls, who sought help for them. They were locked together in the windowless prison for days with nothing but water. Attempts to give the girls bread were unsuccessful. Both cried loud pleas for help but no one could help them.

Not long after, Alyona climbed up to Tasya's bed, her face was grey.

"Tasya, they're gone," said Alyona, shaking.

"Who's gone?" Tasya asked, sitting up. She had been quietly chewing a small hunk of bread that she had hidden in the mattress.

"Stefa and Vera. They are gone. I was just at the penal barrack, and it's empty. They're gone."

Tasya slid another small chunk of bread to Alyona, who slipped it into the pocket of her jacket without even looking at it. "They're gone. Sent away. That guard, he told me. They were sent to a KZ camp."

Tasya froze. They had heard stories of the KZ camps from the guards. These were the death camps where prisoners and Jews never came back. After word spread about women sent to a KZ camp, most of the escape attempts stopped. Boys still snuck away from the factory to find food and risked beatings or whippings if caught. Escape attempts by the girls stopped.

The German workers, feeling sorry for the forced workers, brought in more food from home. Alyona came into a bit of luck when she was assigned to another department. She found herself working with a quiet old German man. Unable to communicate with one another through language, they slowly settled into a routine where each day the man shared his lunch with Alyona. Tasya was relieved. As Alyona relied less on Tasya for extra food, Tasya had more to herself.

Alyona's new arrangement worked well until March, when the German man was ill for nearly two weeks. Tasya worried as the strain of missing him showed on Alyona, both through worry and lack of food. She lost weight immediately, and became withdrawn, worried for his health and safety. The man eventually returned to work when he recuperated, and even presented Alyona with a slice of cake for her birthday. It was the only gift that Alyona received that year, and Tasya watched with some worry as Alyona cried and hung onto the old man.

Tasya's own luck ran short a few months after starting her visits with the Bamm family. After a particularly lovely and relaxing day spent with Frau Bamm and Adora, Tasya found herself exhausted as she started her next night shift.

"What's wrong with you?" Alyona asked, snapping Tasya out of a daze.

"I'm exhausted. I didn't sleep during the day, and now I can barely see straight." Tasya eyelids hung heavily. She tried to force them open with her fingers, but gave up. It was as if a tiny weight was attached to each lid.

"Snap out of it, Tasya. That new foreman is looking for any excuse to lose his patience."

The production overseer at Ford had noticed the gradual decline in productivity on the night shifts. He had assigned a new foreman to the night shift in order to raise production, making it difficult for the girls to sneak away for short nighttime naps.

"I don't care about the new supervisor. I have to get some sleep for a few minutes. Cover for me?" Tasya didn't wait to hear what Alyona wanted to say. Nearly as soon as she closed her eyes in the toilet, she fell asleep.

The next thing she knew, Tasya woke up from a pain in her right shin. Her eyes snapped open in time for her to see the foreman coming at her, and she closed her eyes just before his fist hit her temple.

"Get up! Do you think you are allowed to sleep on my shift? *Schweine Russki*!" he yelled at her, grabbing Tasya by one arm as she tried to get her feet under her. He dragged her across the floor of the washroom, then down the stairs, where he shoved her to the factory floor. Tasya cowered in a ball, holding her arms around her face. A number of girls had gathered to watch.

Tasya caught sight of Alyona's worried face. The man punched Tasya. Black creeped in from around the periphery of Tasya's vision, and then the entire world went dark.

Her brain felt like it was being pierced. Bright sunlight hurt even through her closed eyes. She knew that she was lying down. She groaned and tried to open her eyes a millimeter at a time. Peeking through her fingers, she shielded her eyes from the glaring light as her head throbbed with pain.

"You are finally awake!"

Tasya heard the sharp staccato of heels on the floor as a woman moved towards her.

"You've been out for quite a while, and I was starting to get worried about you. I don't think any of your bones are broken, but you are certainly going to have quite a headache for the next few days." Tasya peeked as best she could, and saw a woman with grey hair and sparkling blue eyes.

"That brute of a foreman went at you with much more force than necessary," the nurse said as she put a wet towel across Tasya's forehead. Tasya closed her eyes again to relax. "Imagine, punching a young girl in the head! Oh, wait now...do you speak German?"

Tasya shook her head no. Her head hurt too much to talk.

"But you can understand me, I see. I'm telling you, dear, in the twenty years I've been the factory nurse here, I've never seen such ridiculous behavior. The whole world has gone crazy these past few years, I swear it."

Tasya was sent back to the barrack a few hours later when the nurse decided that she would be fine. When Tasya walked into the barrack, Alyona jumped out of her bunk and rushed through the sleeping girls to give her a big hug, her face flooding with relief.

"Thank God you are alright. I was so worried about you, especially when we carried you over to the medic barrack, and you didn't wake up the entire time! I've never seen anyone unconscious from a beating like that. How are you feeling?"

"Terrible," Tasya answered, holding her temples for emphasis. "I feel like I've fallen out of a very tall tree, hitting every branch on the way down. That crazy foreman didn't break any bones, but my head is killing me from the punches."

"You can see where he hit you," Alyona said as she gingerly touched

Tasya's head, pulling away as Tasya winced. "You have a huge bruise on the one side of your head, and it looks like it's going to look worse before it starts to get better."

The girls lay down together in Alyona's bunk and slept the rest of the day away. At the evening roll call, Tasya was present and said her number with the rest of her group. As they marched through the security gates to the factory, she was pulled aside by a guard who told her that at the insistence of the medical nurse, she had been allocated three shifts off.

The next day, none of the girls spoke to Tasya.

"I just think that it's a bit strange," Tasya pouted to Alyona. "No one seems to care that I was beaten senseless by the foreman. You'd think someone in this place would show that they care."

"Tasya, you have to understand, everyone here is trying to survive. If it wasn't for the extra scraps that you bring back with you from the Bamm's, or my sweet Dirk, you and I would be starving like everyone else."

"I'm hungry too! All the time."

"We aren't like the others, Tasya. They need to take risks for every extra crumb, and many of the girls here have felt the rubber truncheon because of it. Just keep your head down, work hard, and stay out of everyone's way."

VI.

Spring of 1945 arrived slowly, as if Mother Earth was frightened to fully open herself to the misery in Germany, holding back her blooms and new life for as long as possible. Finally, at the end of March, the change of seasons began to show itself in unexpected places. Tasya marveled at the flowers sprouting around the rocks in the factory yard, the buds that appeared around the perimeter fence.

One unusually warm afternoon in late March, Tasya sat with Frau Bamm in the back garden, admiring the early blooms on the trees.

"What is the name of that flower poking through, over there?" Tasya asked, pointing to the edges of the garden walkway. When Frau Bamm did not answer, Tasya saw that she looked to be particularly distracted.

"Frau?"

"Hmmmm?" Frau Bamm sighed heavily.

"The flowers over there? What are they called?"

"Oh. Those are the daffodils. They will soon be quite beautiful. Another few weeks, Tasi, and you'll see."

Tasya let another few minutes go by. Worried, she blurted, "Frau Bamm, what is it?"

She didn't feel any better when the older woman reached over to give her hand a squeeze.

"Tasi, I think that the end of the war may be approaching. I've been hearing reports from Herr Bamm that the Western Allies have gained a strong foothold in Europe, and that they are pushing our army back." She turned to look directly at Tasya. "Soon, you might even be able to return home. I'm sure your mother is praying every morning and evening for your safe return."

This was the first news of the Allied armies approaching that Tasya had heard.

"Frau Bamm, you really think the war will be ending soon?"

Tasya thought about the factory. Production had been ramped-down, but the foremen still seemed to be pleased with the quotas.

"Who knows? Herr Bamm has heard reports that I very much doubt have been made available to the general public. Keeping up appearances is very important to the Reich, or to any country during a time of war, really. But appearances are deceptive, and we must be ready for whatever comes our way."

Tasya had never considered the end of the war in any great detail. She and the others hoped for more food, for actual wages, but there never seemed to be the end in sight to the actual conflict.

"Tell me, Tasi. If you were home, right now, if you had never come here... what would you be doing?"

Tasya didn't need to think about her answer. "I would most likely be looking for a husband, and to start my own family, Frau Bamm. Same as everyone else my age."

"You would still be with your mother at home, I imagine."

"Yes. I think so. Unless I was living and working in a house, as a servant. Like here."

"I was just thinking about how much this war has changed lives. Millions upon millions of lives. Women like myself and your mother haven't been directly involved, but so greatly impacted. Isn't it strange how decisions made so far away by people that you do not even know, can change your life forever?"

"Of course, Frau Bamm."

Tasya didn't say more, but she knew very well how the war had completely changed the fabric of life. So much had happened in the three years since she had left home. She had experienced more than she had ever thought possible at such a young age.

"What do you miss the most about home, Tasi?" Frau Bamm asked softly. "What is the one thing that you are most looking forward to when you go home?"

"I miss my mama the most," Tasya said. "I just want someone to take care of me."

Tasya quickly reached for Frau Bamm's hand.

"Of course, you've been so wonderful to me, and I think that if I didn't have you, I wouldn't have been able to survive," Tasya said.

Frau Bamm patted Tasya's hand.

"I'm glad that I've helped you these past few years, but of course I can never take the place of your mama. No matter what happens after this war ends, if you'll be able to go home, then I'll be happy that your family is restored, even if ours will never be."

Though Frau Bamm was kind, the place of her mama could never be filled with anyone else. The thought of the war ending, and being able to go home, gave Tasya a tiny spark of hope, but she was too wary to let her hope grow.

VII.

Ahem," said Lars, clearing his throat. He looked confused. Tasya watched as two soldiers came into the factory, pulled Lars aside, and left the foreman shaking his head.

"I'm not sure exactly what is going on, but we have to stop all work and begin to dismantle the machinery."

Rather than giving them an order, Lars raised his hands into the air as if asking the girls a question. "Someone...go and run and get everyone from the night shift in here to help."

Within fifteen minutes, everybody was there. Stunned silence gave way to chaos as news of the work stoppage brought confusion and panic. Supervisors yelled at the girls to grab one of the large wrenches and to start dismantling machines. Some girls darted about in confusion, asking questions that no one knew the answers to. Others worked steadily, but feebly, trying to record on scrap pieces of paper which parts of the machine attached where. Tasya felt as if everyone had all gone senseless. She pulled and pushed on her own wrench, trying to loosen bolts that had been tightened by men who had been stronger and well-nourished. As Tasya worked in utter confusion with Alyona and four other girls, she prayed that she would not be the one having to put the machine back together, if that ever even happened.

They worked like mad for the rest of the day and overnight, and were allowed short rest periods to nap in the barracks. Over the next few days the confusion persisted. The workers were told that nothing was wrong, but the word got around that the factory was being moved to the east side of the Rhine for safety. An American plane flying over the factory dropped hundreds of leaflets into the compound. It rained yellow leaflets with black printing.

As one fluttered at her feet, Tasya picked it up and read,

APRIL 15TH, 1945
AMERICANS ARE ADVANCING RAPIDLY AND POISED TO TAKE OVER LAND ON EITHER SIDE OF THE RHINE.

The font was large and stark. There was an illustration of American soldiers in jeeps and tanks. Tasya shivered.

The entire city of Cologne was ordered to evacuate. All the Ford-Werke workers were marched to the outskirts, followed by trucks carrying the factory equipment. All the workers, *Ostarbeiter*, *Westarbeiter*, Italian, were packed into an under-supplied and disorganized makeshift camp. There was no food.

For a week, Tasya and Alyona huddled together, starving and shivering on the bare floor of their temporary barrack. They had absolutely nothing to do but sit and wait for orders that didn't come. Tasya could sense everything starting to unravel. Thoughts of trying to escape to the Bamm's home drifted away. Tasya began to lose her grip on life.

After a week of starvation and cold, three girls from the factory died. There was little the others could do besides drag the stiff bodies outside, and hope that somehow, they would be saved. That God would look after them.

After a week, the workers received their orders; digging useless ditches. When the sounds of airplanes, then shelling, came closer, they ran, staying as close to the ground as possible. Tasya imagined that if she died and went to Hell that it wouldn't be worse than what she was surviving. Starvation, squalor, people dying all around her, some digging senselessly in the mud; either she'd gone mad, or she'd actually died and gone straight to Hell.

"The end is coming, and with it, something good. We can all feel it," Alyona said reassuringly to Tasya one night as they tried to sleep among the masses of girls propped up against each other. They both shared a thin blanket brought from the barracks. Huddled underneath it for warmth, Tasya was exhausted.

"The end is coming," she said to Alyona, "that's for sure, but what comes after that is what scares me. Things just keep getting worse and worse." Tasya began to cry. "What will happen if the Americans come in here and find us all like this? I'll tell you what they are going to do. They are going to shoot us like dogs!"

"Shhh. Don't worry." Alyona hugged Tasya. "I think that the Americans are good."

Nearly three years to the day that she left Horayetz, on April 28th, 1945 the last small group of *Werkschutz* guards got into three Maultier trucks and drove south. Everyone who was still able to walk got up from the filthy, mud-caked floor of the barrack and went outside in time to see the last of the trucks pulling away.

"They left us alone?" Alyona asked. She began to cough, and Tasya put her arm around her waist. They both slowly sank into the mud that surrounded their temporary jail.

"They left us," Tasya said, watching until the last truck was no longer visible. She was too scared to move, terrified of what the future might bring. Had Frau Bamm known this is what would happen? Was she feeling guilty that last time that Tasya saw her? The sounds of vehicles rolling towards the makeshift camp filled Tasya's ears. "Thank God. They're coming back."

"Someone's coming, but it's not the guards. That sound is coming from the other road," Alyona murmured. She leaned further onto Tasya. Jeeps appeared along a different road than the one the guards used. More jeeps than Tasya could count. She pulled her feet from the mucky foundations that they were in, and tried to prop up Alyona to stand on her own.

Fighting her way through the other workers and mud back into the barrack, Tasya retrieved her filthy white pillowcase. Returning back outside, she found a shovel abandoned on the ground, and tied her pillowcase to it.

"C'mon," Tasya said, tugging Alyona, hard. She dragged them over to a mound of damp dirt at the side of a ditch, and waved the improvised flag up high.

"What's this? Surrender?" Alyona asked.

"Celebration!" Tasya cried.

SOLTAU

1945

I.

"In any time through history, the end of war signals a period of great confusion and uncertainty. This reality is true of both the defeated and the victorious."

The American General had a completely captive audience; there were hundreds in the square. He paused to allow his words to be translated into Ukrainian and Polish.

"We are at the end of this war that has revealed to the world atrocities that we could never have imagined. Right now, we are in a time of great change. Of great upheaval. There is much uncertainty, but one thing I can assure you is that we are working as quickly as possible to get each and every one of you settled. First, in one of the Displaced Persons camps that we are creating, then home."

"Home, but when?" Tasya whispered to Alyona. "Here we are, still in Cologne, living in a church basement."

For weeks the freed workers, now officially titled Displaced Persons by the Americans, had been in limbo. Germany was in chaos. No one knew what the future would bring. The Allied Forces struggled to handle the hundreds of thousands of young people from Russia, Ukraine, and Poland.

"I'm sure he doesn't know, either." Alyona shrugged. "Germany is broken and it's anarchy here, total anarchy. Everyone is out for themselves."

If there were two certainties to life under the Allies, they were boredom and self-preservation. Many Germans were in no better state. The girls had witnessed this first-hand just the week before. Food was still scarce as the

Allies organized themselves. Roaming the streets in search of extra food, Tasya and Alyona spotted a tidy-looking row house not far from the church that looked to be occupied.

An old woman answered the door. After one look at the girls, still wearing their Ford-Werke uniforms crusted with weeks' worth of grime, she flew into a rage.

"You Russian pigs! You dogs! Get away from my house. Get back to your own country. You people make me sick, begging door-to-door while we starve in our own homes. Get away before I get out my gun and shoot you!"

Frightened, the girls scuttled away. Moments later an American soldier on a motorcycle roared up beside them.

"Girls!" He called out in a heavily accented Polish. "What just happened? Did that woman just turn you away?"

Sheepishly, they relayed the incident. The soldier then jumped off the motorbike and strode up to the front door. Taking out his gun, he took a step backwards; he shot the door handle right off. Both Tasya and Alyona jumped a foot into the air at the sound of the bullet ripping through metal. The soldier then kicked the door right through the frame, went into the house, and accompanied the old woman back outside.

"Frau, you understand that German citizens must help support the liberated labourers in any way possible. Yes?"

The woman nodded. She went into the house, and emerged carrying a half-loaf of bread. Tasya saw the woman was shaking when she handed over the loaf.

As soon as the soldier rode off, Tasya and Alyona ran and didn't stop until they regained the relative safety of the church.

In addition to thousands of refugees looking for ways to get home, many Germans were fleeing as well. There was a constant sense of low-level panic. An American soldier explained the mass exodus as one of guilt. Anxious for their personal safety, anyone who had taken any small part in the Nazi war-machine had fled. The roads were filled with people and jeeps and cars. There was disorganization and fear. Many Germans had left their shops and houses; groups of young workers roamed free.

Boredom grew quickly in the unstructured spring. There was little for either Tasya or Alyona to do but walk around the city during the day and spend as little time as possible in the over-crowded and noisy church shelter as possible.

Tasya realized that the Bamm's would not be immune to the uncertainty and chaos of post-war life. Finally allowed to travel, Tasya and Alyona got a ride by an American GI to Jüchen. Tasya found the house empty, the curtains drawn. Neighbors said that they had not seen the family since the end of April, and suggested trying back in a few weeks. Eventually, Alyona took Tasya by the arm, and led her away, back to the musty church basement on the other side of the Rhine.

In June, Tasya and Alyona were placed again. They were assigned to the American zone, moving often from one temporary shelter to another. The only constant was that the conditions were poor; however, the Americans tried to make up for it by providing everyone with much-needed food.

From the moment that Tasya and Alyona were in the care of the gracious Americans and their doctors, they basked in the glory of incredible food. All former prisoners and labourers were put on diets of gradually increasing caloric intake and instructed to avoid eating foods that were difficult to digest. In the canteen of a Displaced Persons camp, Tasya made friends with a Ukrainian prisoner-of-war named Oleksander.

"Oh, Americans learned that lesson, alright." Oleksander laughed as they ate a dinner of beef stew. "It's funny, in a hideous sort of way." Oleksander turned serious. "When the Americans went along liberating the death camps, they were obviously horrified when they saw what kind of condition we were in. Imagine, I was eighty pounds when I left Dachau. Well, the Americans, they are generous, good people. They were eager to feed us starving skeletons and brought in huge sides of beef. You know, I was one of the lucky ones with only some diarrhea and stomach ailments. The unlucky ones? I swear to you, Tasya, I saw one Jew die right there on the spot after he ate a piece of beef the size of his head."

That same month, Tasya and Alyona registered with the International Refugee Organization as Ukrainian. Over and over, they recited their information to American administrators. They waited in long lines with other Ukrainians, Poles, Romanians, Czechoslovakians, and Russians for their life histories to be documented. It was at a crowded temporary holding camp outside of Düsseldorf that they first heard about the scheme to have all Soviets citizens repatriated back to their home countries. Alyona was ready to go home.

"Let's register to go home now, Tasya. I want to be back in Ternopil." The dark circles under her large eyes made Alyona look more tired than Tasya had ever seen her. "I'm tired of all this moving around, sleeping on the floor, not knowing what the next day will bring."

Tasya agreed.

"I'm ready to go home, too. I'm thinking every day of my mama and sister. I need to see them again." Tasya desperately needed to be in the arms of her mother again, and to kiss the small face of her new niece or nephew. "I want to know what happened to the Bamm family too, but there isn't anything holding me back here."

Soviet Army repatriation agents were working with the Americans in Düsseldorf. Tasya and Alyona had listened to their speeches over the past few weeks. Every other day, a new soldier came to whatever temporary holding camp they were in and encouraged everyone to go 'home' to the Soviet Union. Gathering curious onlookers like street magicians, the agents made it seem as if they could be entering paradise.

"Listen! All young men and women from the Soviet Union, your motherland needs you. We will work together to build up a great country, where everyone is valued for their contributions. Everyone is equal! Come sign up with us, and we will put you on a train to get you home as quickly as possible!"

The girls registered with the Soviet agents in the American camp, and signed up for a transport back to Lviv for July 15th.

Now the days went by quickly. Food provisions and wooden suitcases were donated by the Americans, and on their assigned day, Tasya and Alyona were again at the main train station in Düsseldorf. With their suitcases waiting next to a proper passenger car, they stood in the shade of the building.

"Thank God we're leaving this nightmare!" Alyona cried out.

"Sshhh. We are on our way, Alyona. We are on our way."

Two young men were also standing on the platform. Both were watching Tasya and Alyona carefully.

"Let's move over to the side of the station. It's too hot over here." Tasya said loudly. She didn't like the way the two men were eyeing her. But, as they moved over, so did the men. Tasya pulled Alyona further down the platform, but the men edged their way down.

"You are both Ukrainian?" One of the men asked, quietly. As he got closer, Tasya could see they were not much older than she was. Tasya and Alyona ignored them.

"Listen, girls. We are telling people what we have heard. The Soviets are accusing Ukrainians of treason, of being German spies." When Tasya didn't make eye contact, the second man stepped closer. "They are interrogating, then they are sending people to Siberia."

At the mention of Siberia, Tasya and Alyona looked at each other. Tasya wasn't sure what to believe.

"Are you joking with us?" Tasya asked.

"Yes, and why are you telling only us? Why not tell everyone standing on the platform?" Alyona asked, narrowing her eyes at the two men. "Don't listen to them," she said, turning to Tasya, "they have no idea what they are talking about."

"No, listen to us!" One boy said, grabbing Tasya's arm. "Don't go. I've seen the Russians bribing people with food and liquor, meat and bread. They want to make it seem as if there is bounty after all this starvation that we have gone through. But, you must understand, bounty is not what you will find."

"We tried to go home, just like you," the second young man said, this time focused on Alyona. "We went and registered at the Russian camp. The man who registered us was not a soldier. He heard us speaking Ukrainian to each other. Then he told us in our language that we could sign up to go home, but that we would never make it there. They are taking everyone to Russia, or Siberia."

Tasya didn't know what to say, but Alyona was getting upset. "Why would this man tell you that? Does he really know what it's like back home?"

"We don't know why he was trying to help us, but we believed him. As should you!"

Tasya felt her blood run cold, but Alyona didn't flinch. A long whistle sounded, and everyone started towards the train, including Alyona. Now uncertain, Tasya felt a tug of loyalty to her friend, following her reluctantly, while the young men stood back.

As she dragged herself up the stairs to the train car with her heavy suitcase, Tasya felt a sensation creeping its way up from the pit of her stomach. Memories from the past three years flooded back, and she fought the rising panic she felt, remembering her first train ride that brought her to Hell. The brick factory, the bombings, and the stench of fear flew through her mind.

She remembered how she and Hanya ran for their lives during the bombing of Düsseldorf. She thought of Ford-Werke, and could nearly feel the sensation of starving. Tasya thought about the cold that permeated her every moment, asleep or awake. If what the boys were saying was true, Tasya had a terrible fear that she would once again experience the cold, the constant orders from soldiers, and the total lack of food.

As she walked down the aisle, Tasya realized that, to this point in her life, she had never been in charge of her own destiny. She had been forced to go to Germany by Daria and Kateryna. She had been forced to stay by the Germans. She had been moved around Germany on what seemed to be no more than a whim by some distant administrator. Now, she didn't have a good idea of where her mother and sister were, or if they were even still alive.

"Where would I be going to?" Tasya asked herself. She felt as if she could see clearly for the first time in years; everything was finally totally clear to her.

As they got to their seats, Tasya made her decision – that she would no longer allow anyone to dictate the shape of her life, ever again. Heaving her suitcase up from the floor, Tasya leaned out the open window, calling to the two young men who still stood in the shade of the building.

"Boys," she called, easing the wooden suitcase out the window, "Come take this!" and half-dropped, half-threw the suitcase out the window.

"Come with me?" Tasya desperately asked Alyona, grabbing her hands, and trying to pull her friend out of the seat.

"No, Tasya - I'm going home," Alyona replied, pulling her hands away, and then looked ahead of her.

"We can't let anyone tell us where to go, or what to do. Never again should we follow like sheep other people's orders. Come with me, and later we can figure out how to get home, or at least, be sure that we can find your family before you head back!"

When Alyona didn't answer or make eye contact, Tasya knew that there was no changing her mind. A second long train whistle sounded.

Grabbing Alyona by the shoulders, Tasya whispered, "I'm sorry. I'll find you," then embraced her friend. Tasya ran down the aisle, and out the open door of the train just as it began to roll. The two boys ran over to the door, each grabbing one of Tasya's arms and swung her down as the train began to move. Running beside the train as it pulled out of the station, Tasya watched Alyona's stoic face become smaller as the train picked up speed on its journey east.

II.

The two young men took Tasya to a British camp. She was in shock, and never asked their names. She never saw them again.

Tasya was settled to a semi-permanent camp. The camp, called Münster-Lager, was nestled among the pines in the northern part of Germany, near the town of Soltau, far from Cologne, and even further from Jüchen. Though over-crowded, Münster-Lager was a vibrant community. A few thousand Ukrainian Displaced Persons had established more sense of normal life there than Tasya had seen anywhere aside from the Bamm house.

Tasya's heart ached. She didn't know where to go, or what her next move would be. Many nights, Tasya woke up in a panic in her bed, sure that she had made a bad decision by letting Alyona go. Alyona was her only friend, her only family. Now there was no one. By the time that early morning light began to creep in through the windows of the women's barrack, Tasya would begin to feel as if she could continue to live in the camp. Yearnings of returning to Horayetz began to quickly decrease when Tasya had heard that Soviet agents roamed the streets in open-top jeeps and took young Ukrainians by force back to Russia. Stories went around the camp of people who had been captured by the Soviet agents, but committed suicide after being registered to return to the USSR.

Münster-Lager was so large a camp that Tasya could remain anonymous. While the British military was formally in charge, the day-to-day running of the camp and policing was left to the Ukrainian residents. A community sprang up. There were makeshift churches, schools, and even a newspaper.

Every day, a new poster would appear on the bulletin board in the barrack. A primary school for children started first, then a few weeks later, a trade school. A roughly erected hall became the gathering point and heart of the camp. She was comfortable in the bustle of the women's barrack, and found that helping in the kitchen barrack of her area of the camp was a good way to pass the time and to ease her mind away from thoughts of all those who she had lost. While peeling vegetables in the crowded and lively kitchen, Tasya would stay in her own corner, hiding amongst the mountains of potatoes and carrots that were delivered each day. The other women of the kitchen tried to draw her out of her self-imposed shell, but Tasya politely kept to herself. She preferred to spend her time in quiet contemplation, allowing herself to indulge in thoughts of her mother and sister, of Hanya, of Elzbeta, and of Alyona.

Tasya found herself struggling to adjust to the hierarchies in the female barracks. Tasya was among the lowest social level in the barracks; she was poorly educated, young, and from a family of low background. She had no one with her, no friends, no family. She wore her loneliness on her face like a mask, keeping others away. Her one advantage was that she was able to adjust quickly to camp life. Many of the women in the camp were political refugees. This awarded them a higher social status, but Tasya saw how they struggled with the responsibility of cooking and washing, and especially how they were not adept at vying for provisions.

Shying away from the various women's groups that were sprouting around the camp, fewer women reached out to Tasya to invite her into their social fold. Lonely and bored, Tasya only felt like she could be herself when playing with the young children who lived in the camp. Even in the middle of a transient Displaced Persons camp, she preferred the company of small children to their parents, who were intimidating and sophisticated.

It was a sunny day in September. Tasya was sitting on the edge of the football field waiting for a match that was scheduled to be held before dinner preparations in the kitchen. She held one of the many young girls in her lap. They watched the team of Ukrainians play against British soldiers. As one of the players on the Ukrainian team jogged to the sidelines to strip off his shirt, Tasya found herself staring. He was obviously still recovering from time spent in starvation conditions. His ribs stuck out and his knees looked knobby, but beyond the slimness, she could see the lean build of muscle and a powerful edge to him. Tasya blushed and looked away when he caught her looking.

A few days later, as Tasya helped to serve the midday meal of soup, she looked up, and straight into the eyes of the man from the sports field.

"Ah, it's you!" He said, flashing her a wide grin. "You were watching the match a few days ago, yes? With your daughter?"

Tasya thought her heart had stopped. She tried to return the friendly greeting, but felt like she was making more of a grimace than a smile. "No, ah, that girl isn't my daughter. I just spend time with her now and again."

"Ah, good. I was worried that you were taken," he said, continuing his grin.

Tasya was now positive that her heart had completely stopped beating. She worried that she would soon faint if it didn't start back up again. She took a small gasp for air, and realized that she had been holding her breath. She struggled for something clever to say. "I'm far too young for a daughter that age," she then added a forced giggle, regretting it instantly as it came out sounding like a donkey.

"Since you are too young for children, and are free, why don't you spend a bit of time with me, this afternoon? How does that sound?" He took back the bowl that Tasya had filled to the brim, and tried to balance it on a chunk of bread he had in his hand.

Tasya blinked rapidly. No boy, much less a man, had ever shown her even one iota of interest. Even in the camp, where it seemed as if spring fever had attacked everyone else, Tasya remained solitary. She nodded, speechless.

As he walked away with his soup, the man turned back over his shoulder and called out, "My name is Stephan, by the way!"

That same afternoon, with the late fall sun warming their backs, Tasya and Stephan sat on the edge of the sports field. They talked about everything from their homes to what brought them to Münster-Lager. Stephan smoked cigarette after cigarette, always offering Tasya one before he lit up. She finally accepted after being offered a half-dozen times, coughing till her lungs nearly came out with her first full inhale of smoke. Stephan roared with glee as Tasya coughed and coughed. Once she recovered, Tasya began to laugh herself. Soon, both were chuckling in the warm autumn sunshine. Tasya silently could not recall the last time was that she had felt so happy.

Recovered, they watched a group of women who looked to be in their mid-twenties, corralling a group of children towards the community center. Soon after, the sounds of a children's choir practice floated through the air.

"Look at those women." Tasya said. She had been so nervous that she had hardly said a word the entire afternoon. "They are so organized, so driven to create a community here in the camp. I admire them."

"That's one thing you can say about Ukrainians – they love to organize themselves into groups and committees! It seems like everyone here is part of five organizations," Stephan nudged Tasya playfully with his elbow, grinning. "Me? I like to stick to one, maybe two. One being the sports club, of course."

"Were you a part of many organizations at home, in Peremyshyl?" Tasya was eager to show Stephan that she remembered the details of his life.

"Nah. I left that stuff up to my father. He was a teacher. I stuck to sports and left home to join the army as early as I could."

Tasya learned over the course of the afternoon that Stephan was older – much older – than she was. He was born a full decade before, and his maturity level reflected it. The age gap was further made evident when Tasya learned that Stephan had been in the Polish army even before war broke out, and that he had been captured in the early months of war between Poland and Germany.

"See that?" Stephan asked, rolling up his right arm shirtsleeve. "That's my prisoner number. Buchenwald. Ever heard of it?" There was a crudely stenciled six-digit number tattooed on the front part of Stephan's forearm, reading '83439'.

"No. I've learned about the death camps since coming here to Münster-Lager, but I hadn't heard of that one."

"Your factory was bad, but I'm certain that Buchenwald was worse."

Tasya nodded. Compared to the men from the now-notorious death and work camps, she felt as if she had been sheltered and coddled during the war.

"I was in a prisoner of war camp for a year or so, before I got transferred to Dora, Bergen, and then Buchenwald. I was meant to be worked to death, not gassed like the Jews there. The Jews went quickly once they arrived. Prisoners of war seemed to last longer."

Tasya didn't know how to respond; she never did when hearing about these stories.

"Now they want to send us back to the Ruskies? Can you believe that?" Stephan stood up, gesturing in a general direction around the camp. "I survived this long, and now the British want us to be repatriated back to the Soviet Union."

Reaching down, and helping Tasya get to her feet, he grinned again and his anger faded as quickly as it had arisen. "They can forget it. I'm a follower of Bandera. We stand for self-determination. We fight against the Russians! I am Ukrainian, not a Soviet."

Stephan pulled Tasya along and they fell into an easy stride together. Tasya's heart skipped a beat when Stephan reached out and held her hand as they strolled around the perimeter fence. If she had been unsure of his feelings until then, Stephan had made them clear.

III.

Over the winter months at Münster-Lager, Tasya and Stephan began to spend more time together when Tasya wasn't busy in the kitchen. He was her first kiss. With a beating heart, she let him take her to a newly empty barrack, and there, they first made love.

Emboldened by her budding romance with Stephan, Tasya made an effort to become more oriented to the other adults. Gathered around the tables of the community hall late into the night, there were lively discussions about politics and of Ukrainian identity. While the others argued, yelled, laughed and drank German beer, Tasya quietly tucked herself into Stephan's side. She was a country mouse, unable to join in, invisible to the others. The more Tasya spent time away from the kitchen and children, the more she realized that she had little experience in the skills she needed to thrive in the social aspects of camp life.

The most heated discussions occurred when Stephan and his friends debated the Ukrainian identity in their Russian-controlled homeland. Both men and women argued about the changes that needed to be made. Before these talks, Tasya had no idea that this type of dialog about identity even existed; she had certainly never heard her mother or sister speak in such a way. Too old to be considered a child, and too young and inexperienced to understand the intricacies of politics, Tasya floated uncomfortably in a half-existence within the Ukrainian camp community, tagging along, silently absorbing everything about her homeland that she could. She sat next to Stephan as he laughed and argued with immense vivacity during the charged political debates. Slowly, she gained confidence in herself, and found that the odd time she was able to contribute to the charged discussions that were going on all over the camp. The few times that she did speak up, she felt tremendously proud of herself, and watched as Stephan beamed.

"I just can't figure out where I fit in!" Tasya cried to Stephan one cold spring evening. They were huddled by a fire in one of the common-area barracks. It had taken days to convince Stephan to spend an evening alone with her, away from his huge group of friends.

"What do you mean? You fit right here, with me," Stephan said as he pulled Tasya over to him and gave her a squeeze.

"You know that's not what I mean. And anyway, I'm getting tired of being your lap dog, Stephan. None of your friends care about me or my opinions. Why am I even bothering to come with you to your discussions?"

"You have opinions?" Stephan teased. When Tasya got up to walk away, he pulled her back into his arms. "So you aren't that interested in the same politics that I am. So what? Figure it out. What are you interested in?" Stephan asked.

"I don't know! That's the whole problem. Compared to others here, I barely went to school. Everyone else here had lessons in this and that, but I did what every other child in Horayetz did with their free time…I played outside." Tasya wanted to cry.

"Well, did you play some sort of instrument? What books did you read?" Stephan asked when Tasya shook her head. He was gentle, but she shot him a dirty look anyway. "No? There must have been something that you learned that you can find in common with the other girls. Women."

Tasya desperately wanted to hit Stephan.

"The only thing that I learned was how to embroider. A little."

"There! Now, why didn't you say so?"

"Because, who cares about embroidery in the middle of a camp? Look around you, Stephan. All the women are busy, organizing this, organizing that, teaching, arguing. I just don't fit in."

"Then do something about it, Tasya. Stop acting like a child, and take responsibility for your own life!" This time, when Tasya stood up, Stephan didn't pull her back towards him.

As Tasya stormed away from Stephan, back to the women's barracks, she knew he was right. She realized that she had not only been silent through camp discussions, but she had been idly waiting for something to come by and save her from her own uncertain destiny.

The next day, Stephan arrived at the periphery of the women's camp, a small and sad-looking bunch of spring flowers in his hands.

"I have an idea, my Tasya," he said, handing over both the flowers and a yellow flyer. Tasya slowly read the Ukrainian text. The British were offering their own classes to the adults of the camp. Among the courses listed: English language, arithmetic, history, and geography.

"School?" Tasya said as she handed the flyer back to Stephan. "I haven't been in school for years. I don't think this is for me."

"Oh come now, Tasya! At least try it. Take the courses, then maybe you can teach me and my friends a thing or two." Stephan laughed.

With immense nervousness, Tasya started classes the next week. She quickly found that she didn't particularly like any of the courses, except for English. Much to her own surprise, she *loved* English.

Münster-Lager was still administered by the British army, and whenever she could, Tasya listened in on their conversations. The soft pronunciation of vowels, and the ease with which the soldiers conducted camp business in the exotic language was fascinating to her. They were in Germany, but English was the universal language for post-war business. She was curious, and thrilled to be able to take a class to learn a language that might eventually give her status and power. There was the language of inside the camp – Ukrainian, and then, there was the language of the world – English. If the language of oppression and the devil was German, Tasya decided to go into the world of the British camp administrators, running into the arms of the language like a lost child.

One afternoon in April of 1946, Tasya huddled over a discarded London *Daily Mail* newspaper in the women's barrack. She was reading about India; slowly, carefully, sounding out the words, trying to understand their meanings. She jumped when she felt a tap on her shoulder.

"Tasya?" A woman stood next to her. Tasya recognized her as one of the women who was constantly working and organizing the schools for the children. Tasya nodded.

"Hello, my name is Olia. You look familiar now that I see you in person."

Tasya looked at her, confused.

The woman continued, "I hear that you can embroider. Is that true?"

Tasya nodded again.

"Are you any good?"

Tasya nodded a third time.

"Can you speak?" The woman asked, laughing. "Stephan didn't say that you were mute."

"Sorry. Yes. No. I can speak. And, yes, I can embroider. I used to at home, anyway."

"Wonderful! There are many women here who can do it, but they seem to lack…talent. We need many embroidered shirts for our boys, and blouses for the girls, but most of us are too busy to dedicate the hours necessary. Not to mention, we don't have very many patterns with us here! Oh, also, can you teach it?"

The woman pulled out a chair and sat at Tasya's table. Tasya had never had such attention from any of the women of the barrack. Olia must have mistaken Tasya's stupefied silence for reluctance.

"Listen, Tasya. This is a very important job." Olia placed her hand on Tasya's sleeve and squeezed. "We are putting together a campaign to promote Ukrainian culture in Germany and Austria through an exhibit of folk art. Organizing displays of artifacts of Ukrainian culture, showing different regional costumes, and providing lessons on how to incorporate the styles of Ukrainian culture into the contemporary clothing that we have on hand."

Flattered by the attention, Tasya barely let Olia finish before she blurted, "Of course I'll help!"

The act of embroidering allowed Tasya to escape from camp life. She traveled back to her childhood, when her mother would sit near, patiently teaching her how to use a simple cross stitch to create intricate and detailed patterns. In Horayetz, the style that was favoured by most of the women was traditional to the region of geometric ornament and used sharp contrasts of colour. In the camp, Tasya preferred to keep her use of colours simple, sticking mainly to a pleasing combination of red and black threads against a plain white fabric. She loved the clear lines, the repetition of patterns, and how putting together seemingly mismatching patterns could result in a garment that once worn, was striking.

After Tasya taught other women to master her patterns of choice, they began to request ornamental roses and other expressions of plant life. Women, especially from the Poltava region of Ukraine, also requested that she use other colours like blue, green, or a pale palette.

As Ukrainians left the camps to scatter around the globe, there was a desire to keep traditional patterns alive. Some of the women who organized the folk exhibit encouraged Tasya to perfect her patterns on paper. Curious of the project that suddenly mobilized many of the women of the camp, the British administrators were quite taken aback at the beauty of embroidery, and the skill that Tasya possessed. She blushed when Ukrainians complimented her work, but even more so when the British officers praised her. Through the act of remembering and documenting her own culture, Tasya's strength and resolve improved. For the first time in her life, Tasya held a small degree of power.

IV.

How many is this, Tasya?"

"The seventh. This week."

"Seven! Is that a new record for us?"

"No. Two weeks ago, we went to eight."

Tasya watched Stephan straighten his tie. A bead of sweat pooled at his temple and eventually broke away to run down his cheek. It was stifling in the common-area barrack, yet it wasn't even yet ten a.m.

"Is there a lunch after this one?" he asked. Tasya shook her head.

Stephan stopped fussing with his tie.

"What's wrong? Why are you staring?"

Tasya smiled and blushed. The way sweat ran down his face. The way he made her laugh. The way he held her tight in his arms. She loved him.

"No party, then? That's a shame," he said. "When you and I get married, Tasya, a party is a must!" Tasya giggled. He hadn't even officially asked her.

Nearly all the young people in the camp had coupled off, getting married as quickly as possible. There was a makeshift Ukrainian Orthodox church set up in a spare barrack. Religious wedding ceremonies were held there. For those who turned up their noses at the notion of being married by an Orthodox priest, a German justice of the peace came into the camp five days a week to perform the ceremonies. Everything was paid for by the British government. The marriage boom that began in the spring had resulted in a rash of pregnancies.

Even though it was already hot that July morning, Stephan had his only jacket with him, thrown over the back of the chair, ready to be worn with mismatched trousers. As Tasya picked it up, ready to help him put it on, she caught a glimpse of a familiar white package.

"No, Stephan! You can't do your selling at the ceremony," Tasya said, pulling out three packages of US-issued cigarettes.

"What, Tasya? It's new customers! How else am I to make us money?" Stephan snatched the packages back from Tasya and glanced around before stuffing them into his trouser pockets.

Illicit goods were a booming marketplace in the camp. Cigarettes, liquor, women's stockings, cosmetics. Even some caviar stolen from a General's stash had made the rounds in the cramped barracks. Selling these goods was dangerous and against camp laws. Stephan didn't care. Once he had set his mind, Tasya was unable to change it.

Stephan planted a kiss on the top of Tasya's head, then picked her up and spun her around until she laughed.

"I'm not that easy, Stephan. No selling. Not today."

"*Ach*, fine! Not today, my darling." He kissed her intensely on the lips.

Only a week later, Tasya returned to the woman's barracks from a visit to the camp doctor to receive word that the British authorities had arrested Stephan. Tasya's hands shook and she was heady with rage when she attempted to see him in the camp prison barrack. Looking apologetic, the British soldier told her that Stephan was sentenced to solitary confinement for two weeks.

When Stephan emerged from the prison barrack one warm, fine day in August 1946, Tasya was waiting for him. She had her arms crossed in front of her chest, ready to explode. He came out squinting and grinning. He grabbed Tasya for an embrace. She pulled back and hit his chest as hard as she could with both her fists.

"Ow! Now that's no way to greet me!" Stephan laughed.

"I told you that you would get caught! But, no, you didn't listen to me, and had to be locked away for two weeks!"

"Aw, it wasn't that bad, Tasya. I've been through worse. At least they didn't get my money, plus, it was a nice break from your nagging." Stephan playfully ducked away.

"Stop goofing around, you fool. There's something I have to tell you. I've had to wait two weeks."

"That you missed me? Can't live without me?"

Tasya looked at Stephan with tears in her eyes.

"No. I'm pregnant."

Her long and eloquent speech was out the window. Instead, she burst into tears.

Stephan's face went through a range of emotion. He looked stunned and was silent for once.

Then, confused.

A smile began to grow across his entire face. He let out a long whoop of joy as he jumped up in the air. He embraced Tasya a second time. He let her go as quickly. He reached for her hands and held them tight.

"How long have you known for?"

"For two weeks I said! The very same day that you were caught."

"And you are sure?"

"I went to see the doctor when I suspected, and he said that I'm about three months along."

Counting quickly on his fingers, Stephan looked up, "February?"

"February." Tasya nodded, her lip trembling.

"This is great news!" Stephan whooped again.

With much seriousness, he knelt down on one knee, holding Tasya's two hands firmly in his. He looked up at her.

"Anastasia. Will you marry me?"

A weight lifted from Tasya's shoulders. Something within her broke, another swelling of love, and even relief. Still crying, she nodded her yes.

V.

"Me, married at the Orthodox church? Have you gone mad?"

"I know it's not ideal, but we need to be married by a priest. What are you thinking to do, get married by that German *chaplain*?"

It was a week after his release from the camp prison when Tasya and Stephan had their first major argument. Stephan had exploded at the very mention of the Orthodox Church for their marriage.

"I'm not going to be married by a priest who is practically Russian, and who doesn't even believe in the authority of the Pope! Tasya, how do we know that he's not a member of the Communist Party?"

Tasya rolled her eyes.

"If he's a Communist then why would he be here, in a camp full of political refugees?"

"I'm not going to do it, so you can forget about it. It's the chaplain, or we aren't going to get married, and that's that."

At first, Stephan's explosions of anger had caused the blood in Tasya's veins to run as cold as ice water. Stephan's moods swung as wide as a pendulum; however, with some effort and finesse, they could be controlled.

"Alright, just calm down. Our priority is getting married, and if you want to be married by a chaplain, then so be it. I won't have a real wedding." Tasya turned away, angry at the tears of frustration that welled up.

"You'll see, it's better." Stephan softened and took her into his arms. "We'll have a real church ceremony as soon as we can get to a Ukrainian Catholic church. I promise."

Their marriage was witnessed by two of Stephan's friends from Peremyshyl, a couple who were Stephan's age, already married for ten years. Initially, they took Tasya's side in the ceremony battle, but Stephan eventually also wore them down with his stamping, child-like tantrums.

After a small celebratory party in a café in Soltau, Tasya and Stephan spent their first married night together in a cramped and dusty room in a local Inn. It was Stephan's idea of a wedding gift to his new bride. He paid at the front desk with a wad of crumpled and dirty American bills. Tasya looked at the pile warily, but the clerk was overjoyed to accept the hard currency. The entire day – the ceremony, the small luncheon party, the shabby Inn with worn-out furnishings - wasn't ideal. Her dream wedding would have been in a proper church, with a priest. A proper party that lasted well into the night, spilling out onto the dark village roads, like in Horayetz. Though it wasn't ideal, Tasya was happy.

Lying in the semi-darkness of the room, light coming in from the glow of the street-lamps between the shutters, Tasya relaxed as Stephan stroked her belly. He was there to support her and the baby. For the first time in many years, she could rely on someone besides herself.

Stephan cleared his throat, shifting awkwardly.

"I've been thinking about something. Your name." Tasya turned to look at his face. He looked as nervous as he sounded.

"What about my name? I'm going to change my last name to Bykovsky with the camp authorities tomorrow," Tasya walked her fingers over Stephan's hand playfully, "unless you don't want me to."

"Of course I want you to take my name," Stephan said, as he gently pushed Tasya's hand away and sat up. "No, it's not about my last name. I want to talk to you about your name. Tasya, I mean."

"What about it? I can't change that, if that's what you mean."

"I don't want you to change it, exactly; I just want to call you by something different. Well, uh, you know that my oldest sister also goes by Tasya, and I've been finding it...strange to call my wife by the same name."

Tasya also sat up.

"What? You knew that was my name when you first met me."

"Of course. It's just that I've been thinking, and I want to be able to call you by your full name, not that nickname. I want to call you Anastasia. Not Tasya."

Tasya leaned back on the flat pillows of the bed. A flare of anger came up from deep within her, but then just as quickly, it died down. Her name was her identity. She couldn't change it, could she? Tasya wasn't her true given name, but it was a nickname that everyone called her. It was her diminutive name of affection, a gift from her father. On the other hand, Anastasia was more sophisticated, more adult. Perhaps it was more suitable for a woman who was about to become a mother.

"I'm not sure," she said, looking Stephan directly in the eyes. "It's my name, after all, my identifier. It's practically the only thing that I have left of my old life."

"Yes, but, it would be something new! Something more grown up. Think about when we go to buy our wedding bands. I can go to the jeweler and say, 'Now here is my beautiful wife, the mother of my son, Anastasia.' It sounds so nice!" He winked at her.

The next day, Stephan announced around the camp that they were officially married, and that Tasya now wanted to be called Anastasia. For her, it had become a gratifying change. Like a lizard shedding its old dead layers of skin, Anastasia was stepping into her new life as wife and mother. The scared and lonely girl from a small village in backwater Ukraine was gone.

VI.

Newly wedded Anastasia and Stephan moved to the barracks reserved for married couples. Anastasia was dismayed to find that even there, there was no greater amount of privacy than accommodations reserved for single persons. Couples had an entire bunk bed set to themselves, but there were as many people squished into a single barrack building with the only semblance of privacy a draped blanket.

Adjusting to life in the couples barrack with Stephan was more difficult than Anastasia had imagined. Living in close quarters with other couples and new families was exhausting. At night, dozens of times, the sounds of a baby wailing would punctuate Anastasia's sleep.

Worse than the crying, the silence. Anastasia was mortified in the quiet to hear the strains of couples' lovemaking in the bunks around her. She and Stephan had always snuck off to empty barracks or into the forest when they wanted to be alone. Stephan slept like a rock, and his snoring was the other constant but more welcome disturbance in her attempts to get a good sleep at night.

As the autumn season passed, boredom among the refugees grew to new heights. Political rhetoric was at an all-time high, and those with liberal ideologies or even those with no ideology at all, found themselves to be the target of right-leaning bullies.

By January of 1947, the British and Americans seemed to lose their enthusiasm for repatriation to home countries, and the talk turned to the labour shortages in Allied nations. With post-war economies in the West booming, displaced persons were welcomed to other countries as citizens, starting what the British dubbed 'resettlement fever'.

Stephan grew increasingly bored in the camp. He joined the Organization of Ukrainian Nationalists, a group gaining popularity in the camp with its mandate to protect the Ukrainian population against oppression from the Polish and Russian governments. Even as the threat of Soviet repatriation diminished, the group's appeal to the refugees grew by leaps and bounds. Stephan's involvement made Anastasia nervous. He went to meetings, and came back to their barrack keyed up and full of radical nationalism.

"Even Eleanor Roosevelt is against our repatriation to Soviet territories! Numbers have dropped for the Soviets, and they are getting more and more desperate to trick people into 'coming home.' Eleanor Roosevelt agrees with us!"

"Who?" Anastasia asked, irritated that Stephan had woken her up. "Is she Jewish?"

"I don't know! It doesn't matter who she is, except that she's important." Stephan bellowed.

"Stop shouting at me!" Anastasia yelled, rolling over on the narrow bed they shared, uncomfortable, bloated, and impatient for the baby to finally be born.

When it was Anastasia's time, she found labour painful. Flashes of red appeared before her eyes as she pushed the baby out. As she looked down at her daughter nestled in her arms, she decided that while giving birth was painful, yes, it was certainly not the most difficult thing that she'd had to endure in the world. Her place as mother, wife, and the matriarch of a small family was established.

While Anastasia took her first nap after the birth, Stephan insisted that the nurse leave the baby with him. When she awoke, she watched Stephan as he made cooing sounds and silly faces, not caring that the baby girl could not yet see him, nor that every woman in the hospital dorm room was laughing quietly at him.

The two weeks in the hospital were like a vacation for Anastasia. She was waited on hand and foot by the nurses and doting Stephan. Assisted by Stephan on her right arm, and a lovely German nurse on her left, Anastasia took her first steps across the cold beige tiles of the hospital floor with the unsteadiness and caution of a baby deer. She was practically having to learn how to walk all over again.

Still in the hospital, they played with the new baby during the day, with Stephan returning to the camp each night. He returned early each morning, ready to give his undivided attention to his small family.

"Anastasia, I've been thinking about what we should do next, where we should go."

She nodded. She had been considering the same thing.

"What do you think of this resettlement?"

Anastasia fiddled nervously with the baby's blanket and looked at her daughter's tiny fingers curled around her own. Baby Alya.

"Anastasia?" Stephan reached down to stroke the baby's cheek. "I know you haven't been sure what to do either, but now that Alya is here, it's time we made a decision. For us. All of us."

Anastasia knew he was right. She had been putting off any decision about the future, stalling Stephan, and locking the options away in a cabinet in her mind. She hadn't been ready to truly consider anything. She had been biding her time, waiting for a sign. Something. Word from her mother, or sister. Word from Herr or Frau Bamm. She had been waiting for word from anyone in the world to show that they cared about her.

Anastasia nodded. "Yes, it's time. Everyone is moving on to Allied countries and starting over again."

"That's right." Stephan grabbed a hold of Anastasia's hand. "I know you've been dragging your feet, waiting to make a decision. But, my darling, I don't know if you'll ever be able to find your mother again. I'm sorry."

Anastasia began to cry. She had carried in her heart the knowledge that she might never see her family again, but had been too terrified of the truth to really face it.

"We are your family now. The baby and I. Anastasia, I have to get out of this place. Everywhere I look, I can still sense those death camps all around me, like they have their own stink that never goes away."

"Then, what?" Anastasia asked through her tears.

Stephan grinned, "I have an idea! I was thinking that I would write a letter to my sister Tania in Canada. She's as red a communist as they come, but Canada might be a good choice for us. The Ukrainian communities are strong, and the country is crying for hard workers."

Anastasia knew as soon as she heard the name, that Canada was the right choice.

"They speak English there, yes?"

VII.

"It's here! Her reply!" Stephan burst through the thin blanket that surrounded their bunk. He ripped open the envelope with trembling hands as Anastasia watched with anticipation. He read the first few lines of the letter from his sister to himself. His eyes turned from sparkling with excitement, to dark and confused.

"The stupid sons-of-bitches! May they rot in hell!" he yelled.

"Hush! You'll wake the baby," Anastasia scolded. Their daughter was nestled in her arms, napping with the great peace that only babies can.

"Tania writes that the Communist Party in Russia needs us." Stephan scanned the letter further. "Her idiot husband agrees that we should forget about Canada and return to our motherland to help in promoting the cause. Unbelievable." Stephan spat on the wooden floor in rage, again cursing his sister and her husband.

Anastasia looked into the envelope and saw something else inside. She reached in a pulled out a fifty-dollar American bill.

"This is what is supposed to help us, to help me, her brother?" Stephan snapped up the bill. He looked like he was going to tear it apart. Anastasia grabbed it back from his hands.

"You might be angry, but don't be a fool, too," she chided. "We need this. Think of how it can help us, wherever we may end up." She tucked the precious currency away under her pillow for safekeeping.

Floating in a sea of other increasingly desperate refugees, Stephan and Anastasia didn't give up on their plan to resettle. Stephan stepped up his efforts with the OUN. Anastasia was embarrassed to see him take his frustration out on other men from Western Ukraine who refused to join their cause, bullying them until they joined in.

Anastasia focused her efforts on helping other refugees who were actually from the eastern reaches of Ukraine. These individuals, fearing repatriation, had destroyed their documentation, posing as Ukrainians from the west. To assist in the machinery of forged documents and screenings performed by the British and Americans, Anastasia tried to help these nervous people by tutoring them in a variety of aspects of daily life in Horayetz. Anastasia coached them in Horayetz street names, church names, describing what the landscape looked like, and sharing plausible childhood memories.

The screening process for these Ukrainian refugees was stressful and traumatic; Anastasia thanked God several times that she had legitimate German paperwork issued after her liberation showing that she was from inter-war Poland and that she did not have to attempt to create an alternative identity for either herself or Stephan. The refugees never knew what questions would be asked during the screenings, and the Americans often allowed the presence of Soviet officials. Ukrainians from various groups who usually did not get along bonded over the efforts to get past the screening committee. Stephan learned to respect and use passive resistance as a result of this process, and Anastasia became better versed in camp and Ukrainian politics. Through the camp grapevines, they heard how frustration and anger mounted within the refugee groups all over Germany and Austria. In another German camp, one Soviet officer was even stoned by an enraged mob.

Within the uneasiness of camp life, Stephan and Anastasia nurtured and cared for their small family. They relished the opportunity to dote on their baby Alya. They took the time to rejoice in her every giggle, every cry, and watched her intensely as she slept, marveling at the rise and fall of her small chest. All around them, family life flourished in the camp. Most single people had now married, and most married couples had at least one infant in their arms. Anastasia waited as patiently as she could, wishing for news, any news, that would give her direction.

VIII.

The summer of 1947 came, and Anastasia was still not able to get the idea of Canada out of her mind. Canada was a compelling dream. More terrifying was leaving Europe, and her mother and sister, forever. Wherever they were, there would be an even smaller chance of ever finding them. Anastasia kept her dreams privately in her heart, hoping that Stephan would find somewhere for them to settle. One summer day, Anastasia and baby Alya were playing outside the barrack. Stephan rushed over to them.

"Anastasia, I have a plan!" He threw himself onto the grass, tickling Alya. "There are finally agents coming to the camp, looking for workers."

"Oh, yes. Where from?"

"England...and Canada!"

"Canada," Anastasia said softly, looking at the wispy downy hair on the top of her daughter's head.

"I'll see what they are offering, and then we will make a decision. Looks like we might be going somewhere English-speaking for you, my darling! Plus, Canada loves Ukrainians!"

"Really? Why is that?"

"Well, you know, it's all about politics!" Stephan jumped up and waved his hands around. "Ukrainians have strong communities already established there, plus they love how much we hate the Commies! It's a good way to bond – hate of those Ruskie dogs." Stephan grinned; it made Anastasia happy to see it.

A few weeks later, Stephan, Anastasia, and Alya joined a queue to speak with and hear presentations from the three company agents who had traveled from Canada to recruit workers. Transatlantic passage to Canada would be paid for by the International Relief Organization, and then from port to place of employment, the passage would be paid for by the company. Stephan would be required to sign a contract that he would give ten months employment at Canadian prevailing wages. In order to qualify, men had to be within a certain age bracket, qualify for an industry health certificate, and also pass the company's medical examination. Stephan was cleared that very same day by a British doctor for employment in both the lumber and mining industries.

Discussing their options that night in bed, Anastasia knew exactly which choice she wanted to take. "The lumber industry looks to be a lot further away from any major cities than the mining does."

Stephan made a face. "Mining? That's dirty, not to mention dangerous work. I would rather work outside in the fresh air, not underground like a mole."

Going to Canada only to be isolated in a lumber village sounded to Anastasia as bad as a sentence in Siberia. Over the next few days, they fought over their choices: Stephan threw tantrums, yelled, and made a fuss. Anastasia pouted and went silent around him, keeping Alya to herself.

After three days of arguing, Anastasia decided to play her most valuable card. She had waited to use it. She cried in their bunk until Stephan finally asked her what was wrong.

"Oh, it's just that I've had to change so much for you! My name. I've given you a beautiful daughter..." Anastasia peered at Stephan through her tears. "And the worst? We were married outside the church!" Anastasia sobbed loudly.

Stephan looked around as the few remaining couples in the barrack watched them.

"Ok, Anastasia. Fine, fine. Just stop this carrying on."

"You'll do the mining?"

Stephan exhaled.

"Fine. Mining. We'll be going to Sudbury, then."

"Sudbury," Anastasia said dreamily, pleased with the soft sounds the word made as it rolled off her tongue. "That sounds like a very nice place."

Stephan left Münster-Lager on the morning of September 15th, 1947. Both he and Anastasia cried. For the first time, they would truly be apart, half a world away from each other. Like every other male who signed a contract of employment with a Canadian firm, Stephan would be traveling to Canada first, saving up money and sending for Anastasia and Alya as soon as he could. Anastasia was terrified that something would happen to Stephan, and that she would again be alone. As the men gradually disappeared from the camp, the women embraced each other. For the few remaining at Münster-Lager, camaraderie and support was never more valued by the women of the camp, no matter what their social status.

Anastasia received her first letter from Stephan in December, as good a Christmas present as she could wish for. Another winter passed. By April, he was able to afford a third-class ticket for his wife.

In June 1948, the USS Eisenhower set sail from Hamburg. Anastasia found comfort with several young women and children from the same barrack. They arrived in Halifax harbour on the night of July 1st, 1948, with the women huddled together on the deck of the ship, toddlers in arms. With tears in their eyes, they looked up at the pops of white and red fireworks that welcomed them to Canada.

TORONTO

1970

I.

Alya crunched her way through the fallen oak leaves carpeting the sidewalk of Shaw Street. The early October sun was still warm on her back. Ducking down, she didn't break her stride as she scooped up a perfectly formed and blazing-orange oak leaf. Walking the entire way home from the Moderns Building at The University of Toronto was unusual, but Alya had energy to burn. Her mind was open, ready to absorb the beauty of the city all around her. Her usual route home via the crowded subway hadn't felt right, so she walked. Plus, she saved herself the fifteen cent fare.

Only a month into her fourth year at the university, she was thoroughly enjoying every minute of her classes that semester. No longer a stranger in huge survey classes of five hundred students, Alya had found her place among her classmates in small history seminar-style classes. Today, it had been the 'Europe and the Post War Economy' seminar. Her good mood for the afternoon had been cemented when Professor Moores returned her paper with a nearly perfect grade. She had worked diligently researching the resettlement of Jews in the five years immediately after the Reich collapsed. Tucking the paper carefully into her backpack at the end of the seminar, she couldn't wait to show her good mark to her parents. They were always so suspicious of her choice of academic major. History was too vague a topic of study – what kind of career could it possibly lead to? Alya's parents themselves had been resettled to Canada by the British. If she showed them her paper, they would surely realize that history is as real as it gets. Totally legitimate and a good choice.

Was it her imagination, or had Dr. Moores been much more friendly with Alya than the others in the class?

She was lucky to have such a popular professor to guide her seminar. Not yet forty, the Doctor of Philosophy in History was closer to her mother's age than Alya's, a fact that she could hardly fathom. Closer in age, perhaps, but a world apart. Tall, with shaggy blonde hair and a full beard, Dr. Moores was often in the student's lounge, coffee cup in hand, spending time with the upperclassmen. The first time that Alya spotted him there, relaxing, laughing, totally fitting in with his corduroy blazer and jeans, her heart nearly stopped. He was at The U of T on a temporary stint, teaching a small specialty seminar class of only twelve students. Every single one of his students was female. Even though he was drastically outnumbered by gender, Dr. Moores never showed any signs of discomfort. Recently, Alya's daydreams were focused squarely on her young professor. She imagined the two of them going out for beers after the last class, exchanging phone numbers. Or him calling, asking her to join him at the poetry reading of a friend, or to go and see a new exhibit at the Royal Ontario Museum.

Her entire life, Alya had sailed with ease through school. From her first days in her kindergarten class in Sudbury, she had proven herself to be a quiet but perceptive pupil.

"What a bright little girl you have here," her grade one teacher, Mrs. Smith, proclaimed to her mother. Anastasia nodded her head and smiled, but hadn't said a word.

The teachers did most of the talking at parent-teacher conferences, with Alya translating as necessary. Even in Toronto, at Harbord Collegiate, Alya studied regularily. Most of her classmates went straight to work after high school was complete, but Alya was a shining star.

Opening the rickety wire gate to the path that led up to her house, Alya was careful not to trip on the uneven concrete walk. Her father had been promising to demolish it and pour a new walkway for the entire seventeen years that they had lived in the house on Shaw Street. She took a detour off the crumbling concrete to the left, onto the well-worn dirt path snaking through the long grass to the side door. Using her entire body weight, Alya pushed to open the wood door that was perpetually swollen too big to fit the frame. She half-fell, half-stumbled into the tiny side landing, dragging a pile of leaves with her.

As she regained her balance, Alya watched her mother from the corner of her eye, leaning in, cigarette between her lips.

"Why can't you be more lady-like?" Her mother asked in Ukrainian.

Alya heard clucking sounds.

"You've brought in half the leaves from the yard with you!"

"I'm cleaning them up," Alya muttered back in Ukrainian as she stooped down, her backpack sliding towards her head, setting her off balance.

She peeked up the short flight of stairs that led into the main area of the old house. Alya caught a glimpse of one of her mother's famous looks of disapproval – the one that her brother had dubbed 'Platypus Face'. Anastasia wore her daily uniform: cooking dress and apron, topped off by reading glasses barely hanging onto the tip of her nose. She looked to be elbow-deep in dinner preparations, holding a potato in one hand and peeler in the other. While the reading glasses were not necessary for cooking, Anastasia liked to read while preparing the food. Books, newspapers, flyers, leaflets, information sheets from the local Ukrainian organizations; any form of literature was fair game while dinner was prepared. English or Ukrainian.

Alya shrugged off her jacket and hung it on top of the mountain of coats already occupying the four hooks at the side of the landing. She tried to place her army boots together neatly, but the pile of shoes in the cubby under the hooks made neatness a losing battle. Each family member had taken at least one fall from a stray shoe that found its way out of the mess. One time her father tumbled all the way down the steep stairs to the basement floor.

After getting her things organized, Alya ran up into the kitchen, where she plunked her book bag down on an empty chair.

"Ma? Guess what? I got a perfect grade on a paper today!" Alya said as she retrieved the copy of her paper from the book bag and waved it in the air. Turning from the stove where she had resumed her peeling, Anastasia peered over her glasses.

"Oh yes? That's good, Alya. Keep it up." Anastasia turned her attention back to the potatoes, taking a drag of the cigarette that sat burning on a dish.

Alya came up beside her mother, and shoved the paper between her mother's head and the boiling pot of water on the stove.

"See? I'll read it to you: *You showed great maturity in the analysis of the Jewish condition post-war, and should pursue this topic in greater depth.*"

Anastasia cut the potatoes into tiny chunks, one landing directly on

Dr. Moores' comments. Hardly missing a beat, Anastasia picked up the stray piece and tossed it into the water. Its moisture left a smudge of red ink.

"*Nu*. As I said, that's great, Alya. You can tell me more about it when your tato gets home, and we sit down to eat."

Anastasia planted a quick and dry kiss on Alya's forehead. This was the usual sign to get out of her mother's way.

Alya grabbed her book bag, stomped down the hallway and up the narrow staircase to her second floor bedroom. Each time she brought home a test or assignment with a good mark, it was the same. Indifference. Her parents never really bothered her too much about school. They were happy that she was doing well, but didn't do much to encourage her like the parents of the Canadian kids did.

With little education from a foreign country, Alya's parents had always worked manual jobs – cleaning houses, offices, doing manual factory work. If she got a B in a class, or A+, the reaction from her parents was always the same – measured satisfaction. Alya knew that her parents understood the difference between achieving an A and a B in school, but they didn't show it to her. A perfect grade or something less, it was all the same. Not like with Henry's parents.

Henry and Alya became friends the first week of ninth grade. Anastasia was less than thrilled that Alya was spending so much time with a boy, and constantly tried to sabotage their friendship. She would 'forget' to pass along telephone messages from Henry, and required that Alya be home by 5p.m. for dinner every single evening. By eleventh grade, Anastasia had softened in small ways. She began to let Henry stay for dinner the odd night, and quietly served the pair homemade snacks as they studied at the dining room table. As Alya watched her mother plunk down plates of honey cookies and glasses of milk, she smirked. Her mother had guessed what Alya knew all along – Henry wasn't entirely interested in girls. Not in that way, anyway.

Henry's parents, on the other hand, were enthusiastically supportive of his friendship with Alya. At their house, Henry's mother, Mrs. Jones, or Jane to her husband, invited her to stay for dinner. Of course, on most occasions Alya was not permitted to do so. The few times that Anastasia let her stay, Alya had been ecstatic to try the new and exotic foods (like beans on toast!) that the Jones's regularly ate.

Alya spent hours staring at the dozens of Jones family photos on display in the house. Every time that Mrs. Jones noticed that Alya was looking at a photo, she dropped whatever she was doing and told Alya the story behind the photo.

"I see you are looking at the one on my wedding day, Alya. Wasn't I quite the blushing bride?" Mrs. Jones teased.

"Yes," Alya said.

Each of the stories behind the photographs was so colourful. Mrs. Jones took such great joy in talking about the details of her life. Such a refreshing change from her own parents who ignored the past with a firmness that made her think twice before she asked about it.

"You were very beautiful. Are, I mean."

"Ah...1945. Such a time of excitement! We had been holed up in our houses for nearly six years, afraid every day that something might happen. The year that Douglas brought me to lovely Toronto. Did I tell you that my sister, Alice, she perished in a bombing raid?" Alya nodded. Mrs. Jones had told her the story many times. "She was the real beauty, that Alice. Gorgeous fiery red hair, like my Henry!"

Mrs. Jones pointed to her belly in the photo and leaned in to whisper, "You know, my dear, that I was already pregnant? The white dress was really just for show!"

Mrs. Jones laughed, which sounded like the beautiful and graceful tinkle of piano keys.

Mr. Jones, Douglas to his wife but Doug to everyone else, brought home his pregnant bride. The baby girl had been stillborn. Scrawny, red-haired, and fair Henry followed a few years later. His mother called him *elegantly slim*. Henry remained an only child, doted on by his parents, even as a teen. More than once Alya had watched with jealousy as his family celebrated his achievements with great fanfare. Henry presented his test or report with an 'A+' written on it as if he was presenting his doctoral thesis to his parents. They smiled, clapped, and showered him with congratulations. Mrs. Jones planted unabashed kisses all over Henry's cheeks, followed by proud pats on the back from his father.

With some encouragement, Alya also showed her grades, but only those that were at least on par with Henry's. In those instances, Mrs. Jones planted a light and feathery kiss on the top of Alya's head, and with great seriousness, Mr. Jones extended his hand for her to shake. All four would then celebrate the young students' successes with tea and Chocolate Snaps from a package.

Alya stomped into her bedroom on the second floor of the house and threw her book bag onto the round crochet rug next to her bed. She slammed her bedroom door, then collapsed onto the bed.

An hour later, still lying on her bed and sulking, Alya heard Anastasia calling her name from the bottom of the stairs. Alya slowly got up, and took a look in the small mirror above her dresser. She was pale and the dark circles under her eyes made her look miserable. Good. That's how she wanted to look for her family. Alya took her time walking down the stairs and back into the kitchen. She gave a curt nod to both her father and brother, Bohdan, already seated at the table. Her father read the Ukrainian weekly paper. He glanced up only for a second when Alya walked into the room. Reading the weekly paper was an activity that fully engrossed her father, and for a few hours each week, he was actually kind of quiet. Bohdan sat at the table, looking like Alya felt.

"Finally. Please set the table, Alya," Anastasia said.

"Why me? Bohdan's just sitting there," Alya said, her outrage at life growing by the second.

"Just do what I ask! *Bozhe*! I'm trying to get dinner on the table." Anastasia pulled a sizzling pan of chicken legs topped with rings of onion out of the oven.

Alya exhaled.

"Ok, fine."

She went to the cupboard that jostled for space along the one wall with the oven and sink. The kitchen was crammed. Alya waited for another comment about her petulant attitude, but Anastasia busied herself with the food. Usually, her mother wouldn't let her go on for so long.

"*Donechko,* what is it?" Her father asked, putting the paper down.

"Oh, you know, the usual. I work my butt off on my school work, do well, but nobody around here cares. Like, what's the point?"

"Wah, wah. Cry me a river, you baby," Bohdan said. What Alya found particularly mystifying was her parents' reactions towards Bohdan's antics. More amused than angry, Stephan yelled at Bohdan for his latest transgressions, then playfully messed his hair, demanding half-heartedly that he agree not to skip Ukrainian classes again.

"Shut up, you creep. Like you know anything about doing well in school."

"Hey! That's enough," Stephan said, raising his voice. "Don't speak like that to your brother. You're lucky to have a brother!"

The family ate in silence.

"So?" Stephan asked, recovered from his outburst, chicken leg hovering halfway between his mouth and plate, "what were my children up to today?"

"There's a marbles club at my school and I joined it today," Bohdan said. He was already on his second chicken leg. "I won two cat's eyes from Jimmy, and an Indian from Sam!"

"*Ah, ho*! That's my boy!" Stephan rumpled his son's hair while Alya tried not to roll her eyes. Bohdan was allowed to spend his free time in random Canadian after-school pastimes rather than the Ukrainian activities that Alya had been forced into.

"And you, *donechko*? What other great things did my professor daughter accomplish today?" Stephan's eyes sparkled. At least her father was proud of her.

"Besides getting my amazing mark?" Alya said while looking directly at Anastasia, "Not much. I showed Mama, but she was too busy to take a look at it."

"*Bah*, don't worry about your mama," Stephan said as he patted Alya's hand, winking at Anastasia, who sighed loudly for a second time. "What was this great paper about?"

"It was about the Jewish experience post-war. I might do some more research and turn it into a major paper. Maybe even look at the topic in greater depth if I want to get my Master's degree."

Everyone else at the table didn't skip a beat, entirely focused on the food, but her father stared at her. He did not like to talk about his early years in Ukraine, but he loved to argue about what was right and wrong with the country. The army, forced labour, and concentration camps were off limits, but everything else political was fair game, and Stephan made sure that his children knew it. Alya felt badly for her tato that he had been though a horrific time, but sometimes she wished that he would just move on.

In one of her history classes, Alya had learned that an estimated 710,000 of the labourers who worked for no pay during WWII came from Ukraine. The majority of those workers came by force; whether or not the German government preferred to call it coercion, it had most certainly been forced in one way or another. Of course she understood well the facts that were written in her Canadian text – she lived with the aftermath every day. Within her research the previous year, Alya had purposely searched out information about the Displaced Persons camp called Münster-Lager, where her parents had met after the war. Alya had done all her research and writing in the university library, nervous. She didn't want her parents to find out what she was reading. Could it possibly be considered snooping if looking through public archives?

Over that semester, Alya had pieced together that in the four years that Münster-Lager was a Displaced Persons camp, there had been an average of 1,500 Ukrainians in it each year. Münster-Lager had been one of many, many camps created to house the millions of displaced people after the war. By the time Stephan, then Anastasia and Alya left the camp, Münster-Lager was in the process of being slowly shut down. As it turned out they were among some of the last people to call it home. It closed in 1949.

Truthfully, Alya was more interested in the Jewish experience. How heartbreaking, how cruel those war time years were for the Jews in Europe! Alya tried to quickly re-direct her father before he truly started to rant.

"Look, Tato, I want to do some research on the Ukrainian experience post-war, but there is not really that much information out there about it," Alya said, and immediately knew as soon as the words left her mouth that she was heading down the wrong path if she wanted to avoid a lecture. "The emphasis on research right now is about the Jews, and documenting the Holocaust. It's a lot easier for me to find books and stuff…"

Stephan, on cue, started huffing and puffing. Alya could practically visualize his nationalistic tendencies rising up.

"*Bah*! Your generation, with your books, you are so lazy! Why don't you write the books? Then, there will be some."

Satisfied with his argument, Stephan leaned back, crossed his arms over his chest, and looked at Alya as if that was the answer.

"Alya, we are proud of whatever kind of work you do," Anastasia interjected. Alya was grateful for the distraction. "You have to understand, your tato and I don't know what your school is all about. Was there university where we came from? Maybe for the rich people, sure. But not for everyday people like us."

When Stephan looked as if he was going to speak, Anastasia waved his attention back to his dinner.

After dinner, Bohdan ran off, and Stephan plunked down in the living room in front of the television set. Alya and Anastasia cleared the dinner dishes without speaking. Deciding that from then on she would keep her small academic victories private, Alya again sulked as she helped Anastasia dry the supper dishes. She fled back up the stairs to the safety of her books and music as soon as it was humanly possible.

II.

"It's always the good that die young," Henry sighed. He was obviously feeling philosophical as they looked as the cover of their favourite Janis Joplin album.

"Or, so they say," Alya agreed soberly.

The news of Joplin's death had hit both of them hard, and they felt the need to mourn together – to do something, anything. Alya had been spending more time than usual at Henry's because she felt like her grieving was not being taken seriously enough by her own parents. When Anastasia found Alya sobbing hysterically in the upstairs hallway nook after Henry telephoned on October 5th with the news, she was totally unmoved by the gravity of the situation.

"Who is this that died? You knew her?" Anastasia had asked, puzzled.

"No, Ma, I didn't know her. She was a singer. Hello? You've never heard of Janis Joplin? I have her poster up in my room, for Pete's sake!"

"She can't be that famous if no one over the age of twenty-five has ever heard of this singer," came Anastasia's retort. "Pull yourself together; it's almost time for dinner."

Both women were often baffled with each other. The death of Janis Joplin, together with Alya's reaction, was just another illustration of the great chasm that existed between mother and daughter. Alya knew that Anastasia couldn't fathom feeling such depths of sorrow for an artist that she called a 'teeny-bopper', and Alya didn't understand how her mother did not grasp that a legend had just died. Both women avoided each other until Alya calmed down.

Since the news of their beloved Janis' death, Alya and Henry had spent time listening to Joplin's music, re-writing her lyrics in their marble-cover notebooks, and reading any magazine or newspaper article that they could get their hands on. That afternoon, Alya sketched a drawing of a flower using charcoal.

Earlier that day, as Alya stomped down the main floor hallway on her way out the door, Anastasia looked up from her post at the kitchen sink.

"You are not staying for dinner?" she asked. She had been more cautious than usual around Alya.

"No, Ma, I'm not staying tonight. I'm going to Henry's," Alya said as she grabbed an apple from the fridge.

"Why does Henry not come here for dinner? I'm making *varenyky*. He loves those," Anastasia said.

Her mother was grasping. Encouraging Henry not only to come to the house but also to stay for dinner was totally out of character.

"Because we want to listen to music and this radio program."

"You can listen to the radio here! What's wrong with the one in our living room?"

"Look, Mama, you won't let Henry and I sit alone in my room. You treat me like a child."

"Of course you can't sit in your room together! You know your tato would go crazy."

Anastasia looked back down at the potatoes she was peeling and shook her head.

"But, you are listening to a radio program? Which one?"

"I dunno, a CBC one. Anyway, I don't think you would approve of this particular program. It's called 'Bringing Back the Future'. It's a talk show created by some kids in university. Anyway, it's all about how some university Profs take LSD or mushrooms for spiritual enlightenment," Alya said.

When she saw the look of shock on her mother's face, she was giddy.

There had been much excitement on campus about the new program. Alya and Henry were eager to listen in, to be a part of what they believed was a change in cultural attitudes about the acceptance of mind-altering drugs. Their evening had been interrupted once, by Mrs. Jones, who offered up two bottles of Coke and a bowl of potato chips before quickly retreating back downstairs.

"It's all about self-awareness, about spiritual enlightenment, man," said Henry.

"Yeah, man." Alya giggled. Henry immediately turned red. "Sorry, Henry."

Alya apologized with sincerity. She should have known better than to tease her friend. The use, or in Henry's case, over-use of the word 'man' was something that Henry had picked up on campus. Not only was he using slang in every sentence he uttered, but Henry had changed from preppy and conservative. He grew out his red hair, wore bell-bottomed jeans, and regularly smoked weed. Alya was actually proud to walk with him around campus; a striking figure who drew looks from both females and males.

When the radio episode began, a young, timid-sounding voice came over the airwaves. As she listened closely, Alya's heart tightened in her chest. The female host could have been her. Different from the old-fashioned announcers on the other CBC programs, the girl said that they had prepared a program on drugs and religion. Alya and Henry listened with rapt attention as a professor from York University spoke about his experiences with mushrooms and peyote in a Mexican desert. They loved every second of the program, especially at the end, when a song by Leonard Cohen was played.

When Alya returned home, Anastasia was still up, reading and smoking under the single lamp in the living room. As she dropped off her backpack in the kitchen, Alya stood to listen. The house was very quiet and still. Bohdan and Stephan were most certainly out for the night, Stephan at a local bar with other Ukrainian fathers, and Bohdan somewhere in the city with his own friends. When she went into the living room, Anastasia looked to be struggling through the front page of the Toronto Star newspaper. These days, every front page in the country was covered in news about the October Crisis. On the arm of the sofa was another embroidery pattern that looked to be about halfway complete. Alya picked it up to look at the small picture-style pattern of a pot of poppies against a background of alternating blues.

"Ah, Alya, you are home," Anastasia said. She put out her cigarette on the coffee table ashtray.

"I'm happy anyway not to have to read this anymore."

"Things getting any better in Quebec?" Alya asked, gesturing to the abandoned paper.

"Not yet, though it looks as if Trudeau is going to declare a state of emergency," Anastasia replied, then laughed.

"What's so funny about the crisis?"

"A state of emergency means that our civil liberties will be suspended, and if our civil liberties are taken away, it will be just like living in Germany again. Makes me nervous, that's all," Anastasia answered. She patted the sofa cushion next to her, and Alya sat down. "And how was your radio program?"

"It was interesting, actually. Some of my professors are very interesting and progressive, but none are quite *that* liberated."

"Yes, I actually listened to a bit of the program, myself. I thought 'if Alya is interested in listening to the CBC, it must be good!'"

"Did you listen to the whole thing?" Alya asked. Could it be possible that they could actually discuss something of interest to Alya?

"If you ask me," Anastasia said, "the kids running the program sounded like amateurs. All that talk about having a visionary experience. It sounds like they don't have enough to do with their lives."

"I'm not surprised, Mama," Alya said, feeling the familiar thud of disappointment in her gut. "I don't know why you would even bother."

The two women sat in an awkward silence for a few moments.

"So..." Alya said. Desperate to change the conversation, she gestured towards the embroidery. "You're working on another poppy design?"

Anastasia shrugged.

"It's not going as well as I had hoped. I love the poppies, but something about the way they are arranged isn't working. Also, I'm having problems tying-in the threads at the back."

"Want me to take a look at it?" Anastasia had taught Alya how to embroider when she was small, but Alya hadn't kept up with it as a teenager.

Alya then noticed the envelope on the coffee table with the airmail markings.

"Did you get a letter from Ciocia Kateryna?" Alya asked, another attempt to re-direct the conversation.

"Yes. Things aren't very good in Poland right now, though I think that they are lucky to be living in Warsaw. It seems as if every little task that must be completed is difficult for them," Anastasia said as she picked up the envelope and took the letter out.

"Like this, for example. Kateryna was telling me about needing eggs to make a birthday cake for her husband, your Vuyko Ihor. Sounds simple enough, right? But they don't have good connections to the Party. They live on very limited rations. Kateryna wrote how she had to ask her neighbour for extra egg coupons just to make a small cake! It's unbelievable that the USSR is sending dogs, people, and God-knows-what into space, but they can't provide their citizens with something as simple as a few extra eggs!" Anastasia tossed the letter back down onto the coffee table and shook her head.

"What else did Ciocia Kateryna say? Did she mention Pavlo or Sonia?" Her two Polish cousins were such exotic creatures. How did they manage to eke out their own lives under the repressions of the USSR? Pavlo was five years older than Alya, but Sonia was only a few months younger. She was also very similar looking to Alya. Two young girls; living completely opposite lives on different continents.

"Pavlo is still working as a streetcar operator in Warsaw. Kateryna thinks that he might get married to a girl that he's been seeing for about a year. We will have to send a good wedding gift over."

"Even though it's sure to be 're-diverted'?" Alya said, making quotation marks in the air at the last word of her sentence. No doubt that yet again, whatever money her mother sent would find its way into the pockets of whoever examines the incoming mail at the post office. Alya imagined this person to be an evil and selfish soul, intent on buying American items on the illicit market. Selfish.

"Out of curiosity, Mama, what would you prefer?" Alya took her time. Her mother was easily scared off by questions that required any small amount of self-reflection. Worse were questions about her mother's childhood.

"What do you think? If you were still in Europe, in Ukraine, or Poland, or whatever country claims your village, would you want to live in the village, or live in a big Polish city like Warsaw?"

She waited, holding her breath.

Anastasia was quiet for a long time – at least several minutes – but Alya patiently waited.

"I don't know. I sometimes think about what my life would have been like if the war had never happened, or if I had been too young to be sent to Germany, or if Kateryna had not become pregnant. I'm not even sure what my life would have looked like if I had remained in Horayetz, especially since there is nothing left of the village now."

"But do you think that it would be better, right now, to live somewhere away from prying government eyes, like in a small village, even if it is backwards, or to live in a city?"

The strains of a male voice, singing, broke the spell. Getting up from the sofa, Anastasia pulled the window curtain aside to look. She shook her head.

"It's that old fool of a father that you have, walking down the street, and singing at the top of his lungs. He'll wake up the entire neighbourhood!"

The voice grew louder as Stephan passed by the front window, and stopped when the side door opened. As soon as it was slammed shut, the house was filled with the sound of a Ukrainian folk song being belted out by a rich and husky voice. When drunk, Stephan sang with a voice that poured out emotion of longing and grief for his home country.

He stumbled up the side stairs and into the front living room.

"Ah! There are my beautiful flowers!" He kissed both Anastasia and Alya on the top of their heads. "You, Alya, are a rose, so fresh and young. You, my Anastasia, you are a lily, also beautiful but tough and strong." Stephan flopped down in an armchair across from the couch. Alya laughed, but Anastasia continued to shake her head.

"You are going to wake up the entire neighbourhood! Do you want everyone to know that you are drunk, again, on a Saturday night?" Anastasia swatted Stephan with her rolled up newspaper while walking by him to the kitchen. Stephan grinned and tried to make a grab for her. Alya wanted to disappear when her parents showed each other small displays of affection. She was also secretly pleased.

Alya picked up the letter from Kateryna and examined the sloped writing. She could read printed text of Ukrainian easily, but she struggled with the written format. Her aunt's shaking writing was impossible to read by anyone except her mother.

"What are you reading?" Stephan asked, trying to focus on the envelope.

"It's a letter from Ciocia Kateryna. I want to try to read it, but it's impossible! Who writes likes this?" Alya said, looking up at Stephan, "Anyway, do you think I'll ever be able to meet them?"

"Ah…who knows?" Stephan said, waving his hand at nothing in particular in the horizon. His eyes began to close slowly as he yawned. "Maybe one day we will be able to go to visit, or they come here to us. Poland seems to be loosening their rules about visas and traveling out of the country. They are a lot less nervous about letting the Poles leave the country on holiday than they are the Ruskie citizens."

"I don't particularity want to go *there,*" Alya said, "But it would be nice to have them come here. Look at Sonia. Here's a chick, exact same age as me, and she's most likely had a bummer of a life."

"Of course she's had a bum of a life, or whatever you call it. It might be unfair, but don't forget that your mama and I sacrificed much to come to Canada. We started with absolutely nothing in our pockets, just the promise of a good job. We had to leave our family behind to start over." Stephan's eyes were closed, and he no longer struggled to open them.

"It's obviously been worth it," Alya said. "Look at all the young people my age – we have been able to go to college or university and get an education. If we didn't want to, then that was our choice. No Party connections or bribes needed."

Alya put down the letter; it was impossible to decipher.

"A small twist of fate, small decisions made by you and Mama made the difference between a good life here, and struggle back home. It was just a small twist..."

The sound of light snoring stopped Alya. Stephan was deep into sleep, head leaning heavily to the side, mouth wide open. Alya left her ciocia's letter on the coffee table and kissed the top of Stephan's head as she walked past him to the hallway. She was partway up the stairs when she heard Stephan mumble. When she looked back, he was still slumped over in the chair.

"A rose is very delicate and beautiful, but you had better be careful, because even though it is very pretty, a rose can also prick you with its many thorns."

Alya hung onto the banister, listening to hear if Stephan had more to say. The only sound that followed was more snoring. Alya smiled to herself and continued up the stairs.

III.

After her fall semester class with Dr. Moores wrapped up, Alya was sad to see that he was uninterested in anything more than a passing hello in the hallway of the faculty building. Alya felt a vague disappointment whenever she spotted him. As the spring semester progressed, Alya saw even less of Dr. Moores, and she realized with embarrassment that she was nothing more than a good student to him. The possibility of anything more was something that she had built up within her own imagination.

On an unusually hot evening in June of 1971, Alya made herself a peanut butter sandwich in the kitchen when she heard her parents in the living room. They were discussing an upcoming concert that was going to be held on the Lakeshore, around Sunnyside Park.

The conversation made Alya perk up her ears. Growing up, she had loved going to the large outdoor concerts that were put on by Ukrainians. They were always all-day affairs, a reunion of sorts for Ukrainians who were spread out around Toronto, and those living in towns and villages around the city. Parents spent the day eating, drinking, watching the entertainment, and then as night fell, they sang and told stories. The children also loved going, because after the long and boring concert, they were free to run around, play games, and stay up very, very late.

Now that Alya was well past her teen years, she found herself distanced from her old Ukrainian friends. Most of them still spent all of their free time together, going to dances, playing in sports leagues, and in the summers, camping at the Plast grounds outside of Toronto. Alya had disconnected from the co-ed group where she had once been an integral part. *Integral*, she had thought at the time, though it wasn't even really true. Noticing the changes in Alya around her selection of friends, Anastasia was forever pestering her, pushing her to re-connect with the community where she'd grown up.

"Why don't you call Danna?" Anastasia often demanded; hand on hip, as she peered into Alya's room with a look of distaste as if she had just eaten something sour. "Why don't you think about joining the dance group again? Have some fun with people that are…ours."

The never-ending script made Alya tired.

"Ma, I told you. I just want to go do my own thing. Stop pressuring me."

Alya often escaped into the company of shy, reliable, and consistent Henry. What he lacked in excitement and glamour, he made up for in his steady friendship, and the easy-going silences that they shared when drinking coffee at one of the all-night dives on Queen Street. Alya loved going to the coffee shops, reveling in the knowledge that Anastasia would die of a heart attack on the spot if she ever spotted Alya in one of the establishments that she called for *chouzhyntsi* – for 'the others'.

When Anastasia said *chouzhyntsi*, she was referring to the shabby, greasy, and sad-looking customers who also visited the all-night spots that Alya and Henry frequented. Anastasia only admired the people who lived a million miles away, but really just across the Humber River. These were those who owned homes on The Kingsway. When Alya was young, and Bohdan just a baby or toddler, the family took leisurely Sunday drives west along Bloor Street to The Kingsway, admiring the stately Tudor-style houses that sat like proud lions on vast expanses of groomed lawns. Even as a child, Alya noted how much her mother loved to murmur the names of side streets that jutted off The Kingsway; names like Wimbelton Road, St. Georges Road, and Kingsgrove Boulevard. The neighbourhood around The Kingsway held a presence that was impermeable, impossible to attain for their family.

Trying to seem nonchalant, Alya strolled into the living room where Stephan and Anastasia sat, munching on her sandwich. Stephan was reclined on the sofa fanning himself and Anastasia was working on yet another embroidery piece, this one, the arm of a blouse.

"It's hot, eh?" Alya asked to neither of her parents in particular.

"So hot your mama isn't even smoking," Stephan said as he leaned back on the couch with his eyes closed.

"I don't know why you let her keep smoking," Alya said, "You know that they are saying it's bad for you."

"*Let* her?" Stephan bellowed, laughing. "There's no *letting* with your mama; she does what she wants."

"It's your fault, anyway," Anastasia said, pointing her needle at Stephan. "You're the one who got me started on smoking."

"*Bah*," said Stephan, waving Anastasia's accusation away with a wave of his hand. "Not like I kept up with the dirty habit myself."

The heat seemed to take all of the intensity out of both Stephan and Anastasia. They sat silent, not continuing their usual banter. It was so quiet that for a few seconds, Alya could hear the clock in the hallway ticking away.

"So, when is that concert that you guys are talking about?" Alya asked.

"June thirty, right before Dominion Day," replied Anastasia. For reasons unknown to Alya, Anastasia loved Dominion Day; sometimes she even participated in the celebrations at City Hall. Many of her references to dates were marked by their proximity to the national holiday.

"Oh, yeah," said Alya, leaning against the arm of the sofa. "I think I might join you this time."

"Holy, moly! Anastasia, call the doctor, I think Alya has a fever!" Stephan joked half-heartedly, still lying down with his eyes closed.

"Alya, get off the sofa arm and stop eating that sandwich like a cow," Anastasia said, looking up irritably as she wiped sweat from her brow. "Since when are you interested in our social schedule?"

"Ha, ha," said Alya. "I'm just wanting to, you know, check it out. See who's going to be there."

"Who do you think will be there? The same people who always go," Anastasia answered, sounding exasperated.

"Well, I haven't gone to anything in a while, and maybe I want to check it out," Alya said defensively.

"Leave the poor girl alone, *zhinku*," Stephan said, fanning himself. "She obviously wants to see her old friends that she's been ignoring. Let's not embarrass her." Stephan cracked open his eyes a bit, grinning.

"Well, whatever, just remember that I'm going to come too," Alya said as she started to side step her way out of the living room. She got away before her parents could see her blush. As usual, they could see right through her.

IV.

Two weeks later, Alya was sitting in her own seat on a Toronto city bus with Stephan and Anastasia directly in front of her. Bohdan had proclaimed that he would rather die than sit together with the rest of his family. He sat at the back of the bus alone, pretending to be independent.

They were riding the bumpy bus that would take them to Union Station, where they planned to take another bus down Lakeshore Boulevard, to the site of the concert. Armed with a picnic basket, flasks of booze, chairs, and their best causal weekend clothing, Alya watched as the hats on her parents' heads bopped and swayed with every rattling bump the bus made. She saw the dampness already gathering around the starched collar of Stephan's summer-weight cotton shirt, and Anastasia dabbed away at the beads that gathered in groups along her hairline.

Alya thought about bringing Henry or one of her Canadian girlfriends along with her, to act as buffer, as if to show that she was not anxious to fit back in with her friends. Her goal was to cultivate an image that projected confidence, as if she was coming along with her parents as an afterthought even though she had better things to do. She thought of the gathered Ukrainians, the boring speeches and overly formal stage performances, followed by the boisterous singing of old folk songs by the drunken fathers. She thought of the smells of kielbasa that wafted from the food spreads with rye bread and cucumber salad, washed down with whatever cheap vodka, or Canadian Club. Then, she had imagined the contrast of red-haired and quiet Henry. She must go unaccompanied, without armour. With each pothole the bus hit, a little more of Alya's self-confidence was jostled.

Hundreds of people had already gathered at the park by the time they arrived but Anastasia and Stephan managed to find a group of friends. They greeted them with kisses on cheeks. The assembled groups headed off to find stretches of lawn in front of the stage to put their chairs down on. Alya panicked when Bohdan also quickly found a group of boys his age, and immediately bounded off with them. Anastasia called out after him to meet at the picnic area when it got dark.

Unsure of what to do and not seeing anyone her age that she knew, Alya followed her parents as they set up their chairs, sitting on the hard ground like a dog.

"Cut it out!" she said as Stephan reached down and patted the top of her head.

The concert started the same way that she had predicted - there was politician after politician waiting to speak to the crowd from the crackling microphone, and on and on it went. A few Canadian MPP's even tried their hands addressing the large crowd with a few sentences in broken Ukrainian. Alya cringed with embarrassment. The politicians themselves appeared smug as they stood visibly perspiring under the beating glare of the summer sun, looking over the huge crowd of potential votes. It was well known that the 'immigrant groups' were often the swing votes in some of the downtown ridings and the political parties wasted no effort in courting the various groups of new Canadians.

Finally, the speeches ended, and the first singer went up on stage. She was a woman about Anastasia's age, clad head-to-toe in the heavy woolen costume of the Hutsul region of Ukraine. The woman was accompanied by a small live band, and her deep alto voice reverberated across the entire field of attendees as she sang. Alya remembered the song from her childhood as one that Stephan sometimes belted out when he was in a good mood.

Just as a line of sweat began to make its way down Alya's back, she spotted at the side of the seated crowd a group of young people gathering, not paying attention to the singer on stage. Right away, Alya recognized her old friend, Danna, as well as a number of other kids.

"Ma," Alya whispered as she poked Anastasia. "I see Danna and some others over there. I'm going to go hang out with them. I'll see you later, ok?"

"Oh yes?" Anastasia said, and turned around, craning her neck to see,

"Yes, you go, and have fun. If you see Bohdan, remind him that he has to meet us around dinnertime at the picnic area."

Alya got up, relieved to be moving away from her post of boredom, a bit dizzy from sitting in the heat. She nonchalantly tried to peel her t-shirt from her back as she walked towards the group. There were butterflies in the pit of her stomach, and with each step, her hands grew sweatier.

Danna spotted her before the others.

"Hey! Alya!" Danna waved and broke into a big smile. "Long time no see!"

They hugged. Relief grew from the tips of Alya's toes and upwards.

"Hi," Alya said shyly. "I saw you guys from over there."

She gestured to the area where her parents sat on their plastic folding chairs; Stephan fanned himself with his summer hat while Anastasia did the same, only with a leaflet.

"I was sitting with my parents..."

Alya didn't know what else to say. From behind her sunglasses she assessed the other girls assembled in the large group.

Alya smiled and tried to relax. They had grown up together, attended an activity most days of the week after school. Even though they hadn't been in touch very much over the past three years – Danna had been one of the few girls who had actually left home to go away to university at Queen's in Kingston. There was a certain level of familiarity in their being together.

Alya and Danna were friends from birth. They had even come from Europe at the same time, as toddlers, making the long journey by ship. Danna's parents had settled in Toronto right away, while Stephan and Anastasia lived and worked in Sudbury for five years before moving to the bigger city.

In the early Toronto years, Alya and Danna were always together. They walked together every Saturday morning to Ukrainian school, where both girls tolerated the history and geography classes that took up half of the time of the morning, and both absolutely detested the grammar classes that made up the remainder of the time.

"Alya!" Alya looked towards the sound of her name being called and saw that Ostap Cheremesh was waving at her. He smiled.

"How are you?" he asked, bounding over, kissing Alya on both cheeks, just like an adult. Alya blushed at the sudden sign of friendly affection, unprepared for how much goofy Ostap had seemed to mature in the past few years.

"I'm good," Alya started, gesturing again in the general direction of her parents. "I'm just with Mama and Tato. They're up front..." she trailed off, seeing that no one cared.

All the guys and girls seemed to be in no hurry to do anything but stand and chat; laughing, joking, with most people holding soft drinks and beers in rapidly warming glass bottles. As Alya looked around, she recognized most of the faces. There was the usual gang that she went to Ukrainian school and activities with, as well as others she recognized who were younger than she, but they had grown up and changed much over the past few years. Alya also found surprising that everyone seemed to have paired off; many girls stood very close to boys, clutching their hands as they stood in special-looking couple groups, laughing and talking. Alya felt a stab of jealousy as she awkwardly stood on her own, wishing that she had a boy who would hold her hand and pay close attention to her.

They stood in one large group together when there was a break in the concert program. Alya turned to look at the stage, and she saw Anastasia standing in a long line of people snaking its way down the side stage steps, out on to the grass area.

"Wow, can you believe that some of the adults are still getting up on stage at these things to see if they can find their families?" Ostap asked, suddenly next to Alya. "My Mama did that like twenty years ago to find her sister."

"Oh yeah?" Alya replied. She was pleased to find Ostap was not apparently taken by one of the other girls there, the ones who looked so confident. "My Mama also did this a few times before too, way back when I was just a little kid. I sort of remember one time, but she hasn't tried in a while."

"Is she looking for anyone in particular?" Ostap asked.

"Her brother, probably. She still hasn't found him. She found her sister and mother, but not the brother," Alya answered.

The line across the stage moved as people took their turns approaching the microphone to announce names and other information they thought might be relevant to finding missing friends and family.

"We get letters all the time from my baba and ciocia because they now live in Poland, but Mama hasn't seen her brother since she was like thirteen years old. I don't know why she even really cares."

"Oh, I'm sure you find Bohdan a pest, but I'm also sure that if you two were separated somewhere across the globe, that one day you would try to find him. Even if it had been a while," Ostap said, teasing Alya. She hoped that he wouldn't notice that she was blushing.

"Well, I guess we shall soon see. She's up next," Alya said, edging slowly back towards the stage. She was pleased to find that Ostap was moving alongside her.

They waited, standing closely together, not talking while the few people in front of Anastasia reported their information. When Anastasia approached the microphone at her turn, Alya was suddenly nervous again; and thought that she felt her heart skip a beat. She also felt incredibly self-conscious around Ostap, like she was vulnerable and exposed, as though it was her on stage.

Anastasia got up to the microphone and cleared her throat.

"My name is Anastasia. Last name Boyko at home. I used to be called Tasya when I was young," Anastasia paused, and Alya worried that her mother might start to cry. Alya had forgotten that Anastasia had gone by a more child-like version of her name when she was young, and wondered for a second when it would be time for her to do the same, to begin to be called by her proper and adult name.

"I lived in Horayetz, which is outside of Peremyshyl, until 1942, when I was taken to Germany." Anastasia paused again, as if trying to think of what to say next and Alya exhaled loudly, realizing that she had been holding her breath.

"I had two siblings, Kateryna, who was born in 1920, and Mychaylo, who was born in 1924. Kateryna went to Germany as a volunteer in 1940, and Mychaylo did the same in 1941. I was forced to go in 1942, to take the place of my sister."

"Sounds like my mama's story too," Ostap whispered to Alya.

"I think that's pretty much everyone's story around here," Alya replied. "Look, everyone is paying close attention. I bet that everyone here has been looking for family members at one point or another since the end of the war."

Anastasia cleared her throat and looked as if she was steadying herself to continue. Alya found that she didn't want to miss another word of what her mama was about to say. Anastasia so infrequently spoke about her life before the war, constantly waving off questions that Alya asked, never participating in reminiscing about her childhood, like Stephan sometimes was willing to do with his children. Anastasia gave the impression of having her feet planted firmly in the present in her life in Canada, and it was unsettling for Alya to see her mother up on stage, emotionally vulnerable, with a thousand people straining to hear the details of the life that she had always kept close to her heart.

"As far as I know, Mychaylo went to Berlin to work in an ammunitions factory. Our family received a few letters from him at first, but they had stopped coming by the end of 1941." Anastasia stopped for a few seconds, and looked like she was thinking of what else to say. "Oh, and I am also looking for a girl, uh, a woman, who would be my age. Her name was…is….Hanya Petrusiv, and she was from Horayetz as well."

Anastasia ended her time on stage with an abrupt "Thank you."

"Who's that last person?" Ostap asked, leaning into Alya.

"I'm not sure," Alya said, surprised at Anastasia's sudden addition. "Maybe a friend who she grew up with? Not sure…"

The next person approached the microphone, and Alya watched as Anastasia made her way back down the set of rickety stairs. Alya had always considered it a fact of life that families tended to spread out across the globe, that not being with your mother, sister, or brother was the norm. 'The War,' and all the uprooting that had gone along with it was the story of most of the families that Alya knew, but now, for a minute, she saw how searching for decades for family could leave a hole in a person's heart that could never be quite filled. She had never really considered issues of displacement and hardship to be anything other than what everyone's parents had gone through in their youth. For a quick glimmer of a moment, Alya saw how far away from normal that way of living life actually was.

"So," Ostap said, breaking the silence, "Awkward transition, but do you want to join us for a game of volleyball after lunch? There's enough people for a small tournament here."

"Sure, but I haven't played since like grade ten phys ed," Alya replied. "Are you sure you want me?"

"Oh, I'm sure you won't be the worst!" Ostap laughed. "I just have to keep the fathers out of the game. They take a few shots of vodka and forget their age. They think they are still young and invincible."

"Yeah, no kidding," Alya laughed back. "I could totally see my tato getting into a game with his usual gusto, then spraining an ankle or something."

"Ok, then meet us over by the washrooms, say in half an hour?" Ostap said, as he waved goodbye to Alya.

Alya was actually a terrible volleyball player but she wanted to get in on any activity that was going on, no matter how much she disliked sports. Alya made her way back to Anastasia and Stephan's seats, just as a dance group was going on stage. As she approached her parents, she noticed a pair of men about Stephan's age heading in the same direction. The three arrived at Anastasia at the same time.

One of the men tapped Anastasia on the shoulder.

"Excuse me? I think I might have some information about your brother," he said as he extended his hand. "My name is Lev Mykolychyk."

He shook hands with both Anastasia and Stephan. Alya watched, waiting for what he had to say. Anastasia must have been surprised because she nodded without saying a word.

"After I was liberated from Dachau in 1945, I was moved to a camp outside of Soltau."

"Soltau? That's near where we were," Stephan interjected. "Which camp?"

"Lager Wolterdingen," Lev answered. "I was at Lager Wolterdingen for two years after the liberation. I met your brother, Mychaylo there. Anyway, I think it was him. Boyko is a common last name. What did your brother look like; maybe it was the same person?"

"I haven't seen him in a long time, but I remember him with blonde hair that was just beginning to darken when he left home." Anastasia paused to think. "He had blue eyes. His eyes were no ordinary colour but very blue, like the sky on a totally clear day."

"Like yours!" Alya exclaimed, but no one paid attention to her.

"He was of medium height, maybe the same as you. But the thing that set him apart was a birthmark on the side of his face." Anastasia traced with her finger an area around her jawbone. "It was around here. It wasn't big enough for anyone to really notice or to make him ugly-looking. It was just there, at the side, but you could see if it you were looking directly on the right side of Mychaylo's face." Anastasia laughed suddenly, "I've been searching for that birthmark on the side of men's faces for years. Everywhere I go, I look."

Though her parents were together for many years, Alya saw there had been some secrets. Stephan looked as surprised as she did. Had her mother really been searching the faces of strangers for years?

Had Alya never noticed?

Lev smiled and looked at his friend.

"Yep! That's him, isn't it, Orest? We decided not to say anything to you about the birthmark, to see if you would say something about it first, and you did!"

"That's him," said the second man, Orest, but didn't add any new information, frustrating Alya further with the glacial speed of the conversation.

"Well? He survived, then? What happened to him?" Alya demanded, and Stephan shushed her.

"Oh, sure he survived. Not like he was in a concentration camp during the war or anything. He was skinny as a rail when we first met, but rounded out again quickly," Lev laughed. "Anyway, anyway, to make a long story short, there was a huge group of us young men who got jobs working in Manchester, in '47."

"Manchester." Anastasia repeated, sounding dazed. Lev thought she meant the word to be a question.

"You know, as in England? All three of us ended up going on the same train – me, Orest, and Mychaylo. We all had wives by then, but we went to England first, and then we sent for them a few months later." Lev looked at Orest, "I sent for my wife only three months later, but Mychaylo took a bit longer to save the money, maybe another six months."

Orest nodded his agreement.

"So, what happened to him?" Alya interjected again, impatient.

"I'm getting to that!" Lev said. "Both Orest and I moved to Canada, to Winnipeg, in '50, but we've kept in touch with Mychaylo. I haven't heard from him in a few years now, but I'm sure he's still living in Manchester with Irina and the kids."

"Irina?" Anastasia asked, still sounding dazed.

"Sure, you know – his wife. They met in the camp and got married. Now they have two kids," Lev said. "No, wait. Three! Three kids. Though I suppose they aren't that small anymore."

Alya had never even considered the possibility of other cousins from her mother's side. Apparently, there were three others, and they were British! Family in England, on the correct side of the Iron Curtain and the Cold War were much more accessible than the family that was on the other side. Alya wondered what her mother was thinking at that very moment.

"Do you happen to have his address?" Stephan asked in the silence that followed after Lev stopped talking. Anastasia didn't seem to be able to ask the correct questions as she stared at the men.

"Well, not right here in my pocket with me, but sure, I have it at home. In Winnipeg, that is." Lev gestured to Orest. "My family still lives in Winnipeg, but we are here in Toronto to visit Orest and his family. We are all *kumy* – I'm godfather to Orest's oldest son, and he is godfather to mine."

"Oh, yes," Anastasia said, seeming to suddenly wake up. "Do you think that if I gave you my phone number and address that you could send it to me when you get home?"

"Of course. I would be happy to, but I won't be home again for another week. We drove out here, and it will take us a long time to get back again. I'll call your house in a week-and-a-half, two weeks, maybe?"

"Thank you, that would be great," Anastasia said.

"Two weeks! That's an eternity!" Alya exclaimed, knowing the time lag couldn't be helped, but she felt anxious, excited. After decades, her mother finally was on the way to finding her brother!

"Alya," Anastasia said, facing her. "It's already been nearly thirty years. I can wait another two weeks."

"That's also if Mychaylo hasn't left Manchester in the past few years," Lev reminded them. "But don't worry, even if he has, I'm sure someone around there in our community know where he and his family have gone."

"Just take your time getting his information to me, and thank you so much." Anastasia stopped, and to Alya's surprise, tears were in her mother's eyes.

"Thank you very much," she said as she hugged both men tightly.

After exchanging information, Alya, Anastasia, and Stephan watched the men walk away, eventually swallowed up by the crowd.

Stephan was the first to break the silence.

"I'm actually shocked that you were able to connect with someone, Anastasia. The last few times you've gone up at these things, nothing became of it. I thought today was going to be the same."

"Let's not get too excited, yet. That man isn't even sure if Mychaylo is still in Manchester. He might be impossible to find, again," Anastasia said. Alya watched as her mother snapped back to her stern and efficient self. "I really didn't think that anything would happen today, but I didn't want to let the chance go. It just goes to show that you never know."

Then Anastasia and Stephan did something that surprised Alya; they embraced. She had so rarely seen her parents show each other serious physical affection, though she could see that they truly loved each other. Alya shifted awkwardly, and waited till they broke apart to tell them that she was going to go join her friends for a game of volleyball.

Walking over to the playing fields, Alya couldn't believe Anastasia's luck that afternoon. As far as Alya could tell, Anastasia had actively looked for Mychaylo during their early years in Canada, then she seemed to stop. But had she stopped looking? Even Stephan was surprised to hear that Anastasia had for many years kept an eye out for the distinctive birthmark of her brother, yet she had never told Alya or Bohdan about it.

Once Alya reached the playing fields, she spotted Ostap right away and gave him a friendly wave. Alya didn't have a chance to tell Ostap about what had just happened with Anastasia because he was busy yelling out directions and instructions to everyone gathered around. Ostap had never been so self-assured, so confident. He seemed to be at ease with being the one in charge, and the others clearly deferred to him, taking his directions with good-natured ease.

As the tournament started, Alya's terrible aptitude for the sport was soon evident to everyone on her team. She bumped, volleyed, and underhand-served with all her might, but she could barely get the ball over the net whenever she had the rare opportunity to get her hands on it. Her teammates came to her rescue every time the ball headed anywhere near her direction, calling 'mine!', and sprinting as fast as possible over to her. Alya just tried to keep out of the way. Once, she saw Ostap watching her, laughing. She waved with embarrassment just as the ball sailed over the net from the other side, nearly hitting her square on the head. She ducked out of the way and the ball hit the ground. Her teammates groaned and Alya shrugged, grinning her apologies.

Later, as Alya lounged on the grass next to a spirited game that Danna was playing, she saw Anastasia and Stephan setting up a picnic area with a few dozen other parents, just on the outskirts of the playing field. The hottest part of the day had passed, and everyone gravitated towards the small grove of maple trees on one side of the field. Alya soon spotted Anastasia sitting in her plastic chair, sunglasses on, and a beer in her hand. Anastasia very rarely relaxed, but at that moment, she looked totally serene.

Alya jogged over to her mother. Behind Anastasia, in the midst of the cool shade of the maple trees, women worked busily setting picnic tables with gingham cloths, and laid out the few dishes they had brought. There were cold-cut meats, pickled beets, cucumbers, hard-boiled eggs, split and sprinkled with dill, and many loaves of rye bread from Future Bakery. Usually, Anastasia would be right in with the others, getting food organized while the men tried to get the BBQ lit.

"Boy, you look like you're enjoying yourself," Alya quipped, sitting down next to Anastasia, braving the waters enough to take the bottle from Anastasia's hand and take a sip of the beer.

"I was just watching you and your friends," Anastasia said, still looking out, reaching and taking the bottle back. "I was thinking to myself, that all of this was worth it. Truly worth it."

"Worth what?" Alya asked.

"Worth everything that I've been though, everything that your tato went through. It wasn't of our choosing, or our doing, and yet we managed to survive and make our way here, to Canada, to Toronto. It was all worth it."

"So, what are you saying, Mama?" Alya asked. "Until now, you weren't sure if your life had been worth all of the trouble that you had gone through?" Alya paused, but Anastasia didn't say anything in response, so Alya continued.

"Look at all you have, all that your children have. Could you have even begun to imagine this life as a teenager in Ukraine? From what it sounds like in Baba's letters, not much has changed in the USSR since you left. Canada is a world away from where you would have been if you had stayed in Ukraine."

"Oh, I know that," Anastasia said. "I think about my life's path all the time. Our lives – mine, yours, Tato's, Bohdan's. Here in Canada our lives are so full of things that were beyond our wildest desires when we were young. But, there was still something nagging at me. On TV once, I saw a woman on a soap opera talk about 'what if.' It's a perfect way to describe the thoughts I have sometimes. What if – I had stayed home? What if – I had tried to return home? What if – I had been sent to another camp? Where would I have ended up, then?"

"You might have ended up right here still, but then you wouldn't have your wonderful and lovely first-born daughter," Alya said, nudging Anastasia's arm as she smiled. For the first time, Anastasia looked down at Alya, and smiled back at her. Alya was encouraged by the conversation. She didn't know if it was the huge news that Anastasia had received about Mychaylo that day, or because of the effects of the beer, but Anastasia was more open and honest with Alya than she had ever been.

"Yes, you and Bohdan wouldn't be here if there was any alteration to mine or your tato's life. It's amazing to think that with a small twist of fate, a small change in the logistics of the Nazis, that you might not even be here at all," Anastasia reasoned.

"Finding a good lead to get in touch with Vuyko Mychaylo is starting to bring things full circle for you, huh, Mama?" Alya asked.

"No, it's not that exactly," Anastasia said, "But I find that I have a sense of relief in even knowing what happened to him. Not knowing if he was dead or alive has been weighing on me all of these years, though I never talked to anyone about it. Not even your tato," Anastasia said as she reached down to touch Alya's hair, as if trying to prove to herself that her daughter was real, was present.

"I was looking out at you," Anastasia continued, "and at the children of friends who are just like me, just like your tato, and all of a sudden, it just seemed worth the years of hunger, cold, and heartache. You are all so young, so fresh and vibrant. I was thinking about when I was twenty-two years old, and how old, how tired I felt. But in you, Alya, there is so much life. You have so many possibilities. Most importantly, you aren't dragged down by bad memories, or heartaches that cannot ever be lifted. You are so lucky to be so free."

Alya didn't know what to say, so she reached up and held Anastasia's hand. They sat together that way, for only a little while, until they were called over by the other women to eat. Then, the spell between them was broken.

V.

"Do you want me to get you something, Mama? Maybe a coffee?" Alya asked Anastasia as they shifted around on the hard plastic seats in the airport waiting area.

"No, I'm fine. Time is ticking by very slowly, and I'm just anxious for them to get here. To arrive." Anastasia stood up from the bank of chairs that she and Alya were sitting on to pace a few feet back and forth in front of Alya.

The women had been waiting for over two hours for the plane from London to arrive. Because of an early snowstorm that had settled over most of Western Europe, flights had been delayed out of Heathrow Airport. Both women were disappointed to learn that she would have to wait another few hours before the plane arrived.

Alya watched as Anastasia sat primly down again, and fussed with the buttons on her coat sleeve for the hundredth time since they had arrived at Toronto International Airport. There wasn't much for Alya and Anastasia to do but wait. In addition to the two hours that they had already waited, Alya saw from the flight schedule that they would be waiting another hour or so.

In little over five months, Anastasia had been able to re-connect with the missing member of her family. Though her baba and Ciocia Kateryna were not able to get permission to leave Poland to join in on the reunion, Alya knew that a piece of Anastasia that had been missing for the past three decades would finally be put back into place that day.

There was one nagging doubt that Alya had about the reunion, but she dared not share it with Anastasia. The night before, Alya sat with Ostap in his car at the end of yet another blissful date. She confided that she was worried the reunion between brother and sister would be anti-climactic. After all the anticipation of waiting, that Anastasia and Mychaylo would find that they had very little in common.

"What would even make you think of something like that?" Ostap asked. "Of course it's going to be as joyous a reunion as it can be, given that they hardly know each other. Why rain on the parade?" He asked as he kissed Alya softly on the top of her head.

"Haven't you ever been let down before?" Alya replied, turning to look at him. "Sometimes, the anticipation is more than the actual event. Like when I started hanging out with Danna again over the past summer. I had missed her, and imagined that once we re-connected, everything would go back to the way it always was. Then reality set in, and I realized that we had both grown up into two totally different people. I'm just saying – it can be a let-down, and I just hope that my mama and vuyko have something to talk about for the entire month that he and my aunt are visiting."

"That's what we third-party 'buffers' are for," Ostap said, laughing. "Even if they realize that thirty years later there isn't much of a connection, you'll be around, your tato, and of course, Bohdan can be counted on to be a distraction!"

"I guess," Alya said. "When that kid is around, he can actually be quite entertaining. Come to think of it, I'm pretty surprised how easy-going he is about losing his room for a month. The basement in the house is pretty dank, but he had no issues with being moved down there to give up his room to strangers."

"What you don't understand about adolescent boys," Ostap said, "is that they like to have their privacy. Know what I mean? Wink, wink?"

Alya had laughed and said that Ostap was gross, that she didn't want to think about her baby brother needing any privacy. Even with all of Ostap's reassurance, she didn't feel less worried for Anastasia. What if her uncle was weird? What if he, or his wife, didn't get along with the family?

Alya had no idea if Anastasia had been thinking the same thing, because for the past few weeks, since it had been decided that Mychaylo and Irina would come to Toronto to visit, Anastasia had been uncharacteristically quiet. She criticized Alya very little in those weeks, though Alya suspected that may have had something to do with Anastasia's obvious pleasure at Alya dating a

Ukrainian boy. In addition to the quiet, Anastasia had also been cleaning the house as if the Queen of England was to arrive at their doorstop at any minute. Anastasia had always kept a tidy house, a skill that she had acquired when she worked as a domestic when she was a teen, but she had truly gone overboard the past few weeks.

While giving the entire house a full dusting and vacuum every single day that week, Anastasia had gone into every corner of the house, clearing out the dusty storage closets, relegating everything that she deemed to be 'junk' to the garage in the backyard. Then she washed down everything, replacing items only where needed. She had also dragged Stephan out to purchase a new chesterfield and love seat for the living room, relegating their old, sagging furniture to the basement, which delighted Bohdan. Bohdan's room was to be used as the guest bedroom for Mychaylo and Irina, and nothing had been spared in the course of getting it ready. All of Bohdan's trophies and posters that he proudly displayed on the walls had come down; the items boxed up and moved temporarily to the basement. Anastasia single-handily painted Bohdan's bedroom a cheerful peach, promising him that she would later help to paint it back a more acceptable colour. She had even sewn new curtains in peach to match the walls. In between her cleaning frenzies, Anastasia had cooked enough *borscht*, *varenyky*, and *holubtsi* to feed any army, imposing on their Ukrainian neighbours for additional freezer storage space.

One night around midnight, Alya had come home from the movies with Ostap, and she found Anastasia at the kitchen counter, working furiously at peeling potatoes for a fresh batch of *varenyky* with a cigarette dangling from between her lips.

"Ma! What are you doing still up? I think we have enough food to last us for a while!" Alya said.

"I need to make more, just in case. What if my brother's wife doesn't know how to cook? I have to be ready to feed my family, plus two other adults for a month, especially since Mychaylo will be here for the *sviato*. I don't want to be making everything last minute!"

"First of all," Alya answered. "Obviously I can help with the cooking and getting stuff ready for the *sviato*," Alya said. "Second, what makes you think that Ciocia Irina can't cook?"

"Because," Anastasia scoffed, "she's been living in England for nearly thirty years! All she probably knows how to make is 'bangers and mash', put beans on the toast, or some such nonsense, then have the audacity to call it dinner."

Alya had to laugh, especially at the way that Anastasia had spit out the words "bangers and mash" in her heavily accented English.

"Uh, hello?" Alya said, laughing. "Ma, you know how to cook all of those foods from home, yet you've been living in Canada for over twenty years, for Pete's sake! It's the same thing."

Alya had a very brief moment of triumph when she saw that Anastasia, knife poised over the potato in her hand, paused to consider what Alya had said and made the connection between she and her brother's wife. Then she immediately began peeling away once more with renewed vigor.

At the airport, Alya kept stealing glances at the Arrivals board, hoping that the flight from London would soon arrive. Anastasia paced for a few minutes, and when finally the card next to the flight number flipped from 'Delayed' to 'Arrived,' so did Alya's heart. From the look on Anastasia's face, she could see her mother had the same reaction.

In the weeks leading up to the day that Mychaylo and Irina were set to arrive, Anastasia and Alya had been coached by Ostap on the ins-and-out of plane travel. Ostap had taken four flights during his lifetime, where neither Alya nor Anastasia had ever set foot on an airplane. He told them that it would take at least half an hour for Mychaylo and Irina to retrieve their bags after the plane had landed. They were instructed not to rush to the Arrivals door. Even armed with that knowledge, as soon as the flight was showing as 'Arrived,' both Alya and Anastasia stood up from their seats, Alya grabbing the bouquet of flowers they had brought, and Anastasia fixed the perfect buttons on her coat again. Together, they walked towards the busy Arrivals door.

"Now I kind of wish that we had brought a sign, like Ostap told us to do," Alya said, looking around her at the throngs of people waving excitedly as friends and family weighed down by luggage came pouring through the Arrivals door.

"I'll recognize him," Anastasia said for the tenth time, keeping her eyes glued to the door, scanning the face of each traveler as they exited into the waiting crowd.

"I can't believe that you are so sure," Alya replied. "It's been so long. How do you know what he'll look like?" Though Anastasia had a few short phone conversations with Mychaylo, and had exchanged numerous letters in which

Anastasia had included family photos, Mychaylo sent only photos of his children – two boys and a girl.

"I'll know," Anastasia repeated again firmly. Almost as if she was speaking to herself, she added, "Not recognizing my own brother would be like not recognizing my children after thirty years. I'll recognize him."

After a few more minutes, Alya became bored and distracted as she watched the newly arrived plane passengers greeting their families. Every single person coming out of the Arrivals area had someone to greet them. Each person corralled outside the Arrivals area had a big smile plastered on his or her face. Anastasia was the exception. Her lips were pressed tightly together. Her face was set into a serious mask. Alya wondered if her mother would ever smile again. Then Alya saw Anastasia suddenly stand on her toes and look up across the crowd. Her face remained grim as she waved her hand in the air. Alya watched as tears gathered in the corners of her mother's eyes before a small smile grew across her lips.

Alya looked to the Arrivals door, but she could not tell who Anastasia was waving to, until she spotted an older gentleman with grey hair combed neatly back in place who was accompanied by a chubby, friendly-looking woman. Both the man and the woman were smiling, and as the man smiled, Alya felt as if she was looking directly into her mother's face, complete with sparkling blue eyes.

Trailing behind Anastasia as they made their way along the outside edge of the crowd, Alya watched as Anastasia and Mychaylo walked quickly towards each other and embraced. They stayed that way for quite a while, both crying tears of joy. Joining in on the celebration, after a shy greeting, Alya and Irina hugged too, watching as Anastasia and Mychaylo broke apart and took a long look at each other. Alya realized that it was the first time that brother and sister had seen each other up close, face-to-face, since they had been children. Since living together in Horayetz.

Next, Mychaylo embraced Alya, "And you look just like your mother when she was young," he said with a voice strained by emotion. He kissed her on both cheeks. "Finally, I get to meet my niece, Alyona."

TORONTO

2015

To: vika2244@gmail.com
From: Dr.Sofiya@BWOrtho.ca
Subject: Hello & Happy Easter
Date: Wednesday, April 30th, 2015 3:22 pm

Dear Viktoria,

Greetings from Canada! I hope this email finds you and your family well. I saw the kids' Easter photos that you posted on Facebook. Everyone looks well, and your youngest one is growing like a weed! You look gorgeous, as usual. I loved your dress – fashion is certainly coming along in Ukraine! Mama tells me that when she visited you and your parents in 1992, there were absolutely no Western brands available, aside from the underground market, of course. That one photo of you with iPhone in hand, carrying a Coach bag, looks like it could have been taken right here in Toronto.

Did you get a chance to see the photos that I put up last week? This Easter was a blast, as it was the first time that Ana really was aware of what was going on. My little *zaichyk* was so excited to go search for hidden chocolate eggs around Baba and Dido's yard! Unfortunately, for days after, the little monkey was constantly searching our yard for hidden treats. Her two-year-old mind can only retain so much, and I think she's finally forgotten all about the magic of chocolate hidden among the backyard plants. Anyway, we also went to a farm to have bunny photos taken of Ana. It's silly, but the photos came out really well. Now that the chaos of attempting to get a two-year-old to sit still with bunnies is over, I'm happy to have a set of very cute pictures, one of which is on its way to you via *snail-mail*.

And now for some unfortunate news. Jeff and I have decided to formally separate. If all goes amicably, we will be formally divorced in about eight months from now. The separation was a long time coming, and of no surprise to anyone, even Baba Anastasia. In fact, she was the one person in the world who I was the most frightened to tell, but she took it very well. That was only about a month or so before she passed away, but she was still quite lucid and actually remained very sharp-witted, right up until the very end. As one of her last pieces of advice to me (of maaaaaaany ☺), she told me to move on and try to be happy. I thought: move on? Be happy? Who is this woman?? But of course, she couldn't let me off the hook too easily. She added that I should find a nice Ukrainian boy to settle down with and marry. Her main concern for me (right until the end!) was that I get on with the business of having a second child. It was an absolute relief to know that she accepted my decision.

Shortly after Baba passed away, I was telling my mother about her marital advice, and Mama started laughing. Apparently, when my own mother was in her thirties, Baba had also pestered her about having more children. Apparently, most women of the wartime age believed that families should have a minimum of three children – the heir, then 'the spare', then another, just for good measure. You know - if one of the kids ends up as a total disaster, there are at least two more to carry on! ☺ Most of my friends have only one child. Actually, it's hard to imagine fitting in another set of sports practices, dance lessons, and another child's worth of private school tuition!

In any case, having a second child wasn't really an option for us. Deciding to end our marriage after only one child was a decision that we were both relieved to finally make. The few years leading up to the separation were terrible, and our home was constantly filled with tension. Abandoning the sinking ship that was our marriage was the right choice.

I bought a small three-bedroom home just north of where we used to live, and Jeff has moved to a condo near his downtown practice. I'm not thrilled at the thought of Ana spending a large chunk of her time in that small condo and I tend to let my own imagination run away on me. I picture her cooped up watching cartoons, eating reheated pizza for dinner. I know I'm not being totally fair, but I think it's my guilt getting a hold of the better part of me.

So, slowly, we are moving on with our lives. When we first separated, I was hoping that all the misery that we both endured over the past number of years would be the end of sadness – that we would both feel instantaneously happy once we no longer lived together. I can see now that it will take some time to move on. For now, I'm grateful for the support of my friends and family, and I know that with time, I'll be okay, as will Jeff.

Now, for the other important reason that I'm writing this email to you - attached to this you will find a transcript of an interview with Baba Anastasia from about two years ago. Gaining a better understanding of where my grandparents came from has helped me to define my own identity and what my role is as a Ukrainian Canadian. I've always had a particular interest in Baba Anastasia's story, not only because I spent so much time with her as a child, but also because she was my last remaining grandparent.

My past is so delicately intertwined with yours, Viktoria. Down from our great-grandmother Daria, and our shared story from our grandmothers. Learning more about my Baba Anastasia and your Baba Kateryna was a turning point in my life. Do you remember that afternoon that we spent driving around the countryside of Poland? That afternoon four years ago was one of the highlights of my life. It was so good of you to act as our tour guide, and to show us around the site of what used to be Horayetz. I can still smell the soil after the rain had stopped that afternoon. Do you remember how we guessed where our great-grandmother may have had her house? I've tried to look into the 1947 massacre of that village, but there's been next to nothing written about it. Although the women of our family were long gone by 1947, I remember how the senseless killing of their countrymen affected my grandmother. To her last day, this massacre was something that deeply troubled her, and as she lost her grip with reality, she often spoke about it.

The transcript that I've attached is of a series of interviews between Baba and myself. At first, it was difficult for Baba to remember all of the facts. The details of her life as a child, then her teenage years in Horayetz seemed to be etched clearly in her memory, but then her recollections of her experiences in Germany were much more difficult for her to remember accurately. I found that she would get her time-lines mixed up, or jump from one part of her life to another without warning. It was difficult to keep all of the facts straight, and understand how the vast and varied experiences of her life were all intertwined. The more Baba spoke about her story, the more that old memories were triggered, and she was able to slowly remember more places, dates, and people. Some parts of her life as a teenager were still so clear to her, even some sights, smells, and sounds. It goes to show what a wonder for storing memories the human mind is. I learned so much about her and about your own Baba Kateryna. This is why I've attached the transcript for you to read. There are many details about Horayetz, about your own grandmother, as well as our great-grandmother. I hope that you will be able to gain a better understanding of your own history, as well as mine.

In the interviews, you will read how I asked Baba Anastasia several times about a friend named Alyona, who Baba met while at Ford-Werke. You know that my mother, Alya, was named after this girl. My mother has never known much about her namesake, as Baba kept the details of that friendship very close to her heart. We only knew that she was also Ukrainian, and decided to go back to Ukraine after the war was over. You'll see that truly, it is because of this young girl that I am even here today.

After I completed the series of interviews with Baba, the voice files remained on my computer, untouched for a year or so. After Baba passed away, my mother finally got around to listening to the interviews that we did. I don't know why she had never actually listened to them while Baba was alive. Perhaps she didn't think there would be any new information to learn? Mama finally listened to the interviews, she cried and cried. Part of it was because she was listening to Baba Anastasia's voice for the first time after she had passed away, but part of it was because she was learning much more information about Alyona than she had ever known.

We've both been quite keen to find out more about Alyona. We have tried to use Google to find information about her, but we have not been able to find even one detail. The records of labourers at Ford-Werke have also failed us. Whatever became of both of the young girls that I now know about, Hanya and Alyona, remains a mystery to us. I reflect on the fate of these two girls often, wishing that I could at least know what became of them. Baba Anastasia was fortunate to be able to piece her family back together, but these two young girls were forever lost to her. I think that she tried to take solace in the fact that at least, the family of Daria, Kateryna, Anastasia, and Mychaylo were together one time before Baba Daria passed away.

Finally, there is one mystery that Mama and I want to ask your family about. Last month, we were sorting through the last few boxes of items from Baba's apartment when we came across a curious small container. Hidden underneath a pile of documents from Baba and Dido's immigration to Canada was a small, square box made of sterling silver. Both Mama and I were together when we found it, and neither of us had ever seen it before. In the box was a thin plain gold band, like one that would have been used as a wedding ring. It wasn't Baba's...as far as Mama can remember; she had worn the same band forever.

The ring itself is unremarkable, and the box itself brown with tarnish. The box is beautiful now that it has been polished, and underneath all the tarnish there is intricate engraving. I wish your Baba Kateryna were still alive, so that she could maybe give us clues as to where this ring and its box may have come from. Can you ask your tato; see if he has any idea? We are absolutely stumped for clues. Both the box and the ring are a total mystery to us.

I'm looking at that ring and box right now as I write this email. I find myself losing vast swaths of time – ten, twenty minutes – staring at it and the silver box, tracing my finger over the intricate details as if a new feature will jump out at me. The mystery behind it is captivating my imagination. The silver box is small and delicate, yet beautiful and strong, just like Baba was. The ring inside is clearly from many years ago, yet remains perfectly unchanged. To think that we nearly tossed it in the trash, as upon first glance it looked like a worthless old trinket box! Dirty and small, what lay beneath the tarnish was hidden. This mystery reminds me that there is so much that we will never truly understand, but that we should do our best to remember what we have learned.

I have to run now to pick up Ana from school, but I hope that you enjoy reading the transcripts of the interview. Who knows, maybe you'll learn something new about your grandmother too! Perhaps there is information that your tato could add to the document, and we could get an even better picture of the history of our family.

Take care, and give your two little ones a kiss from their Ciocia in Canada!

Love,
Sofiya

ACKNOWLEDGEMENTS

Tarnished is largely a work of fiction. However, many of the struggles young Tasya faces during World War II are closely based on the life of my grandmother, Anastasia Chytra. Like thousands of other young girls, she was removed from her home village to work in Germany as a forced labourer, receiving no compensation at that time. While many of the events that Tasya endures were inspired by my own Baba, the stories of her daughter Alya, and granddaughter Sofiya are entirely fictional. My baba, Anastasia Chytra, was raised in the village of Horayetz, worked in Düsseldorf in a factory, in Jünchen as a household servant, and was liberated by the Americans in 1945. She met my grandfather, Nestor Chytra, at Münster-Lager, and they later came to Canada.

My deepest gratitude goes my patient, kind, wise, self-sacrificing and hilarious writing partner, Dave Moores. Without your hours of teaching and editing the "Lesia-ism's", this project would have most certainly been put away in a drawer. I cannot thank you enough for supporting me these years, and acting as my desperately-needed mentor. I'm thankful that our paths crossed, and that you asked me to work with you on *Windward Legs*. I'm forever indebted to you.

Thank you to my early readers – Sarah Sturino and Mary Kebalo-Plata. Trudging through one of the first drafts of *Tarnished* was most certainly painful, and I appreciate your excellent notes and suggestions.

To my dear friend and colleague, Len Bernardo – thank you for the multiple hours that you dedicated to editing *Tarnished*. Always a teacher to the core, you taught me how to write, but also your encouragement meant the world to me. Thank you for suggesting the title of the book.

The haunting and beautiful cover as well as interior layout was created by my friend and graphic designer, Tanya Mykytiuk. I am grateful that you understood my vision, and how to make it real. Most importantly, thank you for reading an early copy of the manuscript, and for your many words of encouragement. Also, thank you to Nadia and Vlodko Brechun – without your notes of support and encouragement, I would not have had the confidence to share *Tarnished* outside of my own circle of friends.

To my parents, Zenon and Mary Chytra. For encouraging me to understand my own family history in greater detail, for helping to provide the time and space needed to write, and for early comments on the manuscript, I thank you.

Writing, working, and being a mother is not an easy balance to strike. Writing is mostly a lonely endeavor, and one that requires much energy. With my whole heart, I want to thank my number one supporter and cheerleader, my husband, Levco Wynnyckyj. You gave me hundreds and hundreds of hours to myself to pursue this project, and encouraged me when I felt completely ridiculous about attempting to write a novel. Thank you for being my sounding board, for your wonderful story ideas, the small touches throughout this story, and your patient eye.

Finally, this book is dedicated to both of my grandmothers, Anastasia Chytra and Anastasia Gurskyj. What these two women had to endure in order to provide their families with a full life in Canada is baffling. This story is for them.

BIBLIOGRAPHY

Bilstein, R. *Working for the Enemy: Ford, General Motors, and Forced Labor in Germany During the Second World War.* Oxford: Berghahan Books, 2004.

Browning, C.R. *Remembering Survival: Inside a Nazi Slave-Labour Camp, 1st ed.* New York: W.W. Norton & Company, 2010.

Isajiw, W., Senkus R., Boshyk Y. (ed). *The Refugee Experience: Ukrainian Displaced Persons After World War II.* Edmonton: Canadian Institute of Ukrainian Studies, 1992.

Luciuk, L. *Searching for Place: Ukrainian Displaced Persons, Canada and the Migration of Memory.* Toronto: University of Toronto Press, 2000.

Luciuk, L., Hryniuk, S. *Canada's Ukrainians: Negotiating an Identity.* Toronto: University of Toronto Press, 1991.

Subtelny, O. *Ukraine: A History, 3rd Ed.* Toronto: University of Toronto Press, 2000.

47112212R00169

Made in the USA
Charleston, SC
06 October 2015